HOW TO FALL

REBECCA BROOKS

Entangled Publishing, LLC
2614 South Timberline Road
Suite 109
Fort Collins, CO 80525
Visit our website at www.entangledpublishing.com.

Select Contemporary is an imprint of Entangled Publishing, LLC.

Edited by Alycia Tornetta
Cover design by Heather Howland
Cover art from Shutterstock

Manufactured in the United States of America

First Edition November 2015

For Robert

Chapter One

Julia heaved her bag off her shoulder and rang the small silver bell. There was no one at the front desk, but she'd already learned that in Brazil, life had a way of taking its time. She set the backpack on the floor and twisted her long hair up off her skin, welcoming the breeze on her neck.

It had been nicely air conditioned on the bus, the first time she'd felt cool since her plane touched down two days ago. The evening heat hit her as soon as she stepped into the street, laden with luggage and unsure where to go. Clutching the map in her guidebook, she'd finally found the turn-off for the hostel hidden behind a row of palm trees, long fronds rustling as she passed. After the twelve-hour ride from São Paulo, through rushing greenery and endless fields, she wanted nothing more than a cold drink and a long dip in the pool.

The pool was why she'd chosen this place. "A delightful

option," her guidebook said. "Pousada Iguaçu may be off the beaten path, but with a steady stream of travelers looking to unwind, relax, and explore the waterfalls—the main reason to come to this border town—you'll be sure to leave with new friends from around the world."

New friends? She was sold. Just having someone to *talk* to would make Iguaçu a major step up from São Paulo. The most social contact she'd had in two days was when an elderly woman waiting for the bus pointed out that Julia had been holding the map upside down.

She took a deep breath. She wasn't *alone*, she reminded herself. She was a woman traveling solo. Independent. Self-assured. She knotted her hair into a ponytail and rang the bell again.

The sound of a door opening from the garden made her turn.

She told herself that the first thing she noticed were his eyes, clear blue like a tropical sea and looking straight at her. Maybe his tan. Or the curl in his sun-lightened hair.

But no. She hadn't gotten laid in she didn't know how long, and the man walking in from the garden behind the lobby was shirtless, wearing nothing but cobalt blue swimming trunks slung low on his tanned, narrow hips. She wasn't about to miss a single detail as her eyes ran from his sculpted chest down to the ripples cut into his abs.

"You must be looking for André," he said, and Julia blinked in surprise at his Australian accent. His voice made her think of the beach and diving into the pounding waves. She could practically smell the sun on his skin.

She ran her eyes up and down his body like she could feel him just by looking. Every inch of his muscular torso. The softness of his thick, curly hair. A picture formed of its own accord: her fingers hooked under the band of his shorts, yanking him to her with a take-no-prisoners grip. Her mouth pressed against his before he had time to protest.

There was no one around. She could totally do it.

If she didn't die laughing first.

She couldn't believe how blatant she was being. Was there any chance this guy hadn't noticed how much she'd eaten him up with her eyes?

He flashed her a teasing smile.

Nope, there was no way she was off the hook. She hoped he'd think the deep flush in her cheeks was from walking up the hill to the hostel in the heat and not because she was in the middle of the least Julia-like fantasy to ever pop into her head.

"André?" she asked, trying to regain her composure.

"He does check in. Hang on, I'll get him for you." Before she knew it, he'd hopped over the front desk and was calling through a back door, giving her a shameless view of the muscles in his back as they narrowed down to what she'd already guessed would be a very, very fine ass.

Damn, damn, damn.

She swung her eyes up a second too late as he turned around.

"It's hard for him to hear the bell back there sometimes."

She nodded, trying to stay cool, but her eyes were moving again, completely out of her control. She was a kid reaching into a cookie jar. An addict going for that next hit. Shamelessly she drank in the sight of the man's muscular chest, his tanned skin, the curl in his towel-dried hair.

She wondered if there were any private rooms at the hostel, any chance she could wind up alone with him. Maybe she could "accidentally" trip and fall directly on top of him. Or just happen to lose all the shorts she'd packed. And shirts.

And, apparently, her sanity. She didn't know whether to be relieved or dismayed when at last the door opened and a teenager appeared behind the front desk.

"*Oi!*" he called. "Sorry to keep you waiting."

"*Oi.*" Julia tested out her imperfect Portuguese, feeling even more self-conscious than usual.

"*Muito bom,*" André encouraged her, *very good,* but she was already lost. Two whole days and she'd only mastered that one simple word.

"That's all I've got," she said with a nervous laugh, and the boy shrugged.

"You'll learn more."

"I'm trying," she lied. But it wasn't a mean lie. Somehow in the chaos of packing and leaving and Christmas and celebrating her god-awful birthday with that number she didn't even want to acknowledge, she hadn't once cracked open the books she'd bought.

But there was some luck coming her way—not only did this hostel have surprisingly good eye candy, but there were still a few beds left in the women's dorm. The bathroom was shared, but Julia didn't mind. The place was impeccably clean. She booked two days and two nights and signed her name nowhere near the dotted line, too distracted to look down.

"You'll love it here," the Australian said with a grin, and Julia hoped he wasn't just praising the hostel's shampoo. There was something electric in the way he was looking at her that made her want to know who he was, what he was doing there, and how much she had to actually talk to him before making it clear *exactly* what she wanted.

If she could make it clear. If she could be the kind of person who for once let her hands do the talking instead.

She wasn't, of course. A week in Brazil didn't change anything about her life. But for two days and two nights she was a stranger in a hostel and could be anything—anyone— she wanted.

It was intoxicating, and for a moment she felt dizzy with the rush of possibility. Maybe this simple place to rest her head was going to be a way out of the confusion and uncertainty she felt. Not just in Brazil, but going back further. Two years now. Two years since Danny looked her in the eyes and told her he was leaving, and she was both released and set adrift.

Julia could feel a current pulling her toward this man by her side. Her best friend, Liz, talked about "the spark," but Julia had never believed her. How could anyone feel instantly connected to someone? Suddenly she believed Liz. Sometimes you *knew*.

Julia had always been the careful one, the safe one, the one who stayed strong and steady so she could pick up the pieces when things fell apart for those around her. But this man didn't know anything about her. He didn't think of her as Danny's girl or Liz's protector, there to help her friend through the sadness and fear she faced after a high school party went devastatingly wrong. Even when things started to seem better for Liz, it was hard to let go of the watchful eye, the caring shield. It was hard to believe Liz might really be okay.

This man didn't know that, though. Standing before him, Julia could be anyone she wanted. She could grab him and let herself *go for it*.

But then André counted out her change, and just as suddenly as it had hit her, the feeling was gone.

She looked away, unsure what had come over her and what ridiculous fantasy she'd concocted in three seconds flat. The image of her fingers sliding under the band of his shorts was nothing more than a joke. She had been staring at the man because, yes, he was gorgeous. But that didn't mean he was looking at her or that anything would actually happen. What she'd felt was nothing more than her own desperate loneliness coming back to bite her in the ass.

Which was hardly her preferred form of foreplay, if she could afford to be choosy.

The man scratched at the small of his back as though to remind her of all that she couldn't have. There was no way *not* to notice how his shoulder muscles flexed when he moved. How easily he could hold her against a wall in a dark corner somewhere, pin her wrists over her head, press his hips to hers…

The fantasy made her legs weak. She was afraid of how much she wanted it to come true.

"*Mais cervejas*?" André asked the man, startling Julia back to reality.

"Please, *por favor*."

"I'll bring them out to you. One minute—" André held up a finger to Julia to signal that he'd take her to her room as soon as he brought out more beer.

"No, wait." The man shook his head. "You get her settled first."

Was it her wishful thinking or were his eyes on her, too? She felt herself under his gaze, her too-long legs and arms and hair that she pulled nervously from its ponytail, a habit of fiddling when she was jumpy to give herself something to do. Immediately she regretted it because of the heat. But she told her hands to be quiet. She couldn't very well go putting it back up now that she'd just pulled it out.

"Thanks," she said, unsticking her voice as she bent down for her bag. But he reached across before she could pick it up, and for the briefest moment their skin touched, hers pale and sweaty, his smooth and at ease.

"Let me help you," he said, his accent buoyant and warm.

She tried to cut through her nerves by thinking about how hard she was going to laugh describing him to Liz. This Australian hunk had walked right up to her like he was auditioning for the lead role in some wild South American dream she didn't even know she had.

And? She could already hear Liz excitedly pumping her

for more information.

And nothing, Julia would shrug. What, did Liz think anything would actually *happen*?

In the last few years, Liz had started getting laid like sex was a thing people did on a regular basis and not once in a blue moon. No matter whether she was in a relationship or not, she always had a satisfied smile and a new story to share.

It hadn't always been like that, so Julia didn't begrudge her friend the good times. Liz had been through hell when they were younger and deserved to have fun. But Julia hadn't given up looking out for what could go wrong.

"Totally not necessary," she said primly, trying to pick up the bag first. But he was already there, so close she could see the light hairs on his arms and the thin blue veins where his muscles flexed as he lifted her backpack in one easy stroke.

"You don't have to," she tried again, arms by her side, holding nothing but her light shoulder bag and the hostel receipt as he looked to André to see where they should go.

"I don't *have* to do anything," he said with a hint of teasing in his voice, his smile reaching all the way to his luminous eyes.

"You know what I mean." But she smiled back, despite herself.

"I want to," he said in that delicious accent, catching her eye again, and there was something in that word—in the idea of him *wanting*—that made her breath feel hot and trapped inside her.

"You have some strange desires," she tried to joke, and then immediately wished that she hadn't. Her blush was enough to set the whole hostel on fire.

But there it was—that grin again. "I'd be happy to share more of them, if you're willing," he whispered as he turned to follow André out the door.

Julia stood frozen by the front desk. Had he actually insinuated what she thought he had? Did people really *say* those things?

Quickly she made herself follow the two men out, her face so hot she knew she looked like a lobster boiled alive. Surely there was some kind of snappy response she could zip back, but her voice had left her.

As had her reason. Was he actually flirting with her, or was she so delusional from a long day of travel and an epic dry spell that she was willing to imagine anything to make herself feel good?

They went around the corner, and André motioned them into a long narrow room with two bunk beds on one side and two twin beds on the other.

"So which bed do you want?" the man asked, glancing over his shoulder as he gripped her bag.

Whichever one you're in, she wanted to say, but fortunately her voice still wasn't working so nothing came out.

The two bottom bunks were taken, as was one of the singles, the sheets partway pulled up, bags cinched and leaning against the wall. Someone had left a pink travel toothbrush and travel-sized toothpaste on a washcloth by the pillow. Julia figured it was safe enough to do what everyone else was doing and leave her stuff out; nobody wanted her tank tops anyway. Her passport and valuables she'd give to André to put in the hostel safe.

She walked over to the farthest single bed, back against the wall, and dropped her shoulder bag.

"I guess this one," she said, surveying the room to keep from straying back to the man's chest. It was like there were magnets attached to her eyeballs. It wasn't her fault they couldn't be stopped.

"Good choice." The man dropped her pack next to the bed and extended a hand for her to shake. "I'm Blake."

"Julia." His skin was warm, his whole hand enveloping hers. She couldn't help wondering what it would feel like for him to hold her. Not just her hand, casually like this, but all of her. Completely. To feel his whole weight pressing against her. That *wanting* he'd spoken of—could it be her?

Danny had always held her like she was something fragile, pulling back like he might hurt her somehow. But Julia didn't want to be safe anymore.

She wanted to be shattered.

Her hand rested in Blake's a moment too long, and she wondered what it would feel like to be his for a night. It wouldn't be delicate. They wouldn't worry about breaking each other. It was as though somehow she knew from his handshake alone that there was nothing he did halfway. The thought sent a shiver from her fingertips all the way down her spine, a mix of excitement and nerves.

But it was impossible. Or at least improbable. What she wanted couldn't change who she was. Julia had spent eight years dating her best friend's brother as together they supported Liz through the most difficult time of her life. Even if Liz was better now and Danny, too, had moved on, Julia had been through too much with both of them for her to ever fully let herself go.

Especially not with a strange man, in a foreign country, five minutes after randomly meeting in a hostel so far from home it felt like it was balanced on the edge of the world.

Or maybe that was exactly why, for once, she could.

André ushered Blake out, but before he left, he stopped by the door and turned.

"Care to join us for a beer by the pool?" he asked.

Us. She felt her stomach plummet, her fantasies dashed against the rocks. Obviously he was there with his girlfriend. This was a pity invite, trying to be nice to the new kid who looked so forlorn.

"Oh, I don't want to interrupt," she said hastily, reaching for her bag as though she had a million things to do at four p.m. in a tiny border town where she didn't know a soul and could barely say *hello*.

"It's not interrupting." Blake smiled broadly. "We're just a bunch of bludgers hanging around. Jamie and his girlfriend, Chris, are Aussies like me, Lukas is a Dutch photographer, and Dana's from Ireland. She just left for the bus station, but if she can't get a seat tonight, she'll be back soon." He rattled off their names and Julia didn't hear anything in his voice that sounded like *spoken for*.

"Oh," Julia said. Both her brain and mouth still seemed to be broken. Blake gave her a look that hovered somewhere between a smile and a smirk.

"Tough decision?" he asked, like he could read the thoughts running through her mind. Like he knew *exactly* how good-looking he was and expected her to jump all over him.

Well, not this girl. She'd been on a bus for the whole day and what she really wanted was to relax. To sit by the pool with a nice cold—*shit*.

Yes, she very much did want a beer.

"Give me five minutes," she said.

"Take your time. André's rules about the dorms are strict, so I'll meet you in the garden before I'm kicked out for improper behavior."

"For improperly carrying my bag?" The edges of a smile danced around her lips.

"Improper actions, improper thoughts." He grinned. "You never can tell sometimes."

"André's got a busy job if he's making sure everyone's thoughts are clean."

"Not everyone's. Only the ones who look like they might be up to something dirty."

His crooked smile made the heat rise to her face. Just how far was she going to push this flirting?

But the question was out of her mouth before she could stop herself. "And who might those people be?"

"Oh, I think you'll know when you see them," he teased. It was a good thing he'd stepped away from her bed. Everything he said in that accent sounded like an invitation to fuck.

Julia was about ready to fling herself backward on the mattress and drag him on top of her. But that would *not* be practical, respectable behavior befitting a high school math teacher now one day into her thirties. She smoothed down the front of her tank top, conscious of how thin the material was and how short her shorts. The outfit was perfect for the heat, but now that his eyes were on her…

"I'll keep a lookout. Wouldn't want to run into anyone…" she paused, choosing her last word carefully. "*Dangerous*."

His blue eyes flashed. "I felt it was my duty to warn you."

"And I do appreciate your concern."

The look they shared lasted a beat too long before he closed the door, telling her to come out to the garden whenever she wanted. Julia's long hair crested down her back from where she'd pulled her ponytail out. But it was like he had suddenly blown on the back of her neck, making her shiver in spite of the heat.

Julia grabbed her toothbrush, soap, and bathing suit and made her way to the bathroom, grateful the hallway was clear. She didn't want anyone to see how pink her cheeks were in the bright bathroom light. She splashed cold water on her face to tame the flush and reapplied a trace of eyeliner to deepen the brown in her eyes.

God, what am I doing?

The face in the mirror pouted innocently back. *Just having a drink with some fellow travelers—so what?*

Yeah right, she scoffed. A drink with one "fellow traveler" in particular who looked straight out of a magazine and here she was changing from not much clothing into even less. She tied the straps of the bikini around her neck and back and pulled on the bottoms, surveying herself in the mirror. Sea-foam green with delicate white patches like clouds rode high on her breasts and low on her hips, which she covered — barely — with a thin crocheted sarong. It was the kind of outfit she never, ever would have bought for herself if Liz hadn't insisted on taking her shopping before her trip.

"It's my birthday present to you," Liz had said as she nodded approvingly at her friend in the dressing room mirror. "And a present to all the guys who are going to lose themselves as soon as you step onto the beach."

Sure, it fit her well. But maybe a little *too* well. With almost everything exposed and the rest concealed just enough to let the imagination run wild, she felt more naked than if she were preparing to meet Blake and his friends with nothing on at all.

The thought made her squeeze her thighs together as a tremble rippled down her spine. What was she thinking? It was just a drink. And with a group of people — she wouldn't even be alone with Blake.

Besides, overworked teachers didn't flirt with gorgeous Australian supermodel-type guys. And they definitely didn't get naked with them. On the first — or any other — night together.

She heard Liz's voice in her head. "Overworked teachers get to have a sex life too you know," she'd said as she plunked down her credit card at the register of the swimsuit shop. Julia had shushed her, horrified at the knowing grin of the cashier.

"You should listen to your friend," the woman said as she folded Julia's gift in tissue paper and found a bag. "Wherever you're going, in these suits you're bound to have a good time."

"See?" Liz raised an eyebrow. Julia didn't respond. She was still wondering at how her friend had gone from practically celibate and constantly wary to the authority on all things sex.

"As long as you can get out of Chicago in the middle of winter, you're going to have a good time," the cashier added, handing Liz her receipt, and on that at least, Julia had to agree.

"I want you to have fun," Liz had said as they left the store and headed to lunch.

"I will." Julia clutched the bag. "I just don't want it to seem like I'm bailing on you, you know?"

"Seriously?" Liz shook her head. "First of all, it's a week—so I'm going to assume you're coming back. And secondly, I promise I'll be okay. You've done so much for me, but you can't spend your whole life worrying. Danny and I are hanging out over New Year's, and then before we know it, you'll be back. How much trouble can I get in until then?"

Liz was joking, but Julia hadn't wanted to answer. Wasn't that what she was afraid of—that at any second something could go wrong? A flashback, a memory that came without warning, any number of reminders that used to set Liz into a downward spiral again?

But the worst parts hadn't happened in a long time. So maybe Liz was right. Nothing much could happen in a week. And who could live always preparing for something bad to go down?

Now, as Julia examined herself in the mirror above the sink to make sure her boobs weren't popping out all over the place, she couldn't tell if she felt secretly pleased or beyond horrified that she was even considering yielding to Liz's entreaties to have a good time.

If Blake was even interested.

He probably had a ton of friends and flirted with everyone, which was how he'd managed to meet so many travelers. She was just going to have a beer, she told herself firmly.

Absolutely zero expectations.

Chapter Two

Blake lounged in the shade and poured another round. He'd been in Brazil long enough to do like the locals, ordering rounds of the large bottles called *garrafas* and pouring the amber liquid into cups so small they were hardly more than glorified shot glasses. Ice-cold perfection in the afternoon sun.

"Someone joining us?" Chris asked as André plunked down an extra glass.

"New guest arrived and I told her to come on out," Blake said. "Her name's Julia—a Yank." He pretended to be concerned with making sure each glass was full to the brim. Did he sound normal? He was trying to sound normal. After all, she was just another guest in the random flow of travelers to come and go.

Just another really gorgeous guest with a beautiful smile and bright eyes who'd stared at him like he was dinner and she hadn't eaten all day.

"Uh oh," Chris said, turning to Jamie and shaking her head. "Blake's got that look in his eye."

"I don't have a look!" Blake protested, and took a huge gulp of beer so he wouldn't have to say more.

"Um, you didn't until that," Jamie said, twisting a strand of unruly beard as he stretched out in one of the pool chairs.

"Lukas, doesn't Blake have a look?" Chris called. Lukas heaved himself out of the pool and came over, wringing water from his swimming trunks. A cluster of small holes marred the fabric across the bottom. He claimed they came from a lion cub dragging his clothes off the line one night when he was camping in a ranger park in Tanzania, but Blake thought it more likely he'd worn through them and didn't want to get a new pair.

Still, the pinpricks were a good conversation starter. Lukas had shown up at the hostel the same day Blake met Jamie and Chris. When they were all lounging by the pool, Lukas and Chris struck up a conversation about his near run-in with the unseen cubs. The four of them had been hanging out ever since, with a few other travelers coming in and out as they passed through the town. After so much time on his own, it was nice to have regular company. Blake would be sad to say good-bye tomorrow, especially to Jamie. The two had become close during late nights talking and laughing over bottles of beer. Blake had made an itinerary, though, and he planned to stick with it.

"Blake always has a look," Lukas said as he reached for his glass.

"See?" Blake said. "This is just my face. I'm sorry if you don't like it."

Chris stuck out her tongue, so Blake did, too.

"Such a beauty," Jamie sighed, and pulled Chris onto his lap, planting a kiss on her freckled, sunburned cheek.

She only stayed for a minute, though, before she downed her glass and cannonballed back into the pool. "Are you coming?" she called, floating on her back. Jamie swallowed the last of his beer and made a more modest splash.

Blake lifted his glass, signaling that he'd be in when he finished. He took extra small sips, wondering if Julia would actually join them. Not that it mattered, he reminded himself. He was leaving for Buenos Aires in the morning.

And he'd been looking forward to it, too, until he laid eyes on the raven-haired beauty by the front desk idly sweeping her hair up and suddenly wished this wasn't his last night in Foz do Iguaçu.

Blake had seen more than a few beautiful women in Brazil. He'd even slept with some of them, figuring that after all the years he devoted to his ex-girlfriend, Kelley, he deserved a little fun. The fewer strings attached, the better— both literally and figuratively. Some of the women down here wore hardly anything on the beach. *Flo dental*, they called their bikinis. Dental floss. If they didn't mind that he was gone the next day, then neither did he.

But somehow Julia didn't seem like just another pretty face. Okay, pretty face and long, stunning legs, hips curved in all the right ways, delicate breasts peeking through her thin white tank top like she didn't realize she would drive any red-blooded man wild as soon as he laid eyes on those sweet, pert nipples saying hello…

All of that was enough to pique his interest, but then there was her blush. Of course he'd noticed her checking him out while he stood in the doorway in his board shorts, watching her watching him back. Plenty of girls saw him shirtless on the beaches, decided they liked what they saw above the waist, and eagerly got to work discovering what his lower half had in store. The interest had skyrocketed after he became—it was still hard to wrap his mind around it—something of a recent celebrity in Oz. (Not that he'd taken advantage of it back home. But it was nice to know he could still turn heads in a place where nobody knew his name.)

Yet where he might have expected to meet Julia's brazen eyes inviting him to explore her own body in equal parts, instead she'd quickly blushed and looked away. Those two pink apples on her cheeks and the downward swoop of her lashes excited him so much more than a direct invitation ever had. More than any overt offer ever could. It made him want to find out what was going on beneath the surface of her smile and how he could make her blush like that again.

Before he'd known what he was doing, he'd walked over to help her with her things, even though she was obviously capable of handling her bags on her own. But he'd wanted to hear the sound of her voice. Wanted to see the shape of her mouth as she formed her lips around the words. The thought of those lips made him shift uncomfortably in his seat. Maybe he *should* take a dive in the pool.

Jamie and Chris were kicking on some neon noodle things floating in the pool while Lukas splashed between them. Funny that he had to leave Australia to find anyone from his home who seemed to like him for *him*, and not because of his fame.

Of course there were people who no longer liked him after he'd been publically disgraced by his now ex-girlfriend and his former best friend. But Jamie and Chris seemed smart enough not to believe everything the tabloids said. Being able to hang out with ordinary people who weren't in the entertainment business, order *garrafas* of beer, swim in the pool, take in the sights—he almost felt normal again.

The fact that Jamie was happily settled with Chris made it easier to remember that not all friends were out to steal his girlfriend and stab him in the back.

But he didn't want to think about that. What was taking Julia so long? She probably wasn't joining them. She'd be tired from the bus—it was a comfortable ride from São Paulo but still must have taken her most of the day. Plus he was a stranger, and for all he knew she wasn't looking to meet anyone new.

But surely she wasn't staying inside all afternoon. Not after the way that she'd flushed and glanced away…

Then he saw a pale glimmer catch the sun and resolve itself into two long legs and he had to keep himself—and other parts of him—from leaping straight up to greet her. She'd kept her hair down and it spilled in dark cascades over her shoulders, bare but for the thinnest strings of a bikini top. Those impertinent round mounds looked even more delicious without her thin shirt pretending to cover them, and the wink of her green bikini through that thing around her waist only made the question of what was hidden underneath all the more enticing.

Not that it was much of a mystery as her thighs flashed through the opening of the wrap. *Down, boy.* He did *not* want to give Chris any more reason to make fun of him.

"You made it." He smiled as she gave a little wave. "Julia, these are the very responsible adults who will be your mates here at the hostel. Very Responsible Adults, this is Julia."

He gestured toward the pool. Chris had Lukas in a headlock and was splashing water up his nose while he kicked up a storm. Jamie was pulling on Lukas's leg, either trying to free him or drown him, it wasn't clear which.

They paused in the middle of dunking each other long enough to introduce themselves, then got back into the fray. Blake was exhausted just looking at them.

"It's so great that you have friends to travel with," Julia said, accepting a glass of beer.

"Oh, we met here at the hostel," Blake said. "Although I guess by now it feels like we've known each other for longer."

"You're traveling alone?" She sounded surprised.

"Yep, you?"

"I'm just here for a week, down from Chicago. What

brings you here from Australia?"

That damned accent of his. He screwed up his face. Sometimes it would be nice to have a little air of mystery about him. He had gotten way too visible in his homeland. But at least no one outside Australia seemed to recognize him, even if they could immediately tell where he was from. Julia wouldn't be refilling his glass and then her own with that effortless grace if she realized who she was sitting across from, and he was grateful for the normalcy. If anything about his life could be called normal anymore.

"I wanted to get out," he said vaguely, looking at his friends in the pool while he thought about the subtle difference between the truth and the answer he gave. "I'd always planned on seeing some of the world, but it never seemed like the right time. Finally, I realized there would never be the perfect time—if I was going to go, I just needed to do it."

It wasn't a total lie. It was even more of an admission of his shortcomings than he usually gave when people asked. But something about the way she tilted her head as she listened made him feel like he could talk to her.

Even if he was sure she would never tell him everything about herself—not with the way her eyes locked into him and then darted away.

And then Jamie dashed out of the pool and whatever moment had happened between them was lost.

"Beer, beer, beer," he chanted, making a beeline for the table. "Pleasure to meet you, Julia. So sorry you had to meet these wankers, too."

"We're not wankers!" Chris called, now straddling Lukas's shoulders so he was forced under water again. "We're delightful company!"

"Well, at least one of us is a delight," Jamie agreed.

Lukas managed to push her off and bob to the surface

again, and then the two of them roughhoused their way out of the pool to shake Julia's hand. Chris was wearing a sporty two-piece that showed off a tattoo of a garden snake winding up her side. Next to her sunburned chest and tanned arms, Julia looked delicate and slight, all smooth skin and narrow bikini top straps.

Blake tried not to stare at the string pulled taught across her collarbone. Somehow all that made him think about was the knot behind her neck unraveling in his hands.

"So how long have you been in Brazil?" he asked, trying to make normal conversation that didn't involve spilling his soul or encouraging a raging hard-on.

"Two whole days," she said. "What about you?"

"Four weeks in Brazil, six days in Iguaçu."

"And all of them spent at the pool," Jamie said. "I think I'm turning into a prune."

"Wow, you've been traveling for a long time," Julia said as she accepted a refill.

"Three months so far," Blake said. "I've got another four to go."

Her eyebrows rocketed up, and suddenly Blake realized there was an unscripted woman beneath her composed exterior. It was only there for a second before her calm expression descended once more. But it made Blake want to draw her out again.

"That's kind of how we do it Down Under," he said. "It's so far to get anywhere that when people travel off the continent, they tend to save up their time and money and do it all at once."

"We've been on the road for six months," Chris said. "We wanted to hit up the falls, and when we read about this hostel online, we knew we had to come. Now we just keep extending our stay!" She laughed.

"It's amazing here," Julia agreed. "Where's your next

stop?"

"We're off to Santiago in a week," Jamie said. "A few days in Chile, and then heading home." He gave Chris's shoulder a squeeze.

"And you?" Julia asked Blake.

"I came down through Central America and then across Colombia and northern Brazil. I'm supposed to be heading to Buenos Aires tomorrow."

Julia blinked. "Wow."

Blake had no idea what that look meant, if she was disappointed or impressed—or possibly excited?

Or maybe she just had something in her eye. It was hard to tell when she kept herself so contained. But the point was that he'd said it. No pussyfooting around the fact that he was leaving when the sun came up.

Wasn't that the whole point of being newly single? No problems, no worries, nothing holding him back.

So what was that "supposed to" and how did it creep in like that? He was heading into town tomorrow to get his bus ticket over the border. Nothing was going to make him change his plans.

"Man, Buenos Aires is such an awesome city," Jamie sighed.

"We could always go back," Chris said, and Jamie laughed, even though as far as Blake could tell, Chris hadn't been joking.

"Next time," Jamie said.

"I'll drink to that." She raised her glass.

"To Iguaçu," Jamie said.

"To travel," Chris said.

"To not being on the bus," Julia said.

"To new friends." Blake couldn't help stealing a glance at Julia as he said it. They all clinked glasses, sloshing beer on the table, and he went to take a drink.

"No, no, no!" Chris admonished. "You have to make eye contact, you idiot."

"What?" Blake asked.

Chris shook her head in exasperation and turned to Jamie. "Don't these people know anything?"

Jamie shrugged. "Maybe that's why the bloke's cursed."

"Ouch," Chris said.

"Yeah, man," Blake added. "Ouch."

"What are you talking about?" Julia looked from one to the other.

"Do you Yanks not do this when you say cheers? Your whole country's going to fall down the tubes."

"Chris has this thing," Jamie started to explain.

"You have to make eye contact when you take the first sip. Otherwise…" She paused and put her glass down for dramatic effect.

Chris raised an eyebrow to Blake, and he leaned over to Julia. "Otherwise it's seven years of bad sex," he whispered loudly.

He was rewarded by the pink fluttering in her cheeks, her hand nervously touching her hair.

"Well I'd better try it to be certain," she said with a flush.

"Pretend you haven't had a sip yet," Chris instructed, topping off their glasses again. When she finished pouring Blake's, she winked.

Blake wanted to protest that he did *not* need help being set up. But Julia was standing between him and Lukas, and when Chris turned to Jamie, he felt a surge of—was it pride or adrenaline?—when Julia turned to him.

"Ready?" Chris asked.

"I don't have anyone to look at," Lukas complained.

"The curse of the odd numbers," Chris said. "I've got enough years of luck backlisted with Jamie, but from the looks of it, your skinny photographer ass could probably use a good streak." And so although she first clinked glasses with Jamie, it was Lukas's gaze she held as she drank.

Jamie didn't seem to care about the ritual, and Blake knew it was nonsense, but he felt a sudden stab for his friend.

Not for long, though. Julia was holding his gaze, open and unblinking, and he couldn't look away. Her eyes were deep brown, flecked with lighter bits that sparked in the sun. There was something unreadable in her, something hidden below the surface that he couldn't see. Like her blush, it made him want to find out more.

It was the writer in him, the one who made his living figuring out people and their situations. Looking at Julia, he wanted to dive right in.

"To good sex," he said.

"To good sex," she echoed, and lifted the glass to her lips.

Julia took a sip, and then she put the glass down slowly and pressed her lips together. The move wasn't so pronounced as to be obvious, but enough to make Blake wonder if she was intentionally playing with him. She smiled with her eyes, even as her mouth barely curved.

Definitely a tease, he decided. How could they be eyeing each other, talking about good sex when they'd only just met?

He really did need a jump in the pool.

But Julia had settled back in her chair, still nursing her beer, and Blake couldn't pull himself away even after Chris, Jamie, and Lukas returned to the water. He was just being nice to the newcomer. Just making friendly conversation. Not at all glad that the two of them had been left alone again under the shady palm trees.

"So what brings you here for seven whole days, Ms. Julia?" he asked.

"Ugh, don't call me that." She made a face. "That's what my students call me."

"You're a teacher?" Definitely not what he would have

guessed. "I thought teachers usually got a last name."

"They try to be progressive."

"I bet your students love you."

"Nope," she said cheerfully. The laugh escaped him before he could stop himself. "I'm strict. You have to be."

"Well, I'm sure they're lucky nonetheless." He grinned. God, to have had a teacher like her… He would have paid a lot more attention in class.

Maybe.

"High school," she went on, ignoring his attempts to compliment her. "Math, all levels. They're hellions, but I love them." She paused. "Most of the time."

"Oh my God—calculus?"

She nodded like it was no big deal. Blake whistled. He wanted to admit that he was terrible at math and was sure to embarrass himself in front of her trying to figure out a bill or something. But that might open him up to questions about what he did for a living, and *that* was something he didn't want to talk about—at least not yet.

Not to mention that it implied some future meeting during which he might be paying said bill, and that wasn't going to happen because even if he got lucky enough to do more than chat by the pool, he was leaving first thing in the morning. He swallowed his comment and tried a different approach.

"So a week is what you get for, what, Christmas holiday?"

She nodded. "I can't even remember the last time I took a real vacation. It's a new school, and I've been there since it opened. I adore the teaching part, but I do way too much of the administrative work because most everyone else is still learning the ropes. I'm supposed to be leading a training this week over the break, but at the last minute I just said fuck it, I can't."

The sudden curse surprised him coming from her delicate mouth but he liked the contrast. Put that down on the list of more things he wanted to elicit from her. Preferably followed by the sound of her crying out his name.

"So what made you say *fuck it*?" he asked, not trying to hide his smile as he took the opportunity to test whether she liked the word on his lips as much as he liked it on hers.

She looked up at the sun beginning to dip toward the trees as though it held the answer, and that was when he saw it again, that hint of something else beneath the exterior she wore for the world. Now that he knew what she did for a living he could see the distinction between the self she put on as a teacher, keeping all those kids in line, and the other woman struggling to break through.

"I guess I'd had enough," she said softly, and suddenly it wasn't the voice of flirty, easy confidence. Suddenly, she was telling him something real.

He leaned forward and listened. "Enough of what?" he prodded as a shriek from the pool rose over a volley of splashes.

"I had a birthday," she admitted.

"These things have a way of occurring."

She rolled her eyes. "Thanks for the reminder."

"It can't have been that high of a number," he said.

"Turning thirty when your whole life revolves around your job and a bunch of hormone-soaked teens is sort of depressing." She sighed into her glass.

"Well, I can tell you from the other side that life does go on, and the view from the ripe old age of thirty-one isn't so bad." He smiled warmly. That he'd spent his thirty-first birthday trashed out of his skull, depressed as hell over Kelley, didn't need to be shared. The fact that Julia was so distressed about the big three-zero was pretty adorable.

All the more reason for him to show her how good her birthday could be.

He drained the last of his cup. "How about a birthday

swim?"

"Too late for that—it was yesterday."

"A belated birthday swim, then." He stood and extended his hand.

She hesitated for a moment, fingers resting on the knot of that thing around her waist. Drops of water from Chris and Lukas's splashing stained her bathing suit and trickled down her stomach. He had to stop himself from trailing his finger along that same path.

And then she seemed to decide something and let the cloth fall. Blake barely had time to appreciate the sway of her hips before she'd jumped in. He laughed to himself at how she'd already left him behind.

Blake dove in and popped up alongside her. "Not bad," he grinned, shaking water from his hair. The temperature was just right, cool enough to be refreshing but still warm enough to stay in for what felt like forever.

"It's pretty much perfect," she agreed.

She closed her eyes and floated on her back, drops of water clinging like stars to her lashes. Blake forced himself to swim a few laps to get his brain back. He wasn't supposed to be noticing things like eyelashes, and the little curve of her nose, and the way her lips parted when she sighed.

He was supposed to be having fun and forgetting anything that might make him linger. Resisting the pull that might draw him to one person, one place for too long.

They swam until they were tired, came out for cold beer until they were hot again, and jumped back in the pool. Then Chris suggested a place in town for dinner, and they piled five into a cab, Julia wedged tightly between Chris and Blake in the back seat.

He could feel her body pressed against his side, his thigh, smell her shampoo and a faint, clean whiff of chlorine. Her hair was still damp from the shower and only the fact that it was too cramped in the taxi to move kept him from brushing it back with his hand.

She sat across from him at dinner, and at first he was disappointed, but on second thought he didn't mind the view. They filled their plates from a buffet laden with grilled fish, spicy sausage, and a thick smoky stew. There were black-eyed peas and empanadas, fresh green beans and pickled beets, and a large fruit spread with mangoes, star fruit, and the pear-like *cupuaçu*.

Julia was thorough about trying everything, sucking on the pulpy flesh of a cashew fruit as she tried to think of what it reminded her of. Blake wanted to be the one licking the juice from her fingers, tasting the fruit on her lips.

For the cab ride back, he announced that his arms couldn't survive another ride being pinned against the door and flagged down a second car. Somehow he wasn't surprised when in all the confusion of who was going where, he wound up alone with Julia in the back seat.

"Good Lord," she moaned, "I hope I get to eat like this every day this week."

"That's what vacation is for." He smiled at her happiness.

"Yet another thing I've been missing out on," she murmured, and looked away at the lights of the town drifting away, lost for a moment in her own thoughts. Blake could hear a trace of sadness in her words and wondered if she even realized she'd spoken aloud.

"Still feeling bad about your birthday?" he asked.

She laughed, pulled back from whatever place she'd just retreated to that he couldn't touch. When she looked at him again, she was smiling. "This has been a great introduction to thirty. I'm beginning to realize life actually does go on."

"Sometimes it even gets better," he joked.

She shook her head. "It'd be hard to top that pumpkin flan."

"I'm sure we could think of something." He slid across the back seat, next to her.

She looked startled, but he couldn't believe that she hadn't been thinking about it all night. Not with the way they'd been looking at each other, pulled into conversations across the table even when everyone around them was talking about something else.

The taxi was climbing the hill toward the hostel. He didn't have much time. It wasn't some grand romantic gesture, but who cared? The night was slipping away and he had to act fast. Before the taxi made the next turn, he lifted her chin with his first two fingers and pressed his lips to hers.

Even in the dark of night she tasted like sunlight and fruit, and he felt the warmth flood him as her mouth opened to him. He could feel her back arch, her neck tilt to draw him in. She'd been wanting that kiss, he could tell.

The car shuddered to a stop as they pulled up to the lighted entrance of the hostel. There was a volley of car doors as the rest of the crew piled out of the cab ahead of them.

Blake pulled away reluctantly. Julia's eyes were still closed and he remembered the water on her lashes, how she was lost to the world. He wished they could have kept driving, but he knew this wasn't the end.

He wasn't done showing her how good her birthday could be.

Chapter Three

Julia tossed and turned on the narrow bed and tried to make her brain—and her body—stop sparking like fire crackers on the Fourth of July. She lay on her back. She lay on her side. She settled onto her stomach only to find herself rolling over again. She hoped that to anyone else awake, her sighs sounded like someone settling into sleep and not like someone so damn horny she couldn't lie still.

She closed her eyes and tried to relax, but she kept drifting back to that kiss. Blake's warm hands, the press of his lips, the way she'd wanted that taste of him more than she'd ever wanted anyone, anything, before. She'd actually dared to slide her hands over his arm, feeling his muscles through his shirt, remembering how delicious he'd looked soaking wet from the pool.

Everything had been going so well. So how the hell had she wound up lying alone in the dark in a room full of lightly snoring women, frustrated beyond all belief?

Stupid brain, she cursed herself again. Always popping up at the worst possible moments to lecture her on what not to do.

Part of her had longed to stop the car, stop time, and erase everyone around them so that it was just her and Blake and that kiss, with no past or future to stand in their way.

But another part knew she never could.

That was the Julia who yawned and told everyone she was beat from her long bus ride. The Julia who could barely bring herself to make eye contact with Blake when she said goodnight. The Julia who knew the smart thing was to leave.

It had seemed like a good idea at the time. Sensible. Prudent. The only way to keep herself safe.

It was fine to share a little kiss, but then she had to be responsible and go to sleep.

Alone.

Except it wasn't just a little kiss. It was a *great* kiss. An excellent kiss. A soul-shattering, spine-tingling, forget-your-own-name kind of kiss. The memory of his skin alone was enough to make her clasp her thighs together under the thin sheets, trying not to make any noise.

She'd thought the right thing to do was to back away. Stay strong and in control of herself.

But now, in the cover of darkness, alone with her thoughts, smart, sensible ideas looked different than they had in the light. Her whole body was on fire, unable to stop replaying the moment when he slid toward her in the back seat of the car and her heartbeat raced into overdrive. His eyes had searched hers in the darkness and even before he leaned in to the kiss, she'd found herself lifting her lips to his. She wanted it, whether it was a good idea or not.

And now she was kicking herself for letting him go.

She pressed the light on her travel alarm, eyeing it under the sheets so it wouldn't disturb anyone else in the room. When the party petered out and the other assortment of hostel guests returned from their evenings, Julia had stayed curled with her back to the room, eyes closed, pretending to be asleep. She didn't know whether Chris knew anything had happened between her and Blake, but she didn't want to face any questions about what they'd done — and why it hadn't continued.

Now it was well after midnight and instead of congratulating herself for making the right decision — "the Julia decision," as Liz would say — all she could think about was the feel of his body pressing against hers in the cab.

She'd never be able to put herself back in that car and make a different choice. She'd always be stuck wondering, "What if?"

She bit down on her lip to keep from whimpering out loud. There was no way she was falling asleep. Quietly, she slipped out of bed.

If anyone woke up from the creak of the door opening or her flip-flops padding down the hall, she'd look like she was going to the bathroom. Like any normal, sane person might do in the middle of the night when they definitely weren't aching for someone's touch.

But instead of continuing down the hall, she grabbed her bikini from where it was hanging on the line and quickly put it on. She needed to cool down, distract herself, work off this steam so she could finally get some sleep.

She tiptoed out of the hostel, guided by the blue glow of the pool and the halo of garden lights. Doing something was infinitely better than lying in bed driving herself crazy. She just needed to take her mind off —

She stopped in her tracks.

She wasn't the only one who hadn't been tempted by the hostel beds that night. There was someone else swimming in the pool. Someone with cobalt blue shorts, a strong back, and sun-lightened hair.

Her stomach nearly flopped out of her body, all the electricity she'd been trying to hold back zinging straight to her chest.

She thought about sneaking back inside and just, she didn't know, sitting up all night in some corner in the hostel where she'd never be found. But it was too late — he had come up for air and seen her standing there.

And in the instant when his eyes met hers, Julia knew that no matter what she told herself was the right thing to do, she would never forgive herself if she didn't get into that pool.

Blake had lost count of how many laps he'd done without pause, pounding at the water like each stroke was taking him somewhere and not ferrying him in circles, which was exactly how his life felt.

It had been so good. *So good.* She'd wanted it; she'd wanted him. She'd lifted her lips to his and closed her eyes and smiled like she was somewhere far away and taking him with her, and he'd felt like whatever they were doing was right. The way he'd wanted that kiss—it wasn't like the other one-night stands he'd had, where things fell into place and progressed from there. He *wanted* this in a way that he'd forgotten he was capable of.

Sure, it wasn't great timing and there had been a car full of people waiting for them, plus more people in the hostel, and their separate rooms. But they'd figure out how to give everyone the slip and find somewhere to themselves. In a dark corner of the garden they could have done anything. It didn't have to be a big deal.

But when he'd turned around after tipping the driver, she'd immediately looked away. Then she gave some big elaborate yawn, when she'd seemed more than awake just moments ago. Okay, fine, so it was a little awkward, but Julia darted off to bed so fast that afterward, Chris demanded to know what the hell he'd said to her in the car.

"Nothing," he'd said, a little defensively.

"Well that's where you made your mistake," Chris said. "The two of you going off—I thought you were going to make your move!"

"You didn't even pash her?" Jamie echoed.

It would have been worse to tell them the truth—that he *did* go in for a kiss and she went from *yes, please* to *not on your life* in the amount of time it took to slam the car door.

Was he really *that* bad?

He was so sullen the rest of the evening, Chris accused everyone of being no fun and stalked off to bed early herself, Jamie and Lukas trailing behind. Blake knew there was no way he could sleep, so he'd grabbed his trunks and gone straight for the pool. He'd been banging out laps ever since, and it was only when he saw a shadow flicker in the doorway to the hostel that he looked up and realized his heart was hammering from more than swimming.

It was obvious who was standing there, but it didn't make any sense. Nobody claimed they were exhausted and then got up in the middle of the night to go swimming alone. Not even this girl.

But there she was. She was just standing there, not moving toward him or away, so he pulled himself out of the pool and approached.

"I couldn't sleep," she said.

"Me neither."

"I didn't think anyone would be out here."

"I guess we both had the same idea."

She hovered between the hostel and the garden as though caught, unsure which way to turn. Blake wanted to tell her to go back inside if she wasn't interested. But her hair was falling in long, dark streaks down her back and the sleek cut of her bikini barely concealed those two maddeningly alert nubs he wanted to flick with his teeth. It didn't take a rocket scientist to figure out what he wanted from his last few hours in Brazil before a bus whisked him away.

But he didn't know her, and obviously he had no idea what she wanted. As far as he could tell, she didn't know what she wanted, either.

At least not yet.

"What time is your bus tomorrow?" she asked.

"Nine a.m."

He waited to see how she would react. But if she thought anything about it, she didn't even blink. That certainty and calm had descended to shield her like a fortress of steel. He wanted to crack it open and see what was underneath. Run his tongue over the pieces she was hiding. Drink in who she really was.

Then she flushed, even though he hadn't said a word. Whatever she was thinking, he hoped it was good.

"Does that bother you?" he asked.

She shook her head. "No, I just—"

"Then let's not worry about it."

"I feel like I should explain," she started, but this time he was the one who said no.

"I don't want to spend the time we have left talking." He took a step toward her and under the garden lights he could see the pink deepen across her face.

"You don't even know me," Julia said demurely. But when Blake extended a hand, she took it. Her soft skin against his palm—was that all it took to make his breath catch?

"I never got to finish giving you that birthday present I'd had in mind," he whispered in her ear, brushing her hair over her shoulder as he leaned in.

The bulge was growing in his shorts, and the thin bathing suit material did nothing to hide it. Her eyes strayed downward and lingered over the knob straining below the waistband. Then they lifted to meet his face. Goddamn, she was beautiful. Her thin mouth stayed set in a line, betraying nothing.

But her rich, smoky eyes looking up at him? There was definite hunger there. She was hard to read, but not her eyes. They gave everything away.

She stepped toward the pool, tall and lithe against him,

and he wanted to kiss her right then. But still he hesitated, prolonging the moment to make sure she wanted it as much as he did. His desire was obvious, and if she moved another inch closer, she would feel it press against her thigh. She knew what he wanted and this time she hadn't backed away. But he could sense her nervousness, some kind of conflict brewing below the surface of what she let him see.

Blake knew all signs pointed to yes, but he didn't want it to just be yes. He wanted more than that. He wanted her enthusiasm to build until everything in her was screaming for him. Until there was no fucking way she could contain herself anymore.

He liked to be in control, but he didn't just want to take her. He wanted to be taken, too.

Without thinking, Blake turned and jumped into the water, intentionally splashing Julia where she stood.

"Come on in," he called when he came up for air, treading water and swinging his head to get his hair out of his eyes. "It's gorgeous."

"Mmm, I see that," she responded, and then bit her lip as though trying to take back what she'd said.

Her surprise at her own boldness made him want her more. "I think you should feel it for yourself instead of looking."

As he looked up at her, he wondered if maybe he'd pushed too far. She was still waiting, still holding back from jumping in the pool—from jumping into whatever was going to happen with him. She looked down at him, obviously aware of how he was running his eyes all over her.

"I like looking," she surprised him by saying, low and breathy and so quiet he almost didn't hear.

Oh.

She had decided.

Blake flashed her a grin and dove back under the water, taking a few strokes toward the center of the pool. He had to calm his hard-on before he got too far too fast. They hadn't done more than kiss in the back seat of a cab and already he ached like he was ready to explode.

When he came up for air, she was still standing there, watching him swim.

"No sharks in here," he teased, paddling on his side.

"Just one anaconda," she smirked, and this time he was the one who felt the heat rise to his face.

"I don't bite," he protested.

"What if I ask for it?"

That brought him up short. He swam over so that he was treading water below where she stood. "You can ask for anything you want."

"Because it's my birthday week?"

Blake shook his head. "All the time. Don't you know you should always get what you want?"

"Hmm, I do like the sound of that," she mused.

He clasped the edge of the pool and heaved his torso up out of the water. "So are you getting in or what?"

"I'm coming, I'm coming," she said, and dipped a toe in to check the temperature.

"I hope that's not the last time I hear you say those words," he said, just loud enough to be sure that she heard. And before he could read her expression—excited? Shocked?— he pushed off again and splashed into the water, bobbing up on the opposite side.

But he needn't have worried about scaring her off. He came up for air, and she held his eye, making sure he saw her take two running steps and leap into the pool, thoroughly outdoing his splash. She swam over to him, her bright laugh ringing through the garden. *Take that*, she seemed to be saying, and he knew not to underestimate this girl.

It was one thing to put his life on hold for seven months to travel the world, leaving behind demands and deadlines and the barrage of headlines and photos burned into his brain. That was such an obvious move that he almost felt like a cliché for running away.

But it was something else altogether to buy a ticket by yourself for just a week, because you were brave and maybe a little impulsive but certain, at last, of what you needed to give to yourself. Whatever she was looking for, he wanted to provide it tonight.

"The water is amazing," she exhaled, limbs rippling in the underwater glow as her hair billowed behind her.

"That's not the only thing," Blake murmured. Now that they'd plunged into the pool, he couldn't keep his hands to himself anymore. She let herself be pulled toward him with an audible sigh, surrendering whatever had been holding her back before. They were treading water together but with their bodies pressed closer they moved toward the shallow end, until his feet brushed the bottom and then hers. He wrapped his arms around her, feeling the softness of her skin in the water and the delicate pressure of her hips against his.

She hooked her finger into the band of his shorts and pulled him closer. He could feel her breasts against his torso, his aching erection pressing back hard against the base of her belly where the thin line of her bikini bottom hid everything he wanted to find.

"Hi there," she whispered.

"Hi." His lips were almost against her ear and he gently bit her lobe. "Just a little nibble from the anaconda," he said.

Her lips sought his, and then her tongue. Then, to his surprise, her mouth pulled back slightly and her teeth grazed his lower lip. Not hard enough to hurt, but hard enough that he felt the pressure rocket all the way down to his cock, now very much standing at attention to find out what else those lips, that tongue, those teeth could do.

"Just a little bite," she whispered, and he felt his whole body shudder as he clamped down on her in absolute need.

Chapter Four

Julia had never had sex with a stranger. Never had a one-night stand. Ever since the summer after her senior year in high school, when Liz discovered what could happen when boys said *I love you*, Julia had been so, so careful not to get hurt, physically as well as emotionally. But if she'd ever wondered whether there was some piece missing, now she knew exactly what it was.

Because she'd never felt herself fall apart like this, her whole body unraveling from the feel of his strong arms circling her waist and pulling her close as his lips found hers. It was everything she'd felt in the cab, everything she'd let run through her mind as she lay awake. Everything she'd never before let herself dream.

Her back was up against the side of the pool, her legs spread wide and wrapped around his waist. She ran her fingers down his chest and over his back, burrowing into his thick, curly hair.

She couldn't stop kissing him. Literally could not. There could be an earthquake, a fire, an explosion—who would notice? The whole world could come crashing down and it wouldn't be enough for her to pull away. She'd always wondered what other people were talking about when they got that misty look in their eyes, going on about passion and fireworks and how just kissing someone could make them entirely melt.

Now she knew. There seemed to be a direct line from her lips to her thighs, because the deeper Blake kissed her, the more she felt it all the way down.

Her hips pressed hard against his. Ordinarily she would have felt self-conscious about so obviously signaling her desires. But that little voice she always carried around—the one that watched everything while recording a tally of all her rights and wrongs—was oddly silent now.

Or maybe that was the same voice making an unholy chorus of pants and whimpers in Blake's ear as he ran his hands over her breasts. When he slid his palm under the cup of her bikini, the feeling of skin on skin made her moan. Then he twisted her nipple between his thumb and forefinger. Hard. But it felt so good that Julia bucked her hips forward and widened her legs as they wrapped around his waist. The thin strip of bathing suit that ran between her thighs was pressed right against the knob straining out from his shorts and the feel of him rubbing through the fabric between their legs... How could she be this breathless when they were still—technically—clothed?

"God, I'm so hard for you," he groaned into her ear, pressing his erection against her harder.

She groaned back and nibbled his ear, wondering who this new person was who lost control and loved it.

"I want you," he panted.

"Show me," she whispered, and the words thrilled her as much as his touch did. What did it matter that she had never done this before? He didn't need to know how she'd always been good. One night, far away from herself and her actual life, she could say such things. She could be brazen and bold.

Desire smoldered in Blake's eyes. "Find out for yourself."

How was it that she knew what to do? Without stopping to think, she hooked one leg around Blake's waist as he supported her against the side of the pool. Then she reached down and tugged on the white strings at the front of his bathing suit until the ties were undone. Her mouth found his, feeling the warmth and wetness of his kiss at the same time as she slid her hand down his torso and didn't stop.

Under the waistband she skimmed her fingers over the tip of his cock, that incredible part of him hard and soft at the same time. He was so excited she could practically feel him jump into her hand. He returned her kiss ferociously.

"Fuck, yes," he exhaled into her ear. "Just like that."

As if this wasn't already the dirtiest experience of Julia's life, he had to go take it to a whole other level. Danny *never* said anything during sex. Certainly nothing that might be construed as an improper way to treat a lady.

Now, though, she wanted to find out just how improperly Blake would treat her. She shimmied his swim trunks down enough to release his cock.

"Jesus Christ." The words were out of her mouth before she could stop them.

His hands paused in their voracious exploration of her body. "I hope that's a good exclamation?"

Julia tried not to giggle as she wrapped her hand around him and rubbed her thumb over the tip. "What was that you said?" she said, furrowing her brow. "Oh yeah, I think your exact words were something like '*fuck, yes*.'" She stroked his entire length and breadth, hardly able to believe how easy it was to be somebody else for the night, feigning confidence and control.

His knees buckled, and he pressed himself against her,

burying his face in her neck with a groan. "That feels. So. Good."

"Just you wait," she whispered. It was a taunt and a promise and a threat, and as she was hoping, it made him wild. He wrapped her hair around his palm and tugged down, forcing her chin up and exposing the soft underside of her neck to give him a clear path for tracing his lips down to her chest. His other hand was on her ass, propping her up against the side of the pool so he could pull down on the cups of her bikini with his teeth.

The fabric dropped over her breasts and she arched her neck back as he pulled on her hair. He toyed with her nipples with his tongue, biting hard enough to make her squirm. She was no longer grasping his cock but instead had her arms around his shoulders, digging in with her nails while he pressed his pelvis against her. The way his hardness rubbed up and down against the thin swatch of fabric between her legs was so hot she thought she might scream.

But as Blake's mouth worked over her breasts, they heard a door slam and the sound of footsteps across the garden.

"Oh shit." Blake's head shot up.

"Is somebody here?" Julia asked, scrambling to pull up her bikini top, glad it hadn't come completely untied.

"Maybe there's a night guard," Blake said.

"*What*?" she hissed.

"They must not leave the place unattended at night. I wasn't exactly thinking about that right now."

What an idiot—she hadn't even thought about the fact that they weren't really alone. The night had been so quiet when she stepped into the garden, it seemed like they had the whole place to themselves. But she could hear the shuffling of footsteps, the jangle of keys carrying through the night.

Blake was still pressed against her, his cock at attention and his shorts pulled down around his ass, when a face appeared in the doorway of the hostel.

"*Oi*, is someone out there?" a man's voice called. Julia's stomach clenched at the thought of him coming out to the patio and seeing them like this, the stranger the hot Australian had picked up within five minutes of her arrival now wantonly pressed up against the side of the pool, waiting for him to stick it in her.

This was why she didn't do things like this. She should never have come to Brazil. Should never have even *looked* in Blake's direction. Didn't she know better? Under the dark of night, the glowing water rippling around her, she burned with shame.

In front of her, Blake had turned his back to the hostel and was frantically trying to stuff his cock into his shorts as she finished putting her bikini in place. But he was too hard to go down and the water kept him buoyant, making it impossible for him to get in.

"*Oi*," Blake called back, still trying to work on his shorts. "I'm staying at the hostel and thought I'd go for a night swim. Is the pool closed?"

Julia thought he'd be horrified to be caught like this, but it seemed like he was *laughing*. Flushed and breathless, he pecked her on the cheek, splashing water every which way. "Can you believe this?" he whispered.

The fact that he found the whole thing funny was making it hard not to laugh just a little. At least she'd never have to see the night guard again. Or, for that matter, anyone else at the hostel—after the morning, of course, when she packed her bags and found somewhere far, far away to hide for the rest of her life. Like Antarctica. She reached over to try to "help" Blake with his predicament but he swatted her hand away. "I can't get out of this pool until you wrap yourself in a burlap sack and hide."

"One sack girl coming up," she teased, unable to stop

giggling now.

"But then I'd know you were under there hiding, so that's no solution."

Julia grinned and bit her lip. "I guess you're on your own this time."

"Don't do that," he groaned.

"What?" Julia asked, but before he could answer, the man's voice carried back over the pool.

"No, no it's fine, but I'm about to lock the front gate and head out, so let me know if you need anything. The gate opens again at seven."

"I'm all set, thank you, sir," Blake said, his voice so strained he practically croaked. "Have a good night."

"*Boa noite*," the man said—goodnight—and continued on his way. The keys jangled in his pocket as his footsteps retreated toward the gate.

Julia ducked under water, leaving Blake free to move away a few strokes to look like he was actually swimming in case the guard looked back. The reminder that the night was passing and Blake would be gone first thing in the morning pounded in her heart as the water rushed in her ears. She held her breath as long as she could, trying to make sense of the swirling around her, but nothing in her brain would work.

She broke the surface, breathless and dazed, as they heard the key turn in the lock. She barely had time to gasp for air before Blake pounced upon her. She let out a shriek and he clamped one hand over her mouth.

"Shhhhh," he hissed, his voice serious but his eyes mocking and light. "Don't want anyone thinking this poor man is doing anything other than having a lonely night swim."

"Are you sure we should—"

His mouth was on hers before she could finish her thought.

"You're not very good at taming a man down," he teased. She grinned. It wasn't *her* fault he was riled up like a racehorse and in no position to talk to anyone.

He ran his thumb over her lips. When he rested the pad of his finger on the middle of her mouth, she parted her lips and bit down gently on his nail.

"See?" he said, and she felt him shudder against her. "You bite your lip like you did, and it makes me want to bite it." He nibbled her lower lip. "And then kiss you." He pressed his lips to hers. "And then…" He lifted his hips to run the head of his cock down her bare stomach and pressed it in between her legs. "That man said he's not coming back to open the gate until seven. I hope they're all sound sleepers tonight."

The feel of him rubbing against her sent her legs opening again, her fingers diving into the curls at the nape of his neck. Could they really keep doing this? But it was too hard to think when the hostel was quiet again and Blake so close she could feel his heart beating in his chest. She wrapped her arms around his waist and drew him toward her, right back where they'd left off.

"I'll try to be quiet," she whispered, running a hand over his chest.

"I hope not too quiet." His voice caught and she grinned at how she could make him lose it with nothing more than a few words and a slight shift in the pressure of her hips. His hand was at her neck, tugging at the knot holding her bathing suit up. This time he let it come all the way undone.

Julia arched back against the side of the pool as his mouth explored hers. The nervousness from their near-exposure was still there, but now a heady excitement coursed through her veins. If they were walked in on now, she wouldn't be able to get her top on fast enough. Blake wouldn't be able to shield her. She'd be completely compromised.

But no one here knew her, and she'd never have to see them again. The freedom made her heart pound and her blood sing. She dug her fingers deeper into Blake's hair.

She felt him tugging on her bikini bottoms, sliding them over her hips. She had a moment of sudden panic that this was real—she was really doing this, getting naked in a pool with this unbelievable stranger doing unbelievable things to her body—but she was too far gone to stop herself with ridiculous things like thinking.

Blake came up from her breasts to kiss her as he pulled her bottoms all the way down. He had one hand on his cock and was sliding it over her skin, up and down the lower part of her stomach and the crease where her thighs met the curls between her legs. She untied the back of her bathing suit, leaving herself completely exposed. The two pieces of her bikini floated up somewhere behind him. This was so, so not Julia.

And that was why she loved it.

She put her hand over Blake's and took over stroking him. "Hold up one second, tiger," he whispered in her ear, and she thought she'd done something wrong as he swam over to his towel and flip flops by the side of the pool. But then he heaved his top half up and pulled out—yes, that was definitely a condom in his wallet, tucked in his sandal.

"You certainly came prepared," she said as he waded back over to her. Did he just assume there'd always be a willing woman around?

"So you know, I've been tested about a billion times since my ex." Julia raised an eyebrow but didn't ask—no question from the way he said it that the ex had cheated on him. But now wasn't really the time to get into details. "And I've been safe every time since then."

Okay, another thing not to ask follow up questions about. *Every time?* How many times were there?

"I know I'm okay," she said, trying not to think of the vast disparity between their sexual experiences. She'd had unprotected sex for the eight years she'd spent infrequently lying under Danny, but they were each other's firsts. And unlike Blake with his ex, she knew she didn't have to worry about what Danny had been up to.

"But there are other things we can do, if you don't want to—"

She swam over to him, feeling his eyes searching her. Normally it made her incredibly uncomfortable to have anyone try to get too close, but maybe it was the fact that it was just one night with Blake that let her feel so at ease. When he cradled her head in his hands and pressed his lips to hers, the kiss was so soft she couldn't believe this was the same bad boy who'd been saying such things to her with that mouth. She opened her lips and sought his tongue with hers.

His fingers traveled down the length of her body, right where she wanted him to be. When he slid a finger inside her, she spread her legs wider for him, her hands on his shoulders guiding him in. He found her clit, tracing lightly until she couldn't stop herself from pressing down, rubbing against his hand. The feel of him on her thigh as she moved only heightened her desire.

Usually she felt like it took her forever to be ready, but Blake's slightest touch was driving her insane. There'd been so much build up since she first laid eyes on him across the room. She wanted him inside her, *now*.

"You're so wet." His tongue was hot against her ear, his hand moving fast as her hips coaxed him on.

"Because of you." At her words, he guided her toward the shallow end of the pool until her bare ass grazed the steps. He leaned her back, pressing his body on top of her. Julia lifted her hips so she was out of the water, holding herself up with her hands on the edge of the highest step.

"Put me inside you," he whispered. The instructions sent another wave of liquid heat coursing through her. It was a good thing the water was lapping at her thighs or else she might burst into flames.

She wrapped her hand around his thick shaft, sliding the condom on. She was the one with her legs spread, the one completely naked while he still had his shorts grabbing his tight ass. She was the one pressed against the edge of the pool, preparing for him to drive into her.

But she was the one in control.

She slid the tip of his cock up and down between her thighs, slick with desire and aching for him. She was dripping with water but her wetness was different, a slipperiness she could feel. He was bucking his hips now, trying not to rush but wanting nothing more than to be inside her. She knew she was driving him mad and she loved it. She pressed his head against her clit and rotated her hips to feel him rub against the sensitive spot.

"Now," he gasped, and without further teasing, she used her hand to guide him right where she wanted.

For a second, she couldn't move, she couldn't breathe, he was so big and it had been so long that she felt she was being split open all the way to her heart. She gasped, her hips rigid as he held himself over her, shoulders straining with his weight against the step.

"Are you okay?" he panted, and she could feel it was taking everything in him not to move. Not to start in on her until he was sure she could take it.

But as she got used to the feeling, she started arching her hips against him, beginning to move. She laughed a little, self-conscious but suddenly feeling like she needed to tell him. "It's been a long time."

"That's okay," he said, and again she was surprised by his sudden tenderness. He shifted his weight and brushed a strand of wet hair from her cheek. "We can go slow."

Julia shook her head emphatically. "No. Slow is definitely *not* what I want." She almost laughed again at the confused expression on his face. She wrapped her legs around him, grinding her hips up and down, setting the pace. The surprise from having him inside her was gone, and in its place, a need was building up deep inside her. "Take me," she whispered in his ear, trying to make herself sound as irresistible as possible and wondering if she could really pull it off.

"Are you sure?" Blake searched her eyes. She searched him back.

"Can I really ask for anything I want?" she said uncertainly, remembering what he'd said before she'd jumped in the pool. Before she'd gone and found herself completely undone.

"Absolutely." He wrapped his arms around her waist and pulled her closer, grazing her lower lip with his teeth.

"Then what I really want is for you to fuck me."

The taste of the words in her mouth was pure sex and she wondered how she'd ever stayed so quiet in the past. The spark in Blake's eyes was like she'd flicked a switch in him. A tremor shot through her. She had unleashed him, and there was no going back.

In one swift motion, he grabbed her arms and pinned her wrists to the lip that ran around the edge of the pool. She was splayed open to him, her nipples hard and aching, her hair caught in thick wet waves. She gasped.

And then he started rocking inside her.

She tried to press her arms back against his weight but he kept her pinned. The feeling of his body against hers was everything she'd ever wanted—covering her, taking her, claiming her as his. He wasn't holding back any more, his frenzied thrusts growing harder and surer every time he drove himself into her. His breath was ragged in her ear, low groans escaping every time she bucked her hips to meet him as he buried himself inside.

The feel of every inch of him was making her whimper, and he unclasped her trapped wrists to clamp a hand to her mouth.

"Quiet, darling," he whispered, but he punctuated his command with a deeper thrust so hot and heavy it made her cry into his palm. She bit down on his hand and then his fingers as he slid his hand across her mouth, delight and desire dancing over his face. She sucked on one finger, then two.

"Good girl," he murmured, but that made her buck her hips harder, her ass hitting the tiles so hard she knew it would leave a bruise. She didn't want to be good—not tonight. Not now, as the moonlight danced over the waves from their splashing.

She moaned into his mouth, her cries muffled by his deep, hard kiss.

"Julia," he groaned, and then whatever he was saying was caught in the frenzy of his breathing. She ran her nails along his back and through his hair, spreading her legs wide around him.

"Fuck me, Blake," she mouthed in his ear, keeping her voice low and just for him, knowing how much her asking for it had driven him insane. "Fuck me harder, Blake. Please."

See? She was still a good girl—she was polite even when she was begging for it.

His groan caught in his throat and then all of a sudden he was pulling out of her, leaving an emptiness she couldn't bear. But it was only to step out of his swim shorts, which by now had slid down his thighs and were getting in the way. He stood before her in the moonlight, cock standing straight up. Instinctively she lifted her hips to him, inviting him back in.

"Don't worry, darling, you'll get what you want," he said, watching her squirm before him in anticipation.

"I want you inside me."

"Right where I want to be."

Without hesitating he reached for her thighs, holding her legs up and spreading them wide. She had to hold on tight to the edge of the step to keep herself stable while he drove into her. The water flowed up over her legs in little waves.

"You're going to make me come like this," he growled, his hands on her hips to give him more leverage.

How could those words turn her on so much? But hearing him say it made her feel it like it was already happening, his heat streaming inside her as he completely let go. "I want you to," she gasped, gripping the edge of the step. She didn't just want to imagine the look that would cross his face when he released into her. She wanted to gaze up into his eyes and see the pleasure and total abandon and know it was because of her.

With one hand she balanced herself while he held her legs up and used her free hand to rub her clit as he moved inside her. Every touch was electric with pleasure. The pressure from his cock and her hand made Julia squeeze her legs around his waist as he gripped her tighter, his eyes fixated on her hand moving between her legs, the water rising up along her ass, her neck arched back in ecstasy.

"Touch yourself. Make yourself come," Blake panted as he thrust harder.

"Don't stop," she gasped, too swept up in the heat of the moment to be appalled by her command or by how forcibly she had—literally—taken her pleasure into her own hands.

"Not a chance," he said, and bucked even harder against her.

The orgasm tore through her, from her clit all the way up inside. She cried out, whimpering, trying to stay quiet but unable to hold it in, her legs tightening as she told him over and over again that she was coming for him. He gripped her thighs as she clenched and released in waves around his cock. And as she kept running her finger over her clit, drawing out the pleasure, he let go completely and released himself into her.

Head thrown back, lips parted, the muscles in his arms and chest defined in the moonlight as he held her legs up— she had never seen anything as beautiful as Blake's face when he came.

When his thrusts began to slow she eased up on her clit, the two of them moving languidly together, breathing hard, making it last as long as possible before their senses returned and they were two strangers again, whose paths happened to cross in the night.

He slid out of her but didn't let go. Her arms and legs trembled from the force of her orgasm, but he held her up now so that she didn't have to. Then he took the condom off and stepped out of the pool to throw it in the trash can in the garden. He jumped back in with a splash, and they swam to meet each other, feeling the cool water on their heated bodies as they dunked under and came up for air.

Julia didn't have much left in her after what they'd just done, but when he embraced her bobbing in the water, she kissed him with everything she did have to give. His arms around her were strong as he kissed her back.

They stayed like that for a long time in the water, silent together. Eventually they found their stray bathing suits floating down in the deep end and slid them back on. Blake swam over to where she was tying up her top and knotted the strings around her neck.

"Happy birthday," he whispered, kissing her cheek.

Julia laughed. "Maybe thirty's not so bad."

What did one do after an explosion like that, when they were never going to see each other again? He was smiling this sweet, sloppy, satisfied grin she'd yet to see plastered on his face, so she figured it was okay for her to wrap her arms around him again. It would all be over so soon. She wanted to savor the feel of him before she let go.

He nuzzled into her neck, grazing his lips against her skin. She kissed him, slow and soft and deep. "You don't regret doing this, do you?" he asked, pulling away to peer at her as though trying to read the expression on her face.

"I'll tell you when the feeling returns to my legs."

"Just checking," he said, kissing her again, but she assured him he didn't need to.

Regrets? There was no way. She'd never done anything like this and that was totally the point. It felt amazing not being Julia Evans for a night. She couldn't believe she'd tried to run away from this. What would have happened if Blake hadn't been in the pool when she walked out and she'd never gotten to experience the feel of him moving with her?

For all she knew, Blake did things like this all the time. But it was different for her. It was something she would remember for the rest of her life.

In the doorway to the lobby, he pressed her up against the wall where he had been standing when she first laid eyes on him. Just like she had imagined.

His tongue searched hers insistently, claiming her one last time.

She could still feel the heat where he had taken her in the pool. There was no doubt about whom she belonged to for those final hours of the night.

"I guess this is goodnight," she whispered reluctantly, carrying her sandals so as not to make noise when she crept back into her room, everyone else long asleep. "I hope you're able to catch a few hours of sleep." *Before your bus*, she wanted to add, but didn't.

"Goodnight, darling," he murmured, holding her chin to lift her lips to his once again. "Something tells me I'm not going to have any more trouble sleeping tonight."

"I'll see you," she said softly, knowing that she wouldn't. He was leaving for Buenos Aires in the morning, and if the thought sent a pang shooting straight through her heart, she just had to remind herself that the fleetingness of their encounter was the reason it had happened at all.

"I'll see you," he promised, and as she slipped down the darkened hallway, she appreciated the lie.

Chapter Five

Blake had every intention of getting up early and going to the bus station. He was packed. He'd paid for his stay at the hostel. He should have been ready to go.

But when then sun came up and spread its warm fingers over the garden, he lingered in bed a little longer as Jamie and the other guys in the room got ready for the day.

He told himself he was just tired from the late night before. But thinking about why he'd been up so late made him think about Julia and the miracle of her soft, lithe body writhing against his, and he had to roll over before anyone in the communal room saw the tent pitched halfway down his sheets.

It would be shitty to sneak out without at least saying good-bye. And there were more busses during the day. He might as well start the day off with breakfast. It wouldn't hurt to see her one last time.

When the room cleared, he rolled out of bed and pulled

on a gray T-shirt and a pair of navy cargo shorts. He ran his fingers through his hair, trying to tame his curls, and slid his feet into his comfortable leather sandals. He didn't bother shaving, but that was to save time while he grabbed a quick breakfast before the bus—not because he was eager to see if Julia was awake. Or because he happened to know that a bit of light stubble around his jawline had never hurt him when it came to women.

It was a brilliant day, the kind of clear blue promise he had come to associate with southern Brazil. Outside he scanned the tables by the pool, glad to see Chris and Jamie weren't out yet. He only wanted to talk to one person there.

She was sitting on the far end of the patio at a table by herself, and she hadn't seen him yet. On her table was a bowl of granola with yogurt and fruit and a steaming mug of coffee. Her long hair rustled in the breeze as she looked down, intent on a book. She certainly didn't look like someone who'd been up half the night. He figured she was used to being an early riser, even during her holiday.

Blake took advantage of Julia's oblivion to watch her. She was even more beautiful in the morning light, wearing a pale blue sundress that showed off her long arms and legs. To anyone else she might be another pretty face, but he knew what was so ravishing about her—and it wasn't only that gorgeous just-fucked glow radiating off her skin. She looked absorbed by what she was doing, attentive and fully alive. He remembered how she had been so present with him and he wanted her again, right then and there.

But he had to calm himself. They no longer had the whole garden to themselves.

Chris and Jamie came out, carrying mugs of coffee and a basket of toast with jam. He felt a flash of possessiveness rise in him as Lukas ambled out after them. The one unattached guy at the hostel who *wasn't* taking off that morning had better not get any ideas about talking to the woman sitting by herself.

Thankfully Lukas made a beeline over to Chris. But before the rest of the group could move to join Julia or invite her to a larger table, Blake strode over to the empty seat across from her. She was turning the page and reaching for the mug of coffee when she caught sight of him coming her way. She looked startled, then quickly smothered her surprise with an unreadable face he already felt like he knew. She'd said she didn't regret what they'd done together, but did she still feel that way in the morning?

Then she smiled and he had a sudden panic that sticking around to see her again had been a mistake. He should have cut loose while he could. She'd been holding back in the cab, but now she might think there were feelings involved or expect something from him today. He couldn't stand the thought of dealing with her disappointment.

But instead he saw her eyes flick over from him to the pool. He couldn't help it—he was looking that way, too. When he looked at her again, she blushed a bright crimson that made him recall the feel of her lips upon his. She cast her eyes down in a gesture reminiscent of her stance by the front desk when he'd first caught her staring, and once again her sudden nervousness awakened an appetite in him. He was afraid things were going to be awkward, but that inviting look at the pool was anything but. He had to admit it—her bashful teasing got under his skin. That mix of innocence and naughtiness made him want to find out just how far she'd go.

"Excuse me, is this seat taken?" he asked with a wink, resting his hand on the back of the chair. In her eyes he could see a lightness dancing, a quick happiness that he hoped had something to do with him—before he reminded himself that it didn't matter because after breakfast he'd be gone.

She slid a bookmark into her book and closed the cover,

motioning for him to sit down. "I didn't expect to see you this morning," she said as he took a seat.

There she was—blunt and practical even with that coy, teasing look in her eye. Blake tried to shrug like it was nothing. "Can't start the day on an empty stomach."

She flashed him a lopsided grin but was kind enough not to call him out for not catching his early bus. "Have you eaten?"

"Not yet."

"Care to join me?"

"Sure," he said, like it wasn't obvious that was exactly what he wanted. Like she was the one doing him a favor by letting him say hello the next morning, and not the other way around.

Her dark hair was striking against her skin. The dress had thin straps over her shoulders that brought him back to the pool and the string of her bikini—and what he knew was hidden underneath. It took everything in him to sit there with his hands to himself when he wanted nothing more than to graze his lips across her bare shoulders and whisper her name in her ear.

He ordered scrambled eggs, toast, and fresh pineapple juice, plus more coffee for both of them. When André left to put in the order, Blake leaned in close.

"Still no regrets?" he asked, keeping his voice low so no one could hear and glancing over at the pool so she'd know he was still thinking about their night, too.

The heat in her face mirrored his own. "It would be hard to regret a night like that."

"That's just what I was thinking."

André came over with a fresh pot of coffee and the juice. Blake leaned back again, casually. As though they hadn't spent half the night fucking mere steps from where everyone now lounged around eating toast and gossiping. Julia suppressed a giggle as André filled their mugs, and Blake had to try to keep from laughing, too.

"I guess we should try to compose ourselves," he teased when André left. But even when Julia tried—and failed—to stop smiling, her eyes gave everything away.

"Wouldn't want to get in trouble with the management," she said.

Blake threw up his hands. "Well if they'd only let us into each other's rooms—"

"We wouldn't have to go defiling public property," she finished his thought.

"So really, it's everyone else's fault."

"Then I'll be sure to thank them all personally." Julia raised an eyebrow at him as she ate a spoonful of granola.

"Don't get too close," Blake said. "I'm not willing to share."

"Oh, so it's like that now?"

"Maybe," Blake squirmed, not wanting to be called out as the jealous one when he'd started off so clear on where things stood.

"I see how it is," Julia said, but her eyes were light, and he knew she was joking.

"Why on earth don't you have any juice this morning?" Blake asked suddenly, changing the subject before he had to dig himself out of that hole.

Julia made a face. "I'm not really a juice person. Just coffee, black."

"Trust me, you've got to try this." He passed the tall glass of pineapple juice across the table.

"Really, no thanks."

"This is not your mom's Tropicana. One sip, you'll be in heaven."

"I think I've already been there," she smirked, but she reached for the glass. Her eyes widened as the liquid passed up the straw and hit her tongue.

"See?" Blake said, satisfied that he'd been right.

"That. Is. Amazing," she said as she passed the glass back.

"Would I steer you wrong?"

She shook her head.

"Here, we can share." He set the glass in the middle of the table. "I credit myself with exposing you to yet another fabulous aspect of this country."

"What, amazing fruit and Australian men?"

He held up a finger in warning. "Man. Just one." The thought of her going to bed with anyone else while she was in Brazil sent a stabbing pain through his guts. He didn't know anything about her life in Chicago, but he knew that he wanted to be the best thing she remembered from her trip.

She laughed and reached for another sip. "Okay, amazing fruit and *an* amazing man. Better?"

"Yeah, as long as we're talking about me."

"I don't know yet. I'll have to wait until the week's up and I see what the competition is like."

He grabbed her wrist as she put the glass down, then softly traced the pad of his thumb along the tender skin of her forearm. "No competition," he whispered.

"Trust me." She shifted forward. "I don't beg like that for just anyone."

When André arrived with Blake's breakfast, their arms were locked together over the table. They pulled back suddenly, Julia obviously flushed to have been caught touching, Blake equally surprised to find himself acting so intimately so fast.

To scale it back, he asked what she'd been reading as he added salt and pepper to his eggs.

"That?" She looked toward the paperback she'd set on the ground. "Oh, it's nothing. About curriculum development and a new program for teaching algebra."

"A little light beach reading?" He thought of himself as a voracious reader, but taking a break from writing had also turned into a break from books, movies, television...a break from pretty much all of his life. Except maybe for women and sunshine. Those he seemed to have in more doses than he ever could have imagined.

"It's nice to have some time to read. Normally I'm so busy I only get to a few pages each night before I fall asleep."

"Yeah, I can see why that would conk you out."

"It's an interesting book!" She put her hand on the cover protectively.

"I'm not saying it isn't."

"Tell me about you. What do you do?" she suddenly asked.

Shit. That question. *See?* he told himself. *This is why you should have gotten up and left this morning like you planned. No more contact, no more questions.*

No more seeing Julia brush the hair out of her eyes as she crossed and uncrossed her legs under the table. No sharing drinks with her, transfixed by her lips on the straw, imagining he could taste her through the sweetness of the juice. No opportunity to picture her lying in bed at home with a book in her lap and then turning out the light...

He shook the image from his mind. Falling asleep together, waking up together—those were things he didn't do. Not since Kelley, and never again. At least not for a damn long time.

"A little of this, a little of that." He grinned absently.

Julia crossed her arms. "That's no answer."

"I'm in television."

"Acting? Production?" she prodded.

"I'm a writer," he said reluctantly, hoping that would be an end to the questions.

But of course it wasn't.

"Anything I would know?" she asked.

"Not unless you're up on your Australian networks."

"Unfortunately I'm a little behind."

He shook his head. Not unfortunately—it was good for him that she had no idea. "I work on a show. Nothing major."

She narrowed her eyes at him. "You get this funny frown when you're lying."

Blake roared with laughter, so loud he could see Chris and Jamie turn and look at him, no doubt wondering what was going on since—as far as they knew—he and Julia had gone their separate ways last night without speaking. "I'm not lying!" he protested.

"See? Frowning. Lying again."

He composed his face, trying to force his mouth into a smile. "Totally. Not. Lying."

"Lying like when you said you were taking the bus this morning," she teased. "So from your non-answer, should I assume that you're ridiculously famous, or that you work on something so embarrassing you'd die if I knew?"

Blake shook his head, his mind racing to come up with an answer. She was sharp and witty, and he couldn't keep up. Suddenly her eyes widened.

"Shit, that's why—" She realized they were being loud enough to draw the attention of the other tables and dropped her voice to a whisper, leaning forward over their half-eaten plates. "That's why you were so amazing last night."

"Because I'm a writer?" Blake was glad to be called amazing, but he wasn't sure where she was going with this.

"You're in porn."

Blake nearly choked on his eggs.

"C'mon it's okay, you can admit it. We hardly know each other. I promise not to give you a hard time."

"I'm not—" he took a long sip of juice to clear his windpipe. "In porn." He swallowed and tried again. "I'm not in porn."

Julia raised an eyebrow skeptically. "Hot Australian TV 'writer,'" she put the word in air quotes, "is total dynamite and won't tell me what he writes?"

Did she just call him hot *and* dynamite? Blake couldn't keep from grinning.

"As much as I would love for you to go around thinking I'm some stud writer, I actually write and produce a historical drama series called *The Everlastings*. You can, I don't know, Google it or whatever. Except don't," he added quickly. "It's kind of boring."

"There. That wasn't so hard, was it?"

"Why do you believe me now?"

"No frowns, no lies." She sat back in her chair with a smug little smile.

"On the other hand, maybe I *should* be a porn writer," he mused, leaning in close.

"Why's that?"

"Just think of the material I could test out on you."

There, he had it again. That blush. He grinned, satisfied. He was back in charge, even if he knew he wouldn't hold onto the reins for long—at least not while he stuck around to see what she'd surprise him with next.

He didn't have to wait long.

"So, Blake, are you coming?" Chris strode over to their table, fanning herself with a wide-brimmed sun hat. "Catching the first bus out—isn't that what you said?"

"I slept in—no real plans, you know how it is." Blake mentally begged her to keep his cover, but Chris had a big mouth and no reason to protect him.

"You, with no plans? You're the most scheduled Aussie I've ever met!" She turned toward Julia. "I mean, have you ever seen anyone like him? He's got all the timetables and the map planned out like if he quits moving for a single day the world will stop turning or something."

Julia laughed uncomfortably. "Um, I didn't know," she said, and Blake felt a funny pang at realizing how much more Chris knew about him, even though he and Julia had shared something so intimate. He willed Chris to put the pieces together. And then go away.

"Having a good time so far?" Chris asked, still fanning herself, and Blake realized from her smirk that she'd definitely heard Julia sneak out last night.

"It's been nice," Julia said slowly. Blake tried not to snort into his pineapple juice. "Nice" was putting it mildly.

"Well, if you're sticking around, a bunch of us are heading over to the Argentine side of the falls. Blake's already been, but they're beautiful, and we thought if we got a car together it'd be plenty cheap and easier than figuring out the bus."

"That'd be great," Julia said, not even looking at Blake to see what his plans were. He had no idea what to think. Did she want him to be on his way?

"You're invited, too, Blake," Chris said. "But I figured you wouldn't be coming?"

Blake shrugged slowly, trying to appear casual without answering the implied question she was asking. "Well, I don't really—"

"Yeah, I thought you had plans." Blake looked up to meet Julia's eyes and saw that she was laughing, teasing him now that he was irrefutably caught changing his schedule to spend time with her. It wasn't the laugh of someone looking to be rid of him, though.

He threw up his palms. "What can I say? I'm on vacation. Plans change." Chris tousled his hair like he was her little brother—despite the fact that he was twice her size—and went to collect everyone who'd be going with them. He and Julia quickly finished their breakfast together, trying to stop looking at each other the whole time. It was hard to get ready to go when they kept grinning like that.

"Last night," he whispered in her ear before she could slide into her room to pick up her things for the day trip.

"Yes?" Julia asked, spinning around at his sudden touch. He'd been trying to be good at breakfast—just friend stuff, no touching, even if the flirting drove him mad—but he couldn't help brushing the small of her back with his palm. The dress was cut low and then tied at the top, exposing all that skin.

"When I said I would see you later." He looked in her eyes. "Was I lying?"

Julia pressed her lips together, then smiled. She rested a hand on his chest and he felt his blood leap at her touch. She shook her head.

"There was no frown."

"Then I guess it's a good thing I'm here."

He brushed her lips with his before leaving to get his wallet, passport, water bottle, and camera. They met back outside with the rest of the crew. Blake took a step closer to Julia when he saw her waving to Lukas. God, what was wrong with him? Changing his plans, postponing Argentina, revisiting a part of the waterfalls he'd already seen, staking out his territory against the other young and single male—he had to remember this was just another one-night stand.

Or maybe two nights. Tops.

This time they called a van to fit everyone. Blake squeezed into the back after Julia. As the driver took off, she idly rested her hand across his knee while she looked out the window, taking in her first sights of the town by day.

The border was porous here, and it was an easy crossing, tourists constantly coming and going to see the waterfalls that stretched from either side. Waiting in line to cross through, they pulled out their passports. Blake grabbed Julia's before she could protest.

"Julia Allyson Evans," he read. "Nice."

She snorted. "Checking out my address?"

"Nah, Chicago streets mean nothing to me. Here we go." He evaluated her picture. Her hair was pulled back, like maybe she'd come from the gym. She wasn't smiling.

"I like your hair better down," he declared, brushing the long strands over her bare shoulder.

"Noted," she said. "Although to be fair, post-yoga isn't exactly my finest."

"Nope, still beautiful," he whispered in her ear, sure no one could hear him over the hum of the motor and the samba-reggae the driver was blasting.

"But the hair is up," she protested.

"I didn't say it wasn't beautiful," he clarified. "Just that I like it down best. It's like having to choose your favorite ice cream flavor. They're all good. In fact, if you could have them all on one giant cone all at once, you would." She laughed. "But if you have to pick, then you choose something chocolatey with lots of chunky bits of everything in it. And Julia with her hair down."

"So I'm a chocolate chunky bit?" She frowned.

"Exactly."

She grabbed his passport out of his hand.

"Hey, I didn't say this goes both ways!" he cried, but she had already found his picture, too.

She burst out laughing so loudly that the whole row in front of them turned around to see what was going on.

"You have no hair!" she exclaimed.

"Let me see that," Chris demanded. She was sitting directly in front of Julia and the passport was passed over before Blake could stop them.

"Come on, not fair."

"Blake, you didn't tell us you had a buzz cut," Chris said, passing the photo to Jamie beside her.

"I cut it off right before leaving. Thankfully it's grown back."

"Somehow we all missed that stage," Chris said, snatching the picture from Jamie and passing it up to Lukas. "How'd you keep the cameras off of you then?"

Blake cringed. "Solitary confinement," he shot back. Of course Chris and Jamie had known who he was—they lived in Melbourne, not under a rock. Blake had been nervous when he first heard Aussie accents coming into the hostel, and then pleasantly relieved to find out that they were happy to treat him like a normal person and not like the current celebrity gossip course, laid out on a platter for everyone to feast. Obviously they knew about Kelley and Liam, too, but they'd been good about keeping things discreet. It was pretty clear, knowing what the tabloids had said, that he was there to get away.

He willed them to hold on to some of that discretion now. The last thing he needed was for Julia to be curious about why there'd be cameras around and start fishing for more. He tried to change the subject—look at the roadside vendors lined up on the side of the street!—but it was no use. Julia shifted in the cramped space to face him.

"You're actually famous in Australia?" she said, loud enough for everyone to hear.

Blake's stomach clenched. Chris and Jamie had no idea how much he wanted Julia to see him as a regular person and not pursue—or avoid—him because of who he was back home. Nor could they guess how desperately he was trying to hide his humiliation at the hands of his ex. It was just his luck that the two of them burst out laughing as the van inched forward in the line.

"Famous?" Jamie said, shaking his head. "Everyone who

owns a television knows who he is."

Julia's eyes widened. "And you're just hanging out in Brazil at some hostel with the rest of us?"

Blake's mind was racing, trying to find a way out. But the only way to play this was to stay cool. "What can I say?" he said with a shrug. "I'm just a regular bloke."

"Who decided to shave his head and come to South America."

"I started in Central, but yeah."

"Because...?" Julia started, and Blake caught Chris and Jamie exchanging glances he hoped Julia didn't see.

"Because why not?" Blake said carefully, and at last a border official stepped up to the side of the van to stamp their passports, saving him from further embarrassment.

But it wasn't over, because Chris turned around to face them. "Seriously, all you foreigners should get your hands on a copy of *The Everlastings*. No one is doing drama in Oz like this guy."

"He told me it was boring," Julia said, talking about Blake like he wasn't even there.

Chris shook her head. "He's being modest. You should know not to take anything he says too seriously."

"I'll remember that," Julia said, and Blake looked at her in alarm.

"Tell me there's more coming," Jamie said. "You're going back for the next season, aren't you? You can't leave Anderson to untangle the storyline with Celia and Reese—it's just not possible."

Anderson was the writer under Blake, the guy he'd hired when they were signed for a third season and things got too crazy for Blake to handle by himself. Now they were between shootings, and he was supposed to be drumming up scripts for the next two seasons they'd signed for and going through all the scenarios the writers under him were working on.

But instead he was here, in the back of a cramped van, edging past the border into Argentina and then bouncing through the countryside, full of eggs and toast and coffee and juice and the warm touch of a smart, funny, beautiful American by his side.

It was agony to sit there listening to talk about the show and all he'd left behind. But there were worse places to be.

And worse ways to be reminded of Kelley and Liam and the mess he still had to sort out with them on and off the screen. In retrospect, maybe it wasn't the best idea to cast his girlfriend as Celia and his best friend as Reese and make a slow and steady attraction build between them over each episode. By this point, the characters were so enmeshed in the storyline that he couldn't cut one or both of them out. Much as he wanted to.

Chris, though, was shooting daggers at her boyfriend. Jamie looked like he wanted to eat his shoe for letting slip his curiosity about Celia and her love interest, Reese. It wasn't Jamie's fault, though. Blake was going to have to learn how to deal with Kelley and Liam professionally, at least while she and her new boyfriend were both on the show. If he could get used to talking about the characters, then maybe he'd finally be able to face going back.

"Don't worry," he reassured Jamie—both about the plotline and about the slip he'd made in bringing up Kelley and Liam's characters. "I've still got some tricks up my sleeve."

Jamie hit the back of the seat in eagerness as the van pulled up to the entrance. "I knew it! We'll definitely be home for the premier."

"We will?" Chris turned to face him, but whatever they were disagreeing about now was lost in the murmur of their voice and the diesel cough of the van lurching ahead.

I wonder if I will, Blake thought, counting up how long he could spend traveling before his real life beckoned him back.

Julia had been silent throughout the exchange about the show, looking out the window even though Blake knew she was taking in the whole thing.

"Right, you're just a regular guy who breaks his schedule to go to a tourist site he's already seen," she whispered as everyone shuffled out of the van, counting up bills for the driver.

He tried not to flush. He could plan and plan forever, mapping a route, typing a schedule, sketching his future like he was diagramming a scene, everyone blocked in the right place, each action a link in a clear and obvious chain of cause and effect.

But then life happened, and so did people with their messy surprises. It used to feel like each new surprise was a dagger to the heart. Until there was brush on his shoulder, long hair lifting in the breeze, and now none of his plans seemed clear.

"Sure," he said with a grin. "Why not?"

"So you really wanted to come back to the falls today?" She was looking at him skeptically, like she was trying to read him but not sure what she'd found.

He grabbed her hand. "Come on," he said, helping her out of the van. "Aren't there some times you have to say yes?"

Chapter Six

Julia could hear the falls long before she could see them. A roaring, pulsing hiss that swelled like the ocean but without the pause between waves. It was so loud it seemed alive, an animal threading its way out of the jungle to devour them whole. There was nothing for them to do but walk into its grasp, mesmerized by the power it held.

They started off in a dense green forest, deafened by the cicadas chirping in the thick, humid air. The path followed along a snaking river, and they could hear the noise swelling up ahead but still had no sense of what was to come. The current below was swift but beside them the water ran flat and calm. The landscape held onto its secrets until the last possible moment, when suddenly the path opened up and the river dropped away.

Coming upon the break in the stream, it looked like a vortex had suddenly appeared out of nowhere, a hole in the water where everything that once seemed certain plummeted away. They were on top of the world, looking down on the waterfall as it dropped over the edge.

Julia stepped back, feeling the rush to her head.

"Whoa there," Blake exhaled, steadying her with his palm on her back. "I didn't think to ask—are you afraid of heights?"

Julia shook her head. "I never thought so. I just—" She looked up at him, searching for the words, but all she could say was, "Wow."

"I know," he agreed, and it was nice to know there was no need to try to put into words what both of them were thinking.

"Doesn't it make you want to jump?" she blurted out suddenly.

"What?" Blake turned to her in alarm.

"Not like that," she clarified. "It's just... If you could fall and fall forever, and never land." If you could feel the thrill of release, the water and wind, the never-ending weightlessness as every last responsibility disappeared.

She would never do it, of course. She wasn't a daredevil—she barely even rode her bike fast. But to stand there with her feet firmly on land and think about the possibilities made her mind spin.

"All that freedom," Blake said almost to himself as he looked out over the falls, and Julia knew that somewhere inside him, he understood what she meant. "It certainly is tempting."

She couldn't help it. She slipped her hand in his and squeezed his fingers tight. If she'd ever said that to Danny, he would have freaked, thinking she was being morbid or depressed or any of the "bad" states they were forever keeping an eye out for in Liz.

But Blake was different. He could travel and dream and imagine other things. Julia wasn't a writer—she dealt with the elegance of numbers and the way they flowed according to a series of rules, not unlike each drop of water on its path toward the sea. But there was a poetry to the numbers that she could get lost in, when she was able to let herself go. She imagined Blake felt the same about words.

Julia was conscious of not wanting to broadcast some kind of "togetherness" when they weren't a couple *at all*, but the beauty and surprise had made her reach for him without thinking. She felt a buzzing inside her that had nothing to do with the current rushing past or the thrill of gravity when he squeezed her hand and didn't let go.

She could have spent hours standing in that one spot, but there was so much more to see and the rest of the group was moving ahead. They kept walking as the vortex opened into a mouth and the mouth yawned into a canyon.

Below was nothing but blinding, obliterating spray, a thick blanket of white streaked with an enormous rainbow arcing across the falls. It hovered in the mist as the water surged over the edge of the canyon and battered the rocks below. Blake wrapped an arm around her waist and pulled her in front of him as a group of Japanese tourists shuffled past.

"Devil's Throat," he said in her ear, nibbling her own throat playfully. He was close but still had to shout to be heard over the deafening roar.

"What a view." She was completely captivated by the sight.

"I'll say," he sighed, but he wasn't looking at the falls. He'd taken the chance to rest his chin on her shoulder, trying to sneak a peek down her dress. She wriggled playfully out of his grasp and he laughed, catching up to where she was walking down the path to get close to the edge.

"You've already been here," she said, and suddenly she felt disappointed that she was the only one of them experiencing something so incredible for the first time. She'd thought the same thing last night, that this was all old news to him. It wasn't special for him anymore. She was embarrassed about what she'd said about falling. Now he'd think she was twisted or weird.

But he surprised her by shaking his head. "I don't think this is the kind of place you could ever get tired of." And looking out at the view, it was true. She didn't think it was possible to take it all in, no matter how many times you came. "Besides," he added, "I was here on a morning when the rest of them slept in. The company is better this time."

She couldn't help smiling as she slid her hand in his again. Maybe there was something to the view, or to her—or both— that was worth a second look. Maybe she could let the day happen without worrying about where it went.

The whole stretch of the river had two hundred and seventy-five separate waterfalls, and she could see the smaller cascades cutting through the endless green. When she closed her eyes and felt the spray in the air as it hung in the muggy December heat, heard the drum beat of the falls pounding relentlessly in her ears, she tried to imagine the landscape without any people around, just water rushing through time. When she looked down at all the falls from their perch at the top of the tallest, widest part, the water seemed timeless, almost solid. A whole mass constantly churning.

But if she squinted and focused and let her eyes shift, she could almost make out the individual drops in flight. She'd follow one as it hurtled down until she could no longer see it anymore, and then start back up at the top. There was green moss growing on the shiny rock edges, constantly battered by the water. Its whole purpose was to take a beating, to lend color to the impressive sight.

"Doesn't it make you feel small?" Blake asked, breaking the silence as they gazed at the surf.

Julia nodded, smiling to herself. It was exactly what she'd been thinking, too. Small and insignificant, but also desperately, wondrously alive.

It was hard to remember that they were still in the world. Streams of tourists buzzed around them, the rise and fall of voices and snap of cameras and phones adding its own cacophony to the sound of the surge. Blake lifted her hand to his lips and kissed her knuckles.

"Should we catch up to them?" Julia asked. Blake looked ahead to where Chris and Jamie were taking pictures against a railing overlooking the edge of the falls. Jamie waved for them to come over and Blake sighed.

"I guess so," he said, and they weaved their way through the crowds until they rejoined everyone else, busy taking photographs and marveling at the sights. Lukas, laden with camera bags, kept switching lenses as he tried to capture the perfect shot.

"So you guys want to walk around?" Jamie was asking as they walked up.

"I want to get on that river," Chris said.

"Your wish is my command," Lukas declared as he produced a brochure from his back pocket.

Chris squealed in astonishment as she flipped through. "Boat tours! Come on, Jamie, let's do this." She passed the brochure to him.

"Are you sure you want to—"

"They give you ponchos and you go right up under the fall," Lukas interrupted.

"Awesome," Chris exhaled, her eyes shining with excitement. "You want to do it?"

"I'm game if you are," Lukas said with a grin. "I have to keep my equipment dry, but can you imagine the shots?"

"So it's settled!" Chris said.

Blake looked over at Julia, and she shrugged. A boat tour sounded fine to her, and she was happy doing whatever everyone else wanted to do.

But Blake leaned over and whispered in her ear, his voice drowned out by the roar of the falls, "If you'd rather…"

She knew exactly what he was saying. His arm was around her in a gesture that seemed not only affectionate but possessive, and she moved closer to feel the heat of his body against her bare skin. She didn't have to say anything—just a blush she couldn't control, and then the slightest nod.

When Blake looked in her eyes, it was like they didn't need to speak to know what the other was thinking. If she was going to get one more day before her fantasy ended, why shouldn't she take advantage of all that she could?

"The boat ride is great," Blake said to everyone. "You guys should definitely do it. I've already been on one, though, so I think Julia and I will go for a hike. But if you haven't done it, you should. Getting up under the falls is terrific."

"Terrifically terrifying?" Jamie asked with a queasy grin.

"You'll be fine!" Blake clapped him on the back. "Chris will protect you."

"Unless I push you overboard." She stuck out her tongue.

"Not if I get to you first."

Chris laughed. Jamie was such a nice guy that nothing he said could sound mean. They had the kind of relationship where they joked about everything, Julia realized. She wondered if that ever made it hard to know when one of them was being serious.

"You're sure you don't want to come, Julia?" Chris asked, eyeing both of them like she was perfectly capable of taking the hint but simply chose not to.

"I get horribly seasick," Julia said quickly, the lie popping effortlessly out. She loved boats and had plenty of experience sailing on Lake Michigan. But time alone with Blake sounded much more appealing. Somehow she was certain that no matter where they were along the endless stretch of cascades, the view would still be spectacular. Not to mention the time together.

She didn't care today if everyone else at the hostel knew what was going on between them—she was never going to see them again. And wasn't that the whole point? She was a completely different person out here, assured that none of her actions would follow her back to her real life.

"I guess that's not a good idea then," Chris said reluctantly, as though sad for Julia that she'd be missing out. Julia smiled like it was a real shame but reassured everyone that she was fine with staying on land. For a second she was afraid that Jamie would elect to join them and their whole escape plan would be ruined, but at the end of the day he wasn't going to take off without Chris.

It took a little bit of acting from both her and Blake to convince everyone that it was fine to leave them behind. By the time they were heading off on their own, they were buckled over laughing at the performance that had gotten them away.

"You really get seasick?" he asked, concerned.

Julia laughed and shook her head. "Could you think of anything else that would have convinced Chris not to drag me on that boat?"

"Quick thinking," he said. "Poor Jamie should have thought of that first. You're sure you don't want to go?"

Julia might have surprised herself by not waiting for him to make the first move, but she already knew that this Julia, the one who bought tickets to Brazil and traveled by herself and climbed out of bed to fuck gorgeous Australians in a pool was hardly shy about getting her way. She pressed him back against the railing and kissed him as the water from the thundering falls coated them in mist.

"Pretty sure," she said, pulling away. But his hands clasped her arms tightly, holding her close, preventing her from stepping back. His kiss was rough and fierce and made her feel like she was hurtling over the edge of the cliff, nothing but spray and water and the sweet, terrifying fall.

For a moment, lost in his touch, she knew how it felt to not worry about the crash.

But there were too many people around. Kids ran screaming as parents snapped pictures and groups pressed in heated throngs against the railings over the falls.

"Come on, let's get away from here," Blake said in her ear. "Some place quiet. I want you alone."

Julia felt a shudder rise up her body and pulse between her legs. How could one little word do this to her? *Alone* certainly sounded different when it was just her on a plane, on a bus, heading for the unknown. Alone with Blake was turning out to be an entirely different story.

He took her hand and led her away from the masses at the top of the falls, following a trail that snaked away from the impressive *Garganta do Diablo*, the Devil's Throat, and pushed toward the hundreds of smaller waterfalls tumbling over the cliffs.

As soon as they were away from the center the crowds started to thin. The path began winding downhill, cutting under the cliffs to the water below. The shade from the trees offered relief from the beating sun, and they stopped to enjoy the newfound quiet. Julia took a drink from Blake's water bottle and after she handed it back to him she could only watch, transfixed, as he tilted his head back and drank, Adam's apple moving with each glug. The stubble on his chin was blond and light brown, and she wanted to feel it against her cheek, her breasts. The thought rose from somewhere unbidden: the scratch of it against her thigh.

He caught her shameless appraisal and grinned. "Happy?" he asked, planting a kiss on her nose.

"This is better," she admitted, her hands resting on his chest. "Did you come down here before?"

"No, but doesn't it seem like there are all these trails that keep going?" Blake looked to where the path turned and disappeared.

"Let's find out." Julia bound ahead of him, delighted to have uncovered something he hadn't experienced before. When she turned off the paved, main path and crept into a smaller dirt opening, she finally slowed down. "What do you think is down here?" she asked as she peeked through the overgrown foliage.

"Looks like another path, but not one that's really used. Most people probably stick to the paved route."

"If they even come here. Do you see anyone else around?"

Blake flashed her a grin that could only be described as *naughty*. "Not a soul," he breathed, running a finger across her bare collarbone and hooking it around the strap to her dress.

She stood there, brazenly letting him caress her in the middle of the empty path. "Then I guess we should go exploring," she said pointedly, well aware of how different she sounded from the girl who'd been in the cab with him last night. He tugged on the front of her dress to snag the view that had eluded him before. Her cleavage rose and fell with her breath. Yes, it definitely seemed like he wanted to explore.

"Well, what are you waiting for?" He raised an eyebrow, and Julia turned and started down the dirt path, pushing the overgrown brush out of the way with her hands.

The paved route wound farther down to the river but the path stayed level. It hugged the edge of the cliff tightly, turning sharply in as the sun sent dappled streaks of light over the leaves. All of a sudden it came to an end, tangled in vines.

"That was disappointing," Julia said as she slowed to a stop. She'd been hoping for something exciting—another winding path, an unexplored part of the falls, something unique to discover. "I guess there's a reason some paths are more used than others." She turned to head back to the main, paved route down.

But Blake was busy pulling apart the vines, trying to peer through. "What do you think is through there?"

"Trees?"

"No wait, come here."

"You think the path continues?"

Julia peered through the opening he'd made. Blake stood behind her and pressed his body against hers. She could feel the muscles of his chest and stomach pressed against her back, his breath warm in the shadowy air rich with the smell of dirt and green and clear running water all around. She used her hands to open the vines more.

"Watch out for the rocks," she pointed, and carefully stepped through.

He was right—the path did continue, and although it was by no means cleared or well used, it wasn't impossible to walk along. She thought he was going to kiss her—to take her right then and there—but instead he grabbed her wrist and pulled her along, saying he wanted to see what was ahead.

She knew what he was looking for. After they'd passed through the opening they'd made, the sound of water had grown. And now it was unmistakable: the steady rush that said they were heading for one of the falls. Since hundreds of smaller waterfalls cascaded over these cliffs, it wasn't surprising that at some point a path cutting along the cliff would lead directly toward one.

It was around the next bend that the narrow path opened and Julia stopped dead in her tracks. The path probably used to be for tourists, but it had since been closed down and fallen into disrepair. With so many tourists visiting the falls, it was impossible to keep up a winding network of trails that got this close to the water. The trail ended in a flat, round opening where the ground was tamped down and mostly still cleared, bits of green struggling through the soil in nothing but shade.

Along one side of the path was the cliff wall, slick and damp and dark. The other side was open to the river below, but it wasn't really open at all. It was covered with a thick, undulating curtain, a constant stream of water cascading down. They were behind the waterfall, watching it from the inside. Compared to the water rushing through the Devil's

Throat, it was nothing, only six or eight feet wide. But still it rushed over them, surrounding them in the pulse of its incessant drive.

"This is beautiful," Julia exclaimed, her voice echoing against the cliff wall. It was almost like being in a cave, but with the light still hitting them through the sheet of water. A dilapidated wooden railing ran around part of the edge of the opening, the wood soggy and rotting with much of it long crumbled down. Green vines with broad, leafy fans snaked up over the edge, taking over the enclosure year by year.

"I can't believe we found this," Blake said.

"Do you think anyone is coming?" She peered back down the path.

"Not a chance. People go to the Devil's Throat, and then walk around the upper paths or take a boat ride like everyone else. I don't think they're coming down here."

"It's a shame to miss this." She couldn't get over the light dancing over her forearms, the glitter and pulse of the waterfall delicate and deadly at the same time. All that power from nothing but water accumulating into sheer force barreling down.

She could feel his eyes on her as she explored the area, running her fingers along the dirt wall of the cliff, the dark shiny rocks of the edge. Everything was rich and moist and vibrant to her touch. At the fence she felt the pieces of wet wood disintegrate in her hand from the spray that kissed her face more urgently the closer she got.

She extended her hand, as close as she dared to come to the edge. Maybe Blake was right and she was afraid of heights. All she knew was that she couldn't trust herself if temptation got too close.

The tips of her fingers grazed the sheet of water and she gasped. The cold slap was almost enough to force her hand down. Dangerous. Exhilarating. Water splashed her dress, coating her hair in a fine mist that cooled down the heat building within her whenever she caught Blake's hungry eyes.

She felt, rather than heard, his body sidling up behind her. He put his hand under the waterfall and ran his wet fingers across her mouth, kissing the spray that clung to her lashes and beaded on her lips. She collapsed against him, collapsed into him, like nothing was holding her up and nothing could keep her away. Her nipples strained through the thin material of her wet sundress, and she could feel his eyes taking in every curve she knew the clinging material hardly concealed.

When he pressed himself to her, she could feel how hard he was, pushing against the fly of his cargo shorts. She thought about how he had rubbed himself against her bathing suit in the pool and was amazed at how the slightest graze against her thigh threw her into such a frenzy. Melted her. Made her his.

"So here we are," he whispered in her ear, running a hand through her hair, down her back, brushing her ass under her dress that now felt so flimsy, like nothing on her skin.

"Mmm, so we are." She put her hands in his pockets and pulled his hips against hers to better feel that tantalizing bulge.

"We're under a waterfall. There's no one around. Our comrades won't be off the river for another hour at least. Whatever do you think we should do?"

"I guess I can think of a few things," she said sweetly, tracing lazy circles with her finger down his chest.

He grabbed her tighter. "Such as?"

She undid the button at the top of his shorts, not breaking eye contact with him. Watching him pant for her touch.

"Such as anything you had in mind."

But he wouldn't let her off that easily. "Tell me what you want," he breathed as he ran a thumb over her breasts, making her nipples stand up and take notice.

It was hard to know what to say to a request like that. The whole idea of saying what she wanted was totally foreign to Julia. It took so much to get herself to say something, like she was still afraid that even now, when they were both so obviously aroused, he might laugh or say she'd misunderstood or he wasn't interested and wished he'd taken that bus to Buenos Aires instead.

But of course that was ridiculous. She took a deep breath and made the words come out. "I want you," she admitted, shy to be put on the spot even though they'd already done it all before.

"You want me what?" he asked, feigning ignorance.

She rolled her eyes.

"Say it," he urged her. Soft and somehow sweet, despite what he was asking.

She chewed on the corner of her lip, trying to think of something good. She remembered what he'd said about how she shouldn't do that because it drew his attention to her mouth and then she knew what to say. "I want you to kiss me."

He brushed his lips softly against her cheek.

She shook her head. "On the mouth."

The touch of his lips to hers was light as a feather, a tickle and nothing more.

"Harder," she whispered, the word catching in her throat.

"What?" He cupped a hand to his ear. "The waterfall, I can't quite hear you."

"Harder," she begged louder, and it was such a strange thing to give commands at the same time that she was completely at his mercy.

She got her wish, though. He grabbed her around the waist and crushed his lips to hers. Immediately Julia opened her mouth, seeking his tongue before he had a chance to pull away. The kiss was so much sweeter, so much hotter, so much more enticing because of how she'd had to build to it.

She had always been well behaved, always done what she was told. She never rebelled against her parents or experimented in college or got in any kind of trouble. Liz had done enough for both of them, and it sort of lost its appeal. Julia was the one who picked up the pieces, not the one who fell apart.

She'd had one serious, significant relationship with the man who was her best friend's brother. They just kind of fell in together, more because they were both there with Liz during her hardest times than because they had any true spark. He'd been kind and sweet and safe.

Too safe.

Julia could take control in a classroom of rowdy teens but that wasn't the same as taking control now, flexing her tongue against Blake's, drawing his hand to her breast to feel the way her nipples responded to the heat radiating from him when they touched.

"What else do you want?" he whispered in her ear, rolling his fingers over the delicate curve of her breast.

"Touch me." Her voice was throaty, hoarse, thick with desire. Thick with the heady, forbidden thrill of asking for what she wanted. Of telling him her need.

Blake bent his forehead down so it was resting against hers, one hand slowly working under the fabric of her dress while the other gently slid the straps off her shoulders, one side and then the next.

"Where?" His voice was quiet, a breath in her ear.

"Everywhere," she exhaled, leaning into him. When she pressed her hips forward she felt him hard and wanting, pressing back. His hands grew bolder, firmer, grasping her around the neck as he kissed her, hard, everything he had kept pent up surging forth with the force of the river rushing around them.

"Like that?" he asked, drawing his lips from hers for a fraction of a breath.

But she could only whimper in response.

She slid her hand down the front of his shorts, reaching for his cock. Wanting the feel of him, solid and real. She couldn't believe how much just touching him through the fabric of his boxers could make such warmth build deep inside her. If he'd asked her right now what she wanted, she would no longer have hesitated with her reply.

"Why don't you find out how wet I am," she whispered, sliding her palm down his shorts. He let out a low moan as she wrapped her fist around his full cock and helped draw his boxers down.

"I can do that," he murmured, running his fingers under her dress, over her thighs, up to her hips, bunching up her dress as he crept north. At the ridge of her hips he stopped, a smile teasing across his face. "Is this what I think it is?" he asked.

She gave a flirty shrug. "Guess you'll have to see."

Slowly he lifted the bottom of her dress to reveal red lace panties hugging her hips. Julia had absolutely not planned to pack anything sexy—what would she need it for? They never got any use anyway. But at the last minute, when she'd been putting her new bikinis in her bag, she rooted through her dresser drawer and found them. It would be only for her, but sometimes it was nice to feel sexy, even if no one else knew. Maybe especially then.

Now, though, the secret was out. And she could see in Blake's eyes that he was more than happy to have discovered her surprise.

"Well goddamn," he said, eyeing her up and down. He ran his fingers over the thin strip of lace and then across the narrow V of fabric that burrowed down where her desire pooled. "I almost hate to take these off you."

She spread her legs apart, granting him further access. He looked deep into her eyes and kissed her.

"Almost," he whispered in her ear, then pulled the panties down.

Behind her, the waterfall roared and roared, a timeless falling. A barrier separating them from the rest of the world. In this tiny circle all their own, they could be anyone they wanted. Julia could be reckless, dirty, stepping out of the little lace things. And Blake? Well, she only knew him as the man who looked at her like he wanted to devour her whole.

This time, he didn't have to prompt her to spill her desires. "I want you inside me," she panted.

Blake squeezed his eyes shut like he was savoring a taste, a smell, a perfect memory he didn't want to forget. "God, I love those words in your mouth."

"I need you," she whispered.

"I'm yours."

The words still shocked her coming out of her mouth, but hidden under the waterfall she could hold nothing back. It was a strange sort of paradox, to be somebody else and yet at the same time to know that in here, with him, she was only capable of truth. It was as though the river washed away all pretense, all hope of normalcy and decency and respectable things men and women did with each another, leaving something naked and raw and devastatingly true in its path.

"Fuck me, Blake," she moaned as he kissed his way down to her breasts.

There were things she'd never said before and things she'd never done. And now that she'd discovered them, she didn't know how she'd ever go back to a more innocent time, when sex happened behind closed doors with people who loved each other, tiptoed around each other, gave but never took, maintained that everything was fine, and never, ever asked for more.

She buried her fingers in Blake's hair as his teeth found a nipple and pulled on her breast. Part of her felt like she was completely letting go but another part knew she was already gone, hurtling herself over the cliff of desire like the water rushing above and all around her, pounding in her head, pounding in her heart, pounding as his body moved with hers in the crevice of the earth they had marked as their own.

Chapter Seven

Blake had been playing, teasing, building up the moment as his hard-on grew from watching her come undone in his hands. He knew from the night before that underneath the demure, proper exterior, light and fun and girlish in her sundress with her long hair streaming, someone else was waiting to be released. He only had to give her permission to let go.

Julia's hair, wet from the waterfall, clung down her back, and her cheeks were flushed from the warm day and the fervor of their touching. The look in her eyes as she begged him to fuck her was enough to elicit a low groan from him, hungry and possessive. He wasn't the only one discovering something hidden deep within that was taking over now. Hearing what she wanted, there was no way he could stop himself from giving it to her. Anything she asked for, he couldn't say no.

He hooked her panties over one finger—goddamn how his dick had jumped when he felt that little lacy tease over her hips. He'd been expecting something simple and practical, the traveler's wardrobe. In fact, he didn't really have any expectations at all. His focus wasn't on her panties but what was underneath.

The surprise and delight that she'd been carrying this secret was almost more than he could bear. Had she woken up knowing she was going to seduce him again? He'd said he was leaving, but maybe she'd already sensed there was no way he was getting away that fast. A night like they'd had could only be followed by an even better day.

Or maybe she'd changed into them when she went back to her room to get ready before they left. The thought that she'd prepare for him was equally thrilling.

He knew, too, that it might have had nothing to do with him. And thinking about her going through her day with that flimsy red lace clinging to the curves of her ass, for no other purpose than the fact that it made her feel sexy even if no one else saw, was perhaps the most arousing possibility of all.

That, and the fact that she wasn't wearing a bra under that dress. Her nipples danced when he pulled the straps down, advertising how turned on she'd become the more time they spent tucked under the waterfall's arm. He wanted to take her like that, her clothes still on but falling off, too close to being in public to risk undressing and too far gone to take the time.

He dangled the panties while she blushed and then, holding her eye, put them in his pocket.

"I don't want them getting dirty," he said when she begged to know what he was doing. He'd decide later whether to give them back.

She was standing before him. Waiting. Wanting. His shorts were unbuttoned, his cock already raging hard and halfway out. He pulled his boxers farther down and saw her breath catch, her cherry lips part. God he wanted to feel those lips around his swollen tip, but the ground was nothing but dirt. And while he figured everyone else assumed by now that something was going on, they didn't need to have their suspicions confirmed by Julia showing up with dirty knees.

Was he already planning more things he wanted to do with her? That would mean more time together—the exact opposite of the one-night stand he'd been looking for.

Delaying his departure to Buenos Aires was one thing. For all that he'd planned out his itinerary to maximize his time abroad, the rest of his travels would still be there waiting for him once she went home. But he didn't want to get carried away. There was no room in his life for anything more than the kind of fun they were having right now.

Sternly he told himself to focus on the situation at hand. Which was looking very, very good. Her dress was wet with spray from the waterfall and clung to her curves, showing off the swell of her breasts glistening and slick with water and sweat. He couldn't hold off any more. It had to be now.

His hands covered her body, her hips, her breasts, pressing between her legs and feeling the heat as she pressed back. He bunched her dress up and ran his hands over her ass. That little noise she made when she was surprised and turned on was to die for. In one swift motion he turned her around so her back was facing him, her bare shoulders pressed against his chest. He worried briefly about whether he was being too rough with her, but she wriggled her ass up against him in a sign that only meant one thing.

He wrapped his arm around her, and she whimpered as he slid a finger over her clit, feeling her wetness as her back arched, sending her ass tighter against him. With one hand he circled her clit while the other hand worked his cock, pulling up her dress so he could slide himself over the soft skin of her ass and her arched lower back. She was so wet and she kept right on whimpering. He knew she was ready for him.

"Bend over," he whispered.

His voice was low. She immediately obeyed.

She supported herself against the part of the fence that was still standing and leaned down. He pulled her dress up so it was draped halfway up her back.

"God, you're so beautiful," he murmured. Julia craned her neck around so she could see him, her hair tumbling over her shoulder and down her back. He'd stashed another condom in his wallet—it looked like Julia wasn't the only one who'd been optimistic getting ready that morning. Now he slid it on and rubbed the tip of his cock against her, throbbing in anticipation. Her legs trembled as she moved her hips to draw him into her, wanting him deep within her as much as he wanted to be there.

"I'm all yours," she said. She closed her eyes, and he touched her hair as he buried himself inside her. She was eager and panting and so soft and wet and warm, he bit his lip to keep from crying out too loudly as she took him all the way in.

Sometimes it seemed like after a while, women should be the same. Wasn't it the same act with each of them? But this wasn't the same at all. It was her body and the blush in her cheeks and the way the muscles in her back flexed and released, flexed and released with every thrust as she braced herself against the fence. And the way the water kept on falling over them, a fine mist over her hands and face but the real power of it thundering just out of reach. It was as though he'd never really felt anything until he felt what it was to move inside her.

She bucked her hips back into him, eager for more, and he built up the motion until he was slapping into her with fast, sweaty thrusts. He kept his hands braced on her hips, holding her dress up and his own shorts low on his hips. He could only think what a sight they'd be if some poor family of tourists were to stumble upon them, half naked and clawing at each other like animals as the water rushed all around.

"Oh God, Blake, yes, right there, oh, *Blake*," she was saying over and over again, in time with his movements. He put his hands squarely on her ass, which seemed to excite her even more, and then he reached around so he could touch her clit like she'd done to herself in the pool. The combination of rhythms was harder to maintain but she ground against his hand, meeting the sensations he was giving her both inside and out. He knew how close she was to coming.

He reached his hand up to her mouth and she didn't hesitate, licking his fingers precisely because it was clear that was what he wanted. He loved the way she played both sides of his game. She told him what she wanted him to do to her, at the same time that she was eager to do whatever he desired. His fingers searched her tongue, pressing into her mouth as he continued to take her, making him think again about that blowjob he was more and more certain that he wanted to stick around for.

He trailed his fingers down her chin, over her chest, and unceremoniously yanked down the top of her dress, running his fingers over her nipples.

"You're going to make me come," Julia moaned, her knuckles on the wooden fence now totally white.

Blake increased the force of his thrusts. If there was one thing he'd noticed from her orgasm in the pool last night, it was that she didn't want him to let up when she was close. She liked it hard and fast, and that was fine with him. He never wanted to stop.

"That's it, baby," he urged her along. "Come for me, Julia. I want to feel you let go."

"I want you to come first," she panted.

He eased up on his thrusts and leaned forward, his chest to her back, and pressed his lips to her ear. "Listen to what's going to happen. I'm going to fuck you, Julia, and you're so close that when you explode, I'm going to know it. And when you're done, I promise you, darling, I'm going to come. And it'll be all for you."

Her cheeks flushed and her eyes shone. "Come inside me," she whimpered, pushing back to feel the full length of him.

"Touch your clit," he commanded, and one hand disappeared under her dress where it fell over her hips while the other hand braced herself. The thought of her pleasuring herself while he was inside her made him take her that much harder. She rocked forward with his thrusts, and if it was beautiful watching her body tremble as her orgasm built up inside her, it was all the more so because they were tucked away in the most gorgeous corner on earth. The Devil's Throat was impressive, yes, but here they were in the belly of the rushing falls and he was so close, he was so close, he was just trying to hold on until she came and he could explode deep inside her.

"I'm coming," she gasped, her hand working vigorously against her clit as his cock kept up the same pace. He could feel her contracting and releasing around him in waves of pleasure.

"Fuck, I feel you."

"Don't stop!"

As though he would ever give this up. He kept drilling her right at the spot that had made her come undone, and then when her hand started to slow, pressing up against her clit to draw the waves out, he grabbed her hips and pounded into her.

"Please," she panted, both hands back on the wooden fence to prepare herself for what he was about to give her.

"It's all for you," he said through gritted teeth. His balls ached as the release grew within him, hot and strong and impossible to stop. On impulse he let out a cry and grabbed her hair in his fists, long and luxurious between his fingers. He pulled and she arched her back, craning her neck. Over her shoulder he could see her breasts half out of her dress. The cloth had gotten all turned around and hung off her waist like an afterthought. She was so fucking sexy. He lost it.

"Right there," she gasped as he pumped his heat inside her, pulling on her hair, making her take it from him. It was like she knew all his secrets—how to make him go insane. It felt like forever before he slowed, completely spent. She ground her hips back against him, bending over so that her head dropped low and her ass was high and pressing into him.

He wrapped his arms around her and slowly pulled out, savoring the feel of every part of her against him.

"That," he exhaled, "was something else."

She straightened and faced him, hair tousled, gorgeous breasts still exposed. She flashed a dirty smile, letting him ravage her all over again with his eyes. Goddamn.

Blake wrapped the condom in tissues to throw out when they got to a trash can. Slowly he buttoned up his shorts, while Julia pulled up the straps to her dress and ran her fingers through her hair, composing herself. She almost looked like nothing had happened. Except for the flush. And her panties still in his pocket.

He pulled them out and dangled them over his finger. She reached out a hand like she was waiting for a gift. He started to pass them over, but on second thought, he yanked them back.

"I'll tell you what," he said thoughtfully, twirling them around. How could something with so little fabric make him go so completely insane? "I'll make you a deal."

She raised an eyebrow skeptically and folded her arms. "Oh?"

"I'll give you your panties back," he said, beginning to pass them to her. "If—" he pulled them back again, making her pout. He grinned. "If you give me another chance to take them off you again."

"So you don't want this to be our last time fucking," she said pointedly, and the way she cut through his teasing to call out exactly what he was saying made him suddenly squirm. They had a great time and he wanted to have another go—why not?

"Or I can hang onto these like some creeper." He went to stuff them in his pocket and she laughed.

"You let me have my underwear back and I promise, you can have me as many times and as many ways as you want."

She reached out her hand, and he passed her the prize. He loved the sight of the bright lace riding up her thighs as she pulled them over her hips and let the dress fall again.

"As many times?" he asked. "That might be a lot." He looped one arm over her shoulder while the other reached out to graze the waterfall as it continued its endless plummet over the cliff.

She rested in close to his shoulder and splashed water over him. "I've got four days until Chicago. You see how many rounds you can fit in."

Chapter Eight

Shit, Blake thought as he stood under the shower, hot water pounding down his back. *Shit. Shit. Shit.*

What the hell kind of post-fuck nonsense had he been thinking? *I'll fuck you as many times as I possibly can in the next four days before you return to your life and I return to mine.* Okay, it sounded good in theory. Great, in fact. But he'd spent the last three months on his own, beholden to nothing more than his calendar and the whims of the local bus schedules. He'd been trying to learn how to do the whole one-night stand thing—stay smooth, don't get attached, and don't ever, ever let your guard down—and already he was ruining everything.

He let the water run until he heard banging on the door.

"You drowning in there, mate?" Jamie called.

"Sorry." Blake shut off the stream. "I'll be out in a sec."

"No rush, just making sure you're okay."

Blake wrapped the towel around his waist and stepped out into the steam. He wiped a streak through the foggy mirror with the side of his fist and looked at himself in the watery stripe. What was he doing? What — *who?* — was he still running from?

The face looking back at him was distorted through the bathroom steam and it didn't have any answers. Slowly he watched the mirror fog over again, and when his face was gone he opened the door to get on with his life, wherever it was leading.

"All yours," he said, passing Jamie in the hall.

"Have a good afternoon?" Jamie smirked as he held open the door.

"I guess." Blake paused, frowning.

Jamie gave him a quizzical look. "Is there some sort of maybe in there?"

Blake tried to laugh, keeping it light. He really didn't know what the problem was. "The waterfalls were great," he said, steering away from any mention of Julia. "What's the plan for tonight?"

"Chris has some bar in mind if you guys want to come check it out."

And there it was, exactly what Blake didn't want to hear. "You guys." Like they were already some kind of a package.

Because packages, he knew, existed to be ripped apart.

But he said, "Yeah, okay," because it would be weird after all this time with Jamie and Chris to say no.

"Leaving at seven," Jamie said. "Drinks out back before then."

Blake nodded noncommittally and walked down the hall to the dorms. He threw on a pair of shorts, ran the towel over his hair, and lay down on his bed, staring up at the wall. It was nearly seven when Jamie came back in to get him, thinking he'd fallen asleep.

"Totally knackered," Blake said, realizing that he sounded like Julia when she'd given her fake yawn.

"That girl's wearing you down," Jamie joked.

Blake gave his best rakish grin, the kind that he'd perfected in his weeks on South American beaches. He grabbed his wallet, rolled up the sleeves of his button-down shirt, and slid on his leather sandals. "Let's go," he said as he closed the door behind them.

The truth was that he hadn't slept a wink. Instead, he'd spent two hours memorizing the spidery pattern of ceiling cracks, and he felt like he could trace their web for two hours more. It *was* a good afternoon, like Jamie had said.

But he couldn't help wishing that he'd gotten on that bus after all.

The bar was a ragtag collection of plastic tables with Pepsi umbrellas on the banks of a wide, lazy lake, dark water reflecting the lights from the makeshift restaurants set up along the path. A leaning wooden structure housed a long table with dark bottles piled high. A grill was set up under a tarp tied between two trees in case it rained, but on this night the clouds were nothing but thin wisps idling by. Every so often a swell of laughter rose from one of the other tables like a ripple of water before falling still.

Julia wondered who these other people were and what they were like and how they had found their way to this hamlet outside of town. She wondered, too, about the man sitting next to her as he brushed her hand with his and then suddenly pulled away, reaching for a menu as though an afterthought.

Was everything okay?

But she was being paranoid. Of course it was—Blake was just tired after the, ahem, *energetic* activities they'd shared. Jamie had said he'd found Blake napping all afternoon, which was why Julia didn't see any more of him when they got back from the falls.

He'd practically promised to spend the rest of her trip with her. She didn't know exactly what that was going to entail since she hadn't booked any more nights at the hostel, but she was pretty sure there'd be space for her to stay on.

Everything was fine.

In the distance, headlights blinked between the trees where a road wound up a hill, rising like a dark stain around the edges of the sky. Somewhere down there was Argentina, and on the other side, Paraguay, but here in the deepening night there were no borders and no boundaries, just the lap of water against the muddy banks.

They had piled five into a cab again with Chris, Jamie, and Lukas, Julia squished uncomfortably on Blake's lap in the back seat over the bumpy roads that twisted and turned to the lake. The whole time he hadn't known where to put his hands, until he basically sat on one and wedged the other between the seat and the door. At first it seemed weird—didn't his arms belong around her? But then she'd decided his awkwardness around his friends was cute. And it was always good to have something in reserve that she could tease him about later, when they found a way to be alone again.

She warned herself that it was dangerous to see her and Blake this way, as a couple that would seek each other out when they could. But she couldn't help it. Hadn't Blake made it clear how much he wanted her? Shouldn't she take in as much of him as she could?

They grabbed two tables, red plastic chairs angled close together on the sandy shore. Chris plunked down between Jamie and Lukas, talking about the view and how she'd heard this spot was a popular place for locals, away from the more energized bars in town. Naturally Julia parked herself next to Blake. He was being oddly quiet, but Julia told herself there was nothing wrong with being comfortable with silence. The rest of the group more than made up for it with their chatter.

She was wearing cut offs and a dark cranberry tank top loose around her hips, perfect for the night breeze coming over the water. The warm air and the hum of conversation washed over her in waves, reminding her that had she stayed by herself in São Paulo, she'd probably be curled up in that closet of a hotel room right now, reading about curriculum development and trying to convince herself she was happy "traveling" alone. She'd been at the falls for just over a day, and it still managed to surprise her that she was here.

"Don't you feel lucky?" Chris asked, perusing one of the plastic menus left on the table. "Other people have jobs and mortgages and kids to worry about and we're like, fuck it, let's go sit by a lake and drink beer."

"I live by Lake Michigan. I can sit by a lake and drink beer any time," Julia said, kicking off her sandals and burying her toes in the sand. "But I guess bringing work there sort of defeats the purpose. Plus it's completely iced over right now."

"All the more reason to stay down here."

"I like how Chris pretends she doesn't have a job." Jamie laughed as he signaled for the waiter, who was bringing another round of beer to a table by the shore.

"It's on hold," she said.

"Yeah, until we get back and pick up where we left off."

Chris shook her head. "How can you say that? It's like six months away doesn't even affect you—you can't wait to get back to early morning meetings and nothing in the fridge for dinner."

"That's why I'm a photographer," Lukas said cheerfully, holding up the camera that was always around his neck. "Travel the world, make my own hours—"

"Be perpetually broke," Jamie teased.

Lukas shrugged. "I'd rather have little money and spend it on this than a lot of money and be trapped by car payments and my dry cleaning bill."

"That's what I'm talking about!" Chris exclaimed, turning toward Jamie. "Don't you like this way of life better?"

"This isn't a *way of life*," Jamie said. "It's a long vacation. You know, a break from the real world."

"This is real to whomever's living it," Chris protested. "It's not like they don't need real estate agents here. We could move to Rio. Or some gorgeous small town on the beach and I could sell land. Or we could run an inn! A little *pousada*—wouldn't that be great?"

Jamie looked pleadingly at Blake. "Come on, you're with me, right? Don't you want to go home? I mean, not right now, obviously. But…eventually?"

Julia looked over at Blake, but she couldn't figure out what he thought of the question. "I'm not looking for a life on the road," he said carefully, and Jamie pounced on the affirmation.

"See? We can't always keep moving, but some day we'll save up enough again and take another vacation. Maybe India. Or Egypt, I've always wanted to go to Egypt. We could tour the rivers of the world."

Even in the darkness Julia could see Lukas smirking, and although he was handsome, the expression didn't sit well on his face. "I'll try and meet up with you on your two-week holiday," he said. Chris laughed. Jamie looked like he wanted to say something but held his tongue.

"Well I for one am glad to have even a week," Julia said quickly. "Not everyone is so lucky to get any time off, let alone can afford to travel."

Chris may have wanted to protest that a week was nothing, but she couldn't argue when everyone else was nodding. Inwardly Julia sighed, relieved that the prick of tension seemed to be dissipating. She may not have been easygoing like Jamie or adventurous like Blake or independent like

Lukas or a laughing, carefree leader like Chris, but she knew how to smooth things over and help make people feel calm.

See? She smirked to herself. Leave it to her not to let bouts of wild sex in semi-public places with a gorgeous foreigner go to her head. She was still the same old sensible Julia, wanting everyone to get along. She could practically feel the force of Liz's eye-roll from across the equator.

Jamie started a headcount for beers to signal to the waiter at the bar but Blake interrupted, saying, "A *caipirinha* for me."

"A what?" Julia asked.

"I need something stronger," he said, which didn't exactly answer her question.

"Make it two," Chris said.

"Three," Lukas added, and Jamie pointed to Julia to see if she wanted to switch her order.

She thought of how she'd finished Blake's pineapple juice that morning and decided that whatever he was having was worth a try. So far, saying yes to Blake had served her well.

Even if right now he was tracing circles on the plastic table with his fingernail, some unreadable expression on his face.

"What's in it?" she asked him, touching his forearm to make him look at her.

"*Cachaça*, way too much sugar, and about as much lime."

"What's *cachaça*?" she asked.

Chris clutched her chest like she'd been hurt. "Nectar of the gods," she said.

"Gift of Brazil," Lukas spoke up. "The cheapest liquor money can buy."

"It'll fuck you up," Jamie said drily, with a look at Chris that Julia didn't miss.

"It's sugarcane rum," Blake finally explained. "Also known as fire water."

"And you're going to subject me to this?" Julia raised an

eyebrow, feeling very much like the newbie at the table. The travel virgin, except for the fact that everything else she'd been doing so far on this trip was anything but virginal.

"It's Brazil's national drink. No trip here could be complete without it."

"We may be underselling it," Chris considered.

"Not the fucking you up part," Jamie warned, rubbing his hand over his beard.

"I'll try to keep my wits about me," Julia laughed. "Count me in."

"Five *caipirinhas* coming up," Jamie said, and went to tell the waiter.

Julia wasn't sure how he and Chris had found each other, since they were so different, but she could see why Blake liked him. His quiet charm helped soften the edges of Chris's brashness, making the other woman easier to handle. Would the constellation of guests at the hostel have gravitated together if Chris hadn't been around? Julia wondered if it was simply the nature of traveling that foreigners found each other wherever they stayed. But she had a feeling Chris liked the attention of people besides Jamie, if the way she bantered with Lukas like they were constantly sharing one long inside joke was any indication.

She wondered what Blake made of their relationship, but she knew that wasn't something they were likely to discuss. Talking about relationships—even if it wasn't your own—probably wasn't on the list of acceptable conversation topics for people just hooking up for the short time their paths crossed.

Maybe talking, period, wasn't part of the deal, judging by how quiet Blake was being, practically giving her one-word answers all night. But what did she know? It wasn't like she'd ever done anything like this before. She was just going to have to make her brain shut up and go with wherever the night took her. It had worked okay so far.

Jamie draped his arm over the back of Chris's chair in an easy gesture, sharing a laugh with Blake about the first time they'd tried the fiery rum drink before realizing its full bite. Chris was hardly paying attention, leaning over to fiddle with Lukas's camera as he explained the different aperture settings he could use for a night like this, where the dark water contrasted with the bright pinpoints of light on land. Julia looked over at Jamie and wondered if he even noticed that anything was wrong with the picture.

The photography lesson was interrupted when the drinks arrived, five oversized glasses floating with ice and a fat wedge of lime.

"Cheers!" Chris raised her glass, and even though everybody groaned, Julia's stomach did a little flip remembering how she and Blake had looked at each other when they clinked glasses—was it only yesterday?—and made a promise they had been more than able to fulfill.

"To the waterfalls," Jamie said.

"To making travel last," Lukas added.

To being someone new, Julia whispered to herself. She glanced up at Blake as they clinked glasses. But this time he blinked and looked away when he lifted the drink to his lips.

The first touch to her tongue burned, and then a burst of sugary lime exploded in her mouth. It was sweet and tart and burning all at once, sour and aching and so strong it brought tears to her eyes.

"That was terrible," Chris commented as Julia coughed from the liquor, and she thought maybe she'd done something wrong and *that* was why it felt like her whole insides were bathed in lighter fluid.

But it was the eye contact, of course, that Chris was complaining about. "Never met a sorrier lot in my life. Every single one of you is going to be doomed to nearly a decade of lousy lays."

So not funny, Julia thought to herself as she recalled the streak of celibacy Blake had broken her of. It wasn't the ritual, of course, that had made them so explosive together. But they had held each other's eyes, and it had worked, and she wasn't about to tempt fate.

Blake didn't seem too worried, though, as he tipped the liquid back, and so Julia followed suit. The second sip burned less and the third warmed her all the way through.

When Chris, Jamie, and Lukas walked down to the water's edge to take pictures, Blake didn't make any move to follow. Julia didn't mind. She was happy to stay admiring the view, sipping on the sweet, tart *caipirinhas*, and reaching for another piece of the fried yucca they'd ordered.

"Did you like the falls today?" Julia asked, breaking the silence between them.

Blake looked up from wherever his thoughts had taken him. "Yeah. You?"

"It was spectacular," she said.

"I didn't mean *us*," he chided, and Julia was relieved to see that familiar, flirty glint in his eye.

"I was talking about the waterfalls! We did a few things today besides have sex, you know." With the quiet around them and everyone else down by the water, she spoke more freely, without worrying about being overheard.

"I'm just making sure that you had a good time during the parts where you weren't quite as vocal about letting me know that things were going well."

She flushed at the mention of how the waterfall had drowned out her cries. There was enough light glowing from the bar that she knew he could see it. "You say things like that to make me blush," she accused, and he held up his palms but didn't deny it.

"I don't want you to get home and feel like you spent your

whole week doing unspeakable things with unsavory men."

"I thought you said it was man. Singular. One." She narrowed her eyes at him. She thought she saw him frown at the reminder of his own words, but it was hard to tell in the dark. "I won't ask how many women you're doing unspeakable things with," she went on, "since you have seven months of travel. And maybe have no interest in ever going home—I don't know, you were a little vague on that part with Jamie."

"What I said to him is true. I'm not looking to live like this forever. I just… I just wanted to get away for now."

"And when you get back?"

She wondered what he was thinking about when he looked over the darkened lake and said, "Maybe things will be different then." She didn't want to push. And anyway… wasn't she thinking the exact same thing?

She noticed he didn't do anything to protest how she'd characterized his months of travel, but she tried not to let that bother her. She wanted him to know that she was okay with the fact that they were going their separate ways. She was even okay with him being lost in his thoughts, without letting her in. These were simply the conditions they had set forth for the few days they had together. It was already more than she should have gotten, since he'd been planning on taking off without a second glance. Then she would have really been alone.

She tried not to think about what it would have been like if she'd gone to the falls with just Jamie, Chris, and Lukas, and whether she would have paired up with the single Dutch photographer instead. But the thought was too weird to wrap her mind around. For one thing, she didn't want to get in the middle of whatever he had going on with Chris, reigning in their flirting just enough so that no one could directly call them out for crossing the line.

And after this time with Blake, she wasn't sure she wanted

to wind up with someone else. It may have opened her up to the idea of random hookups, but it certainly didn't convince her they'd all be this good. If anything, she was sure that now that she knew what it was like with Blake, she'd inevitably be disappointed with anyone else.

The thought didn't sit well with her. It looked like more long, lonely months in cold Chicago. Only this time, instead of telling herself she wasn't missing out on anything, she'd know *exactly* what kind of fire she wished were keeping her warm.

"What's whirling around inside that brain of yours?" Blake asked, shaking the ice in his drink.

She could have asked him the same question, but still she cringed at the thought of telling him what she'd been thinking. "How I'm having a nice time," she said.

"Now you're the one lying. I can see it in your eyes."

She pinched her eyes shut. "How about now?"

"You always wear this perfectly calm expression, but your eyes give everything away."

This time he leaned in close so they were looking at each other, locked into each other like they were making up for the chance they'd missed to wish for more years of good sex— with each other or with anyone, the superstition didn't say.

"What am I thinking now?" she asked, but he shook his head.

"I don't know," he said, and she wanted to reach up and touch the curls tumbling into his eyes because he suddenly sounded so sad. But the sounds of arguing were getting louder as the trio returned from the lake, empty glasses in hand.

Jamie and Lukas came back to the table, engrossed in some debate about the merits of São Paulo versus Rio de Janeiro while Chris peeled off toward the bar to order another round. Julia felt something unclench within her when she realized that they weren't really fighting about anything and that Jamie and Lukas seemed to get along fine. Maybe that stuff she thought she'd observed earlier was all in her head. She was always worried about relationships falling apart. She was probably looking for trouble when everything was fine.

Like she was looking for trouble with Blake, when now he was smiling and laughing along with the rest of them. She had to admit that she hardly knew him well enough to guess what was running through his mind.

"You have to appreciate the architecture of the skyscraper city," Lukas was saying.

"I'm not saying I don't, but how is it unlike so many other cities?" Jamie said.

"That's what I thought when I was there," Julia spoke up. "Like, okay. I'm in another city. Now what?"

Lukas shook his head like she'd told him she didn't like music, or dancing, or anything remotely fun.

"You were in São Paulo before this?" Blake asked. Julia explained how she'd flown into the city before heading to the falls, selectively editing out the overwhelming loneliness and all the time she'd spent reading in her hotel room. Further proof that no matter what they shared when they were naked, they barely knew each other.

"So what did you do while you were there?" Lukas asked.

She shrugged uncomfortably. "I don't know. Walked around, went to a history museum, went to some parks and a really big garden."

"I'm with Jamie. Rio is where it's at," Blake said.

"I'm not saying Rio doesn't have its merits," Lukas interjected. "Just that it's a completely different kind of city — one that has to be evaluated on its own aesthetic terms."

"It's fucking gorgeous, there's a million things to do, you take three steps in any direction and you're either in the mountains or at the beach. Plus you have the culture, entertainment, nightlife, and activities of any major metropolitan area, without the congestion of skyscrapers like you have in São Paulo. What's not to love?" Jamie said.

"Who, you mean me?" Chris asked, sliding into the empty seat next to him.

"It's stiff competition between you and Rio," Jamie teased.

"Oh. Well, I know when I'm definitely beat. Are you *sure* we can't make it there for New Year's?"

"If we have to wind up in Chile, shouldn't we head there from here, instead of going another twelve hours east just to come back again?"

"I know, I know. So practical," she grumbled. "Are you going?"

Lukas shrugged. "I want to head north to the Pantanal for some wildlife shots. The whole region is supposed to be completely different from the Amazon. Because it's so open, you can really see everything."

"You do wildlife photography?" Julia asked.

"Not specifically, but since I'm so close it'd be a shame to miss it. I can go up to the Pantanal and then who knows. I'd like to go to Paraguay and then Bolivia. Maybe up to Ecuador and over to the Galapagos if I can afford it, or else wind back down south through Chile and Argentina, like you said. But I'm open—no time limit except for when the funds run out, but hopefully the photographs will cover that."

"Wherever the winds lead," Chris said.

"Our flight's out of Santiago, so that's where we have to wind up," Jamie reminded her.

"Ugh, I hate planning." Chris rolled her eyes.

"Yeah, well. Somebody's got to do it."

The waiter arrived with another round of *caipirinhas* and plates of food Chris had ordered at the bar. It was nice of her to take care of everything, but Julia couldn't help feeling like that was such a Chris thing to do, taking charge and making everyone's decisions—even what they'd have to eat.

Still, the food was good, and she'd ordered enough for everyone to share. A whole fried red snapper, plus plantains and more yucca to pick at. Plates of rice and beans and sautéed greens. There was shrimp in something fermented and salty and a grain that everyone sprinkled over all the food. Julia dug into a little of everything, remembering how when she'd been by herself, she'd hardly known what to order even when she could figure out some place to go.

"So I guess no one's heading to Rio for New Year's," Chris moped, picking up the conversation where they'd left off.

"What's so special about New Year's in Rio?" Julia asked, flaking the fish off the bone.

"Fucking *everything*." Chris shook the ice in her glass. "Millions of people go to Copacabana beach and party until dawn. Fireworks, music, dancing, champagne on the beach — the works. If you can't be there during *Carnival*, then that's the time to do it."

"If you really want to go, we'll go," Jamie said, always accommodating.

"No, we have to get to our flight in Santiago." Chris sighed in a way that said she wasn't quite as agreeable as the words made it seem. But Jamie ignored the dig.

"What about you?" he asked Blake. "You still heading south?"

Julia bit her lip, waiting to hear how Blake would respond. What exactly were his plans, anyway? She saw him glance over and she raised her eyebrows as if to say, *How should I know what you're doing*?

"That's the idea," Blake said with forced casualness, and even though Julia knew that was what he was going to say, it still dug into her somewhere deep inside.

She could tell Chris was trying not to laugh. She'd already given him a hard time about not following through with his plans. For all that Chris didn't seem to keep her mouth shut, at least she knew the few times when it was better to step back. Instead of teasing Blake, she asked Julia about her plans.

Julia was surprised at the question. That she *could* do something hadn't really occurred to her. At least not until she'd opened up the guidebook to the photo of the waterfalls and decided to take fate into her own hands.

She'd thought she'd stay here for as long as her time with Blake allowed it, and then she'd turn around and head back to São Paulo. But the truth was, she wasn't really thinking ahead. The past twenty-four hours had been such a blissful dream, it was hard to remember that in a few short days, she would have to wake up and fly back to Chicago, where her real life was lying in wait.

"I don't really have any plans," she said slowly, eyeing Blake to see how he'd react. "I fly out of São Paulo really late on the first."

"Really late?" Chris said, slathering her plate of fish with a tangy green sauce. "That totally gives you enough time to do Rio and hop a bus between the cities for your flight."

Julia felt herself freeze. The way Chris said she could *do* Rio made it feel like the city was just something to cross off on a list. But wasn't she right? Couldn't Julia go there, if she chose? Couldn't she go anywhere she wanted?

"You can't be down here and not see Rio," Blake said. "Imagine you planned the trip that way all along. São Paulo to Iguaçu to Rio, then back for your flight. It's not so crazy, right?"

The way he said it did make it sound less wild than if she were hopping a last-minute bus with no plans. Chris might not have thought anything of making sudden changes, but Blake seemed to understand her hesitation. He was a planner, too, even if he disregarded it sometimes.

But hanging out in Rio by herself? She didn't want it to be another disappointment, like São Paulo had been. And she couldn't go into this leg of the journey hoping to meet new people; she felt like she'd tapped out her karma on that point.

And besides, she didn't want to meet anyone else now that she'd met Blake.

But maybe he was telling her something. Making new plans, creating an itinerary that would land her back in São Paulo in time for her flight… Could he actually be offering to—

"You could see the Brazilian side of the falls tomorrow during the day and then take a bus back tomorrow night," Blake said, interrupting her thoughts.

It was so casual, it made so much sense, and yet Julia's insides immediately clenched. Four days to spend together. They'd decided just that afternoon. And now with that little word *you*, he was shipping her off to Rio while he stuck with his plans to head south.

"I don't know," Julia hedged, picking at a piece of fish and fighting the urge to scream. She wished everyone would stop looking at her. She knew this whole thing with Blake had an end date—an end date that was very, very soon. But nothing about their afternoon together had made her believe that end date was first thing tomorrow morning.

She felt the heat rising to her face and even though she knew it was stupid—she was stupid—for the first time this whole trip she wished she were alone so that she could cry.

"It's exactly that kind of once-in-a-lifetime experience you only get out here," Chris was saying, more to Jamie than to her, and as they described the city and swapped tales of what they'd heard about New Year's Eve there, Julia put down her fork.

"Okay, you've convinced me," she declared before she could change her mind. "If there's an overnight bus tomorrow, I'll take it."

Jamie grinned and Chris raised her glass again. "To Julia!"

she cried. "To taking life by the balls."

"You guys should be travel agents, you make it sound so good," Julia said. "I'll write you a postcard and let you know how it goes."

And then they were full of plans for her, where she should go and what she absolutely had to see. Except Blake, who simply told her it was a good idea and then kept quiet for the rest of the night.

Julia wouldn't even let herself look over at him. She didn't know what had changed from Mister I-want-to-be-with-you-for-the-time-that-we're-here to this new, too cool, I've-got-plans-so-you-should-be-on-your-way attitude, but she didn't care.

He didn't want to go to Rio with her?

Well fuck him.

At least she'd gotten her favorite underwear back.

Chapter Nine

Blake cut the cards and dealt another round. They couldn't play Five Hundred with two players, so they'd switched to Ups and Downs, only they kept forgetting the rules.

"No, man, we're in ups now. It has to go up," Jamie said, flicking Blake's three of clubs back toward him.

"I thought the last eight changed it to downs," Blake said. It had been ages since he'd played Crazy Eights, especially with this variation, and he couldn't keep track of what was up and what was down and when his turn was being skipped. Like now, when Jamie played queen after queen on top of his ten.

Or maybe that was the *cachaça* talking. They'd stayed drinking *caipirinhas* until every last morsel of food was gone, and then Chris had produced a half empty bottle of Brazilian Old Eight Whisky. Brazilian whisky seemed like it should be a contradiction, but they claimed to import their malt directly from Scotland. It had a dank, woody taste like something left too long in the rain.

More likely, Blake couldn't tell what was up and what was

down in the game because, as in his own life, the rules kept changing. Julia had headed straight to bed without giving him so much as a good-bye. Not that he deserved one. But still.

He'd been amazed at how quickly she'd picked up his hint to go to Rio without him. He'd been afraid she might read too much into their situation and start assuming things from him, but he'd been wrong. If his disappearing act bothered her, the only evidence she showed was how quickly she'd frozen him out.

That mask was so subtle, though, and the shift so minute that Blake doubted anyone else realized what was wrong.

Or at least Jamie didn't. It was one of the things that made it easy to trust him and their growing friendship. Unlike Liam, Jamie was way too oblivious to be conniving.

"You think the girls are asleep in there?" Jamie asked, playing an eight and switching to downs again. Blake thought he was lucky with his three, but Jamie was ready with a two to beat him. He groaned and added four cards to his hand before coming up with one he could put down.

"What, you think they're up gabbing or something?" Blake tried to picture Julia and Chris staying up late and talking about him—or more likely tearing him apart. But it was unlikely. Julia proclaimed she was going to Rio by herself like she was fine with their twenty-four hour escapade coming to an abrupt close. She'd never admit otherwise.

"Chris doesn't gab," Jamie said, playing his card. "She bellows."

"She likes to make sure she's heard," Blake agreed, but not unkindly. He thought of the two as complementing each other, the quieter Jamie supporting the more outgoing Chris as they hit the open road together. They had been scuba diving all over the Australian reefs, traveled by boat down the Amazon, climbed Mt. Fuji when they were still at university. Sure, now they worked in real estate and law in Australia. But they had put it all on hold to take a six-month trip around the world before they finally settled down and got married. Blake might have had his doubts about whether two people could date for ten years and still have a good time together, but here they were. Living proof.

Once he might have imagined that his relationship with Kelley was like that. They'd made a point to get along well alone and in groups. Too late Blake saw the cracks in the façade. The way they spent time in a group so they didn't have to be alone. The way the friends they hung out with captured Kelley's attention to a degree he never could. The way, at the end of the day, there was really nothing left for them at all.

But Jamie and Chris weren't like that. They didn't seem to tire of each other. Blake didn't know if he'd ever trust anyone enough to be in a relationship again, but it helped knowing that togetherness was out there, even if it wasn't his.

It helped knowing, too, that there were friends who had his back, who wouldn't let women come between them.

"Hey, how did you and Chris meet?" Blake asked, frowning over his cards.

Jamie laughed. "I woke up in her bed—"

"Well that was easy."

"—with my trousers on."

"Wait—*what*?"

Jamie shrugged. "I think we'd been at some party. My memory's a little fuzzy on the details, but I definitely remember talking to some mate of hers."

"But you went home with Chris instead?"

Jamie gave him a helpless look. "What can I say? I wake up in a stranger's bed, ready to congratulate myself for a job well done, when I realize my clothes are on, her clothes are on, and I've never seen her before in my life."

"So *then* you got together?" Blake was thoroughly confused.

"So then she said that if we didn't get to enjoy our night, we might as well have brunch and try again."

"Sounds like true love."

"It took a little while." Jamie grinned. "I kept calling her—you know, keeping it casual. Asking if she wanted to pile on all our clothes and lie side by side for the night. That sort of thing. Eventually I wore her down."

"Something tells me this would be a more interesting story from Chris's perspective," Blake mused.

"She said she wasn't sure about me at the beginning," Jamie admitted.

Blake raised an eyebrow. "Why's that?"

"I had holes in my socks. She called it *unbecoming*, but said she decided to take the risk anyway."

"The risk?"

"You know, in going out with me. Calling me. Seeing me again. It's always a chance."

"Well, either it works out or it doesn't," Blake said, and then wondered if all his months on the road were reducing him to such a pile of platitudes that he'd never be able to write a decent script again.

"The only thing you can do is try." Jamie raised his glass and swallowed the whisky down, making a face. "Or maybe it's better to stick with what you're good at, like making *cachaça* instead of whisky. Yikes."

Blake laughed, shuddering as the alcohol burned down his throat. Jamie made it sound so easy, but it wasn't. Jamie and Chris were the kind of people who took risks. Blake wasn't. It was as simple as that. He'd planned out his whole trip and now he was sticking to it. No more distractions. No more deviations. Argentina was calling to him.

"Rio's a great city," Jamie said after a pause. "Julia's going to have a great time."

"Sure," Blake said. He tried to keep his face impassive as

he picked up cards from the deck. Jamie was creaming him and now Blake didn't have a single diamond to play. "So's Buenos Aires," he added.

"You're sure there isn't anything you'll miss in Argentina?"

"Not pretty girls, I can promise you that." Blake flashed a grin.

"I was thinking more about one girl in particular."

Jamie threw down his last card: six of diamonds. *Damn.* Blake should have changed suits when he could. He swept up the pile of cards to shuffle.

"I've got other plans."

"What, get drunk by yourself in Patagonia? You've got no plans."

"Travel by myself, then go back to Sydney. Emphasis on the *by myself*, you know?"

Silently Jamie pulled on a strand of his beard.

"C'mon," Blake said. "What does it matter if I say good-bye to her now versus saying good-bye to her on Saturday? It's better to stick with the schedule I have. Besides, you heard her—it's not like she even minds."

"If you say so," Jamie said. "You deal this round."

Blake cut the cards, listening to the cicadas in the darkness. The table was lit by the glow from the pool and the pale lamps overhead. Some part of him knew what Chris meant. It was hard not to want to live like this forever.

He knew, too, that he was lying when he told Jamie everything was fine. Julia's face had closed like a screen door when he told her to have a nice trip. But that didn't mean she wasn't thinking something entirely different underneath. Something undoubtedly not very good about him.

It didn't matter, though. They were done. And it wasn't like she'd given any sign that she wanted him to stay with her. She could have said something, too.

Blake sighed. "We're not all so lucky to have someone

who wants to—what was that crazy thing you guys did? Bungee jumping in Panama?"

"Chris was cheering the whole way down. I almost shit my pants. But you find someone you can nearly die with, you hold onto her." Jamie wagged a finger at him.

"Thanks, I'll keep that in mind."

"Sometimes I think Chris wishes she were, I don't know, with some extreme sport maniac daredevil. Someone a little more—"

"Daring?"

"I was going to say crazy, but sure, daring works. A children's advocacy lawyer doesn't exactly scream stud."

"I thought women loved men who care for kids."

"You try telling Chris that." He rolled his eyes as he rifled through his cards, arranging his hand.

Blake set the deck between them and flipped over the top card. "Your move," he said. "I thought this was the big hurrah before Chris makes an honest man out of you and starts hopping on the baby train."

Jamie picked up a card, played it, and groaned when Blake slapped down another heart. He started picking from the deck, looking for a card he could play. "That was the idea. But you heard the woman. Who wants to settle down when you can—what did she say? Open up a beach resort along the Brazilian coast?"

"Yeah, with Lukas as your concierge." They both laughed. It was hard to imagine the Dutch photographer taking directions from anyone, let alone snippy guests in an inn.

"Talk about risky," Jamie said. "You never know who she might run off with. And then—" he caught himself in time. "I'm sorry, man, I didn't mean it like that."

Blake held up a hand. "Don't worry about it."

"We don't have to—" Jamie started.

"Talk about it? No. We don't."

Jamie's mouth shut. He played his card.

Immediately Blake felt bad for cutting him off. He was supposed to be re-learning how to do this whole friendship thing, not alienating people at every turn. It wasn't Jamie's fault that anything that reminded him of Kelley made him want to punch somebody's lights out. And while the list of things that reminded him of Kelley wasn't quite as long as it used to be, it still could fill a few ledgers. Hearing about girlfriends running off with the ones you least expected was pretty high on another list he kept, the one about things he didn't want to talk about. Ever.

But Jamie was just joking around, one bloke to another, the night dark and the cicadas loud and the cards shuffling back and forth across the table, keeping them busy while everyone slept. Blake wondered what Julia was like when she was sleeping. If her little mouth opened as she breathed. How her limbs splayed out on the sheets. Whether her hair fell into her eyes so that he could lean over her sleeping body and brush it from her face. He took a shot so fast it made him cough. That bus to Buenos Aires couldn't come fast enough. Once he was on his way, there would be absolutely no more thinking about another body in his bed throughout the night.

Blake poured another thumb of whisky into their glasses. Thinking about Julia sleeping so close and yet untouchable made the image of Kelley the last time he saw her pop unbidden into his mind. That look in Kelley's eyes hadn't been shock or shame or sadness, but delight that she'd finally been caught.

He never wanted to see anything like it again.

Jamie didn't know that he carried that face with him now, whenever anything came up—even jokingly—about losing one's love. But he would never tell anyone the truth about Kelley. Whatever Jamie wanted to know, he could read about online. He might not think it was true, but it probably was.

That was precisely the problem.

"Chris is just talking about opening up that inn," Blake said. "Everyone loves to fantasize out here."

Another image popped into his mind, this time of the way Julia's eyes crinkled when she was so close to coming, one flick of his finger sending her over the edge.

"To fantasies." Jamie raised his small glass. "And to as many years of good sex as we can possibly get."

They swallowed the shots with a sour face. Blake played his next cards, a two to make Jamie draw two cards from the deck, a queen to skip his turn, and an eight to change the suit to spades, which he had three of left in his hand.

"Fuck," Jamie groaned as he watched Blake make his plays.

"You've been kicking my ass the last two turns. It's time for me to have a go."

But Blake already knew that like all his seeming victories, this one would also be short-lived. Jamie played an eight and changed the suit to clubs, correctly assuming that, of course, Blake was stuck with spades. He flashed Jamie the finger as he reached for more cards, his hand building back up until he finally got one he could play.

Blake wasn't sure how seriously he should take Jamie's concerns about whether Chris really wanted to settle down. Hadn't she talked about their plan to return to their home in Melbourne and start planning their wedding? Even if Chris was having cold feet, it was just the idea of their trip winding down, and he told Jamie that reassuringly.

There were times to step out of your life and jump off a cliff and trust that the rope would hold you. And then there were times when the only thing to do was board a plane in Santiago and go home. Chris would know the difference, when the time came.

"I guess," Jamie sighed as he threw down the last card in

his hand.

When Jamie picked up the cards and asked Blake if he was up for one more, Blake knew he'd better turn in.

"Big day tomorrow," Jamie said as he gathered up the bottle and glasses to bring inside.

"Gotta get to the bus station early," Blake said.

"Don't forget to enjoy it."

"What?" Blake had no idea what he meant.

"The bus ride. Argentina. Wherever you go. You're supposed to be enjoying it, remember?"

"You got it," Blake said. "I'll let you know how it goes."

The last thing he thought of before he fell asleep was Kelley's face, lips parted, eyes flying open at the sound of the door. And the anger—the shock of that anger she held in her eyes. How had he missed that she'd been so angry with him?

But no, that wasn't the last thought. Not really.

The last thought was Julia and her lips on the straw, eyes widening in pleasure and surprise as she sucked up sweet pineapple juice.

Chapter Ten

The sky was turning a deeper blue when the bus pulled out of the Foz do Iguaçu station, heading east for Rio. Julia bunched up a sweater to use as a pillow and tilted her seat back, closing her eyes. She would *not* be nervous. Still, it was going to be a long night.

She couldn't believe she was really doing this. She was really going to another huge and unfamiliar city by herself, this time carrying not only the memory of her loneliness in São Paulo but what was, she had to admit, the most incredible chemistry she'd ever experienced in her life. She wanted to hate Blake, to kick and scream and yell and cry and tell him off for puffing her up and then cutting her down without so much as a good-bye.

But he'd been gone by the time she woke up that morning. And anyway, she had no words for him. Not really.

It wasn't that she was angry so much as resigned. What, did she think that after he fucked her twice, he'd want to stick around and keep doing it again? A night and a day playing at being somebody else wasn't going to turn her into the kind of woman who didn't find herself alone.

The bus jerked out into traffic and shuddered to a stop. She heard the clank of the door opening, muffled conversation, footsteps coming up the steps—some last minute passenger. There were plenty of empty seats. She didn't open her eyes. A whole day convincing herself she was having the time of her life on the Brazilian side of the falls had left her exhausted.

But there were other adventures ahead, she reminded herself for the millionth time that day. The whole point of a fling was that it ended. Period. Full-stop. *Poof* into memory, like a drop of water spiraling away. Like a cloud.

And now it was time to move on.

As if the driver heard her thoughts, the bus lurched forward again. She settled back in to sleep, only to be interrupted moments later by a tap on her shoulder.

"Excuse me, is this seat taken?"

The voice was low and close to her ear. Her eyes flew open and her heart almost stopped.

Then she frowned.

"What are you doing here?" she said crossly.

"I don't even get a hello?"

"You're kidding." Was she supposed to immediately fawn all over him because he had suddenly—what? Felt guilty? Wanted another piece of her ass?

"Well then, don't mind if I do," Blake said like he hadn't heard her and sat down. "Plans change," he added as he reclined the seat and stretched out his legs. "Don't they?"

"I don't know, you tell me. You're the one who suddenly had to get to Buenos Aires, after acting like you were completely free."

"I didn't."

"Didn't say that?" She practically laughed in his face. Julia may have wanted people to get along, but if Blake thought she was going to be some meek, mealy-mouthed pushover grateful for his dick and his non-apologies, he obviously didn't know what it took to make a room full of tenth graders pay attention.

"No, I did, I just mean—" He was getting flustered now. It was incredibly satisfying to watch.

He tried again. "I mean that I didn't have to get to Buenos Aires. I didn't have to be anywhere. I don't know why I said that I did."

"I want to be clear, Blake. I'm not making you go anywhere. You can go to Rio, you can go to Argentina, you can go to the moon for all I care. But on Saturday I leave for Chicago, and that's one plane ticket that's not going to change."

"I know," he said. "Which is exactly why it would be so stupid of me to let you get away before then."

Don't do it, Julia scolded herself, but the heat was rising to her cheeks. It was like her blood vessels were completely disconnected from the rest of her. They went whooshing along for all the wrong reasons, straight from her heart to her thighs, with no concern for her brain.

"I didn't ask you to come with me," she tried again.

"You should have."

"Why, so you could say no to my face in front of everyone?" This time it wasn't hard for her to summon her irritation.

"No. So you could tell me I was being an idiot and to get over myself."

"Yeah, like that would have gone over well," she said, and now it was his turn to blush.

"Okay, I deserve that. I'm just not sure how to do this whole, whatever it is that we're doing. Where it's more than a night but in the end we still leave."

There it was: honesty. Julia turned and looked out the window, where the last bit of light was slipping away. Behind them was the town, ahead of them nothing but dark fields and the deep purple silhouettes of the trees. Every so often the black was punctured by a beacon of light from a lone dwelling or a small cluster marking a village farther off the road.

"I didn't think that was a reason not to enjoy it," Julia said as she squinted at the lights whirring by. She wondered what it would be like to live in those houses—to live anywhere that wasn't the life she'd always known.

"Yeah," Blake said quietly. "That's kind of what I was thinking, too."

He didn't need to know that Julia was never the one who talked about enjoying the moment and seeing what happened. She decided, like everything else on this trip, to just go with it.

His hand brushed the back of hers, as if trying out how her touch still felt. "How were the falls?" he asked.

"Okay," she said, and then laughed. "No, that's a lie. Spectacular, obviously."

The endless chasm, the hurtling spray, the overpowering drumbeat of the falls matching time with her heart had reminded her that she didn't come to Brazil to find a man. She'd come for this: the chance to live a few unscripted days overpowered by something so much larger than her own tidy corner of the world.

If Liz found out that she'd even thought about wallowing in the hostel dorm room eating bad melted-and-refrozen ice cream bars and reading about curriculum development, she'd drag her to the nearest Chicago singles bar and force her to dance, stat. It was only the thought of the depressing neon lights and terrible beats that had made Julia fill her water bottle and hail a cab.

And she was glad she did.

The view from Brazil emphasized the panorama of the

river, crowned by the thundering Devil's Throat. A walkway extended out over the river, and from there the waterfalls looked like slices of white through the lush green trees, piling one behind the other in a never-ending stream. Wringing water from her hair from the spray, the roar of the world in her veins, the rest of her life felt like a far-away dream. It was hard to imagine ever going back to Chicago, bundling up in warm layers, sliding on the ice, surrounding herself with stacks of papers at work, at home, in her bag, constantly reminding her of all she had to do.

And, okay, there was another truth, too. "It was also a little sad," she finally admitted, and gave Blake a shrug as though apologizing for breaking the agreement where they both went their separate ways and neither one cared.

But he had broken it first, by getting on the bus. And then he broke it again, when he gently grazed his lips to her forehead.

"Sad is watching your ride to Argentina pull up."

"That doesn't sound bad."

"And then watching it pull away while you're still stuck on your ass in the station."

"I think the word you're looking for is pathetic," she joked.

"I went to the roadside market that stretches across the border into Paraguay, a hundred and four degrees on the road in the sun and everyone's trying to sell you broken radios from 1993 and refrigerator parts and hashish and, I don't know, probably a child if you wanted. There's no law enforcement there."

"Another word: depressing. Aren't you the writer? I should get you a thesaurus."

"I thought that I could wander around by myself until I passed out from heat stroke and no one would find me or know who I was."

"They'd see your passport."

"I went back to the hostel to leave it in the safe."

"Then yeah, that's a lousy way to bite the dust."

"That's what I figured. So I came back to the station and cashed in my ticket for the bus coming here."

"Rio with Julia: Better than Roadside Death."

"It has a certain ring."

"Thanks. But you were almost late," she said. "You're lucky the bus stopped for you."

"It was a risk," he said. "But a good friend once told me that everything's a chance."

"Everything?"

"Something like that."

She thought it over. "I wasn't planning on coming to the falls in the first place," she said.

"But you're glad you did."

Julia frowned. "How would you know?"

"Your eyes," he said, matter-of-factly. "I told you they give everything away."

"What am I thinking now?"

He leaned in close, peering at her in mock concentration. "That you're so lucky to have crossed paths with this dead sexy Australian guy."

"Don't quit your day job," she snorted in his face. "Your mind reading skills need some work."

But still, as the ride wore on and the bus lulled them with its steady motion, she found herself resting her head on his shoulder. His hand stroked her hair, a sort of absent-minded reflex. Like he was reassuring himself that she was there leaning against him, her fingers idly tracing the contours of his stomach, trying to remember *this is real, this is real* with each strike of her heart.

"I thought maybe I wasn't going to find you," he whispered in the dark.

"When?"

"When I got on the bus and didn't see you anywhere. The best views are in the front, through the windshield, but you weren't there."

"It's nighttime," she said. "I wanted to rest."

"And here I thought it was because all over the world, the cool kids universally know to sit in the back of the bus. How do they figure that out? Is there some code that's implanted in everyone's brain when they turn thirteen?"

Julia didn't know. She'd never been the cool kid. She and Liz always sat together when they took the bus to school, too engrossed in their own world to care what anyone else was doing.

Until Liz decided she wanted to know the secrets of the boys who clustered in the back of the bus, behind the bleachers, under the stairwell after the tinny echo of the last bell faded through the halls. Julia had hovered on the outskirts of those cliques. "Somewhere in the middle of the bus" was how she would have described herself. Neither cool nor uncool. Neither here nor there. She'd gone to the back because she'd wanted to be alone, and now she was grateful for the cocoon of silence that covered both of them as the night rushed past. Even if she didn't understand everything that was happening with Blake, she wanted him here, if only for this moment. For the time that she had.

The bus system in Brazil was well established and the ride surprisingly comfortable. It wasn't crowded for the overnight and the seats were spacious, with plenty of legroom between each row. They reclined far enough that it was possible to get a decent night's sleep without feeling packed in like a sardine. And the scheduled stops along the way offered the chance to walk around and see the countryside, which kept the bus cleaner, too. Julia thought Greyhound could learn a few tricks.

"Are you comfortable?" Blake asked. Julia nodded

against him. The lights were off in the bus and everything was quiet except for the sound of the engine and the subtle snores of the people in the front, already nodding off. He pulled up a blanket to cover them and Julia lay against him, trying to sleep.

But despite the rocking of the bus and the soothing, quiet sounds of nighttime rolling by, it was impossible to doze off. It was too weird, this whole rollercoaster twisting inside her. She had no idea what to expect in Rio or what she and Blake were going to do the whole time. She'd barely been able to think about what she was going to do there on her own, telling herself she'd take it one step at a time. What if, without the rest of the group around them, they didn't have anything to talk about? What if they got tired of each other after the first day and then she was left alone yet again? What if Blake decided he'd made a mistake in coming with her? What if she was making a mistake in spending any more time with him at all?

He kissed her forehead, as though to quiet her thoughts, and as if on instinct her lips searched his. The first kiss was tentative. Then searching. Then it was too much and Blake groaned.

"You're not supposed to be able to do this to me," he whispered, shifting in his seat.

"I didn't know that I came with a rulebook," Julia said, and then had to laugh at herself. If anyone followed the rules, it was her.

And she was pretty sure that her rulebook didn't say "get ditched by your fling and then fall back into his arms on an overnight bus of all places." The thought made her face burn. What would people say if they knew?

But *what* people? Who was she living for?

No one else was in her shoes. They weren't hurtling through the Brazilian countryside at night, feeling the press of a warm body and making absolutely zero plans for what came next. It was scary to think that there weren't any right answers here.

But that also meant that there weren't any wrong answers, either.

This wasn't a classroom. It was her life. There were no rules to follow. Everything was up to her.

It was like Blake had said in the pool. She really could get what she wanted. She just had to know what it was.

For once that part was easy, though. Julia knew there was no option of getting attached, but she was desperate to feel him again. A persistent ache was building between her legs, and knowing that Blake was feeling the same didn't help. Every time she looked at him, every time his fingers brushed hers, she could feel it soft and wanting, a need that couldn't be ignored.

They would finally be alone in the city, and she wasn't sure how much she could hold on and pretend to be in control before she had to give up and throw herself at him completely.

To be in a hotel room, on a bed, no need to be quiet or to worry about being seen... The thrill of being caught had added an urgency to their fucking that reminded her of everything she loved about this trip — the danger and excitement as she tried to be somebody else.

But she couldn't deny that now that she'd been given this last chance with him, she didn't want any constraints. No worrying about time or other people or dirt on her hands and knees. She'd never been adventurous like this, had never done anything unconventional. She didn't have sex standing up, or bent over, or in any way outside of a bed, lying on her back, looking up, wondering what the big deal was. It wasn't that it had ever been unpleasant. It just hadn't been anything special.

Now she wanted to know what else Blake could bring to the bedroom. What would it be like to have him on top of her, as she lay back into fluffy hotel pillows and let him go to town?

What she really wanted, she thought in the quiet darkness of the bus, was so surprising to her that she bit the inside of her cheek, wondering if she really craved what she thought she did. Did she really want to taste him, or was she telling herself that because she thought she should? It was possible that was simply something she wanted to do to check off her "Things Julia Doesn't Do" list. Something reserved for this getaway that she wouldn't otherwise seek out.

But the Julia she wasn't was becoming more and more of the Julia she wanted to be—fun, sexy, spirited, alive. She didn't just want to give Blake a blowjob. She wanted to want it, the way she wanted sex with him, period. The full giving in she felt when she stopped thinking about what she should and shouldn't do, whether it was right or wrong, how silly she looked, how inappropriate it was, how much she was bound to get hurt. The giving in when she wanted more and more and still more of it, until she was no longer herself—but not because she was somebody else.

The thought of what was in store for them was making Julia's pulse leap. In the darkness, she could barely make out the outline of Blake's profile, resting with his eyes closed, his lips slightly open, the faint stubble down his jaw. She wondered if he was sleeping, but when she shifted against him, trying to force her reckless body to stop fixating on sex all the damned time, he opened his eyes to peek over and she felt the thrill that his gaze still had on her.

"I thought maybe you were asleep," she murmured, trying to keep quiet enough not to disturb the other passengers. But none of them stirred.

"Not yet. Just resting. What were you thinking about?"

Julia couldn't stop a smile from escaping, even though he couldn't see it in the dark. "You," she whispered.

The word hung between them, full of the longing she felt.

"I like the sound of that," Blake finally said. "What about me?"

"Good things."

"Such as?" He held her tighter. Teasing. Playing.

Julia glanced up the aisle. There were several rows between them and the next person, an older Brazilian woman traveling by herself. Her seat was back, and she wasn't moving. Soft sounds came from her seat. She was definitely asleep.

Beyond that, Julia could only make out the shapes of heads reclining back, scattered with empty seats between them. She didn't know if anyone spoke English, or whether they'd be able to hear over the hum of the engine, which was louder in the back and drowned out their words. She decided she could risk it.

"Such as everything I'm going to do to you once we're in Rio," she leaned over and whispered in his ear.

She felt him tighten against her. She knew the effect the words had. Her own body was equally on edge.

"Like what?" He shifted, trying to get more comfortable, trying to keep his voice low and relaxed like they were chatting about anything—sports or the weather or the waterfalls.

Anything but how they really felt.

Gently Julia leaned over and bit his bottom lip. That move had been the first thing she'd done that had really surprised herself, showing him that she was game and wanted more. Except that jumping in the pool with him in the first place had shocked her to her core.

Now she felt that same power pulsing through her, flirting and teasing, building the pleasure and anticipation so that by the time they arrived in Rio, there'd be nothing to do but find the nearest hotel room and throw off their clothes.

"Everything," she breathed in his ear. His arm clenched around her.

"Don't promise a man that unless you mean it," he groaned quietly and Julia tried not to stir as she brushed her lips against the sensitive spot on his neck. She paused, but nothing changed in the night except the subtle shifts of their breathing. The bus drove on. The night rolled by.

"There are some things we haven't done yet," she whispered, sure no one was looking at them.

Blake shifted in his seat to face her and slid his arm across her stomach, under the blanket that covered them. His fingers grazed the top of her shorts, finding the edge of her panties.

"I know," he whispered, his breath hot in her ear, making her want him even more. His touch wasn't helping her calm her thoughts, but she had only herself to blame. She had started this. Now the ache between her legs was so intense, she wasn't sure she could take it. Involuntarily she spread her thighs, sliding one leg over his.

"There are things I want to do to you," she said softly, trying to meet his eyes in the flicker of lights from the road and the soft spread of the moon coming through the window.

It seemed like Blake tried to speak but all he could do was groan. Inwardly, Julia danced with delight at the thought that he wanted her like she wanted him. It wasn't that she didn't like giving head; it was more that she'd hardly had the occasion to practice. It always seemed so fraught with her and Danny. He didn't want to do anything that he feared would seem degrading, or that she might not enjoy. No matter how much she insisted that she wanted to—and she did—he remained convinced that she was only doing it because she thought she had to please him. Nothing she could say would convince him that she knew her own desires and was capable of acting on them.

They'd gotten together when they were so young, Julia realized, and he treated her like a child the whole time. Like someone breakable, who might suddenly change her mind.

She realized later, of course, that it wasn't only because of his fears about her. It was also his fears about himself. His fear of pleasure. Of letting go. Of enjoying her body too much. It was only now with Blake, as the night rolled by, that Julia knew how much she and Danny had both missed out on by holding themselves back. Now it was the letting go that she wanted, the loss of control, the terrified, elated surrender of their bodies that was wonderful, not wrong.

She had given Blake her body, had taken him inside her, had felt the pleasure pushing through her so strong it made her scream. She wanted to see how far they could go together, how they could push each other. She wanted to know what he would feel like in her mouth, taste like on her tongue. Under the blanket, she spread her legs wider for him.

They were resting side by side like any two people sitting on an overnight ride, but underneath, Blake's hand was moving. Slowly, imperceptibly, he undid her button and slid her zipper down. She glanced up at him, at his smile, and leaned her head back in the seat. His hand slid under her panties, his knuckle grazing her open fly. She worked her shorts down slightly over her hips, enough to give his hand free reign. Her clit jumped immediately to greet him. Once she had been so shy, so difficult to find, but it was hard to feel anything but open with Blake. He exhaled at her wetness and kissed her ear, sliding in, sliding out, forming the small circles that made her hips dance.

Julia lay back and closed her eyes. She felt nothing but the night wrapping her in darkness and the fine pressure of joy that snaked all the way up her belly, her spine, down her limbs, straight to her heart. Blake had found that perfect spot that kept her at his mercy, and he was working it with a steady, even rhythm, down the sensitive side and over the top, fast enough to build her pleasure, slow enough to make her toes curl.

Her thighs tightened, her leg pressing down on his. Her breath caught and she exhaled, then held her breath again. She gripped the side of the seat, eyes pinched shut, trying to keep her breathing quiet and even. Like someone sleeping, even though she was very much awake.

The circle of pleasure tightened and tightened until it was a pinprick at the very tip of her clit. It felt as though time stood still, the bus stopped moving, her heart stopped pumping, and she floated away. The darkness took her and she gave herself to it. For one brief timeless second she was a drop of water hurtling over the edge, suspended.

And then she crashed.

Into the rocks, into herself, into the night, and into Blake's hand.

He kept circling, vigorously now, holding nothing back as she tightened and jumped against him. Her legs clenched, she held her breath, and she came so hard and so silently it felt like everything turned inward, the waves redoubling on themselves, the pleasure so hot it was searing.

He worked his finger over her clit as the waves came, and when she finally subsided, slack in the seat beside him, he cupped his palm gently over her. She could feel the heat radiating as her pulse leaped between her legs.

After a while, she lowered her leg down from where it had been draped over him and he slid his hand out, resting it on her belly. She rolled her head to one side, trying to keep her breathing steady like she was sleeping. Trying not to keep smiling into the night.

"Did you come?" he asked, so soft the words were more of a shape than a sound in her ear.

She turned toward him, holding his arm, her shorts still unzipped, his hand on her hip, and tried not to look too incredulous.

"Couldn't you feel me?" she asked.

"Yes," he admitted. "But was it good?"

She let a laugh escape. She felt lightheaded, her limbs like jelly from how hard she had clenched—and then unclenched. "I don't think yes is a good enough answer for some things."

"As long as it was good."

She kissed him on the mouth. Slow, wet, deep. "I want you," she whispered in his ear.

"You'll have me," he assured her. "In Rio."

She shook her head. "I can't wait that long."

Blake laughed quietly. "You'll disturb the old lady in row seventeen."

Julia paused, taking the temperature of the night once again. The woman in row seventeen wasn't stirring anytime soon.

Julia slid her hand under the blanket. He was hard as a rock, straining against the front of his shorts.

"Wait," he hissed, grabbing her wrist. But Julia shook her head adamantly. If this were Danny, she would have listened. Sat back demurely in her seat. Held his hand. Done the things good girls were supposed to do instead of taking charge and taking what she wanted.

But this wasn't Danny. And she wasn't the same Julia anymore.

She strained her arm against him, and he had to work to keep her from touching him. "You can't stop me," she whispered. "I want to."

The bid for power over whether her arm was snaking down his shorts or sliding back to her side was turning her on, reminding her of how strong he was when he let go and drove his weight into her, and yet how gentle he remained afterwards.

"I just meant wait a second," Blake whispered, letting her hand drop onto his rock-hard cock. "Switch places so I'm on the inside, away from the aisle."

"Oh. I was afraid you were trying to deny me."

"I know better than to stand in your way." He grinned, and in the cover of darkness they shifted places in the back of the bus. Nothing untoward, should anyone happen to see. Just a woman who wanted the aisle seat, or a man eager for the window instead.

Would the people who saw them think they were dating? A long-term couple traveling, like Jamie and Chris? The thought was sort of exciting. Yet another way she was fooling the world into thinking she was someone she wasn't—or at least had never been before.

Blake settled into the window seat and she sat down where he'd been. Now if anyone looked back, they'd see only her leg visible from the aisle, not anything having to do with his lap.

Julia wondered how much experience Blake had with these sorts of public encounters. She'd certainly multiplied her own several times over. But she pushed the thought from her mind. It didn't matter what either of them had or hadn't done in the past. What mattered was that they were both here, now, and that she was about to give him a surprise.

Julia slid her hand back down his shorts, and this time he didn't stop her. Instead he spread his legs slightly and leaned back as she had done, preparing to enjoy what was to come. She worked him out of his shorts, marveling at how bringing her to orgasm had made him so incredibly hard. She stroked his shaft, running her thumb across the sensitive tip, and then worked her hand down to cup his balls, bringing a sigh to his lips.

"Shhh," she whispered, teasing, flicking her tongue over his ear while she stroked him. A broad smile spread over his face, his eyes still closed.

And then she bent over and lowered her mouth to the head of his cock standing straight up in his lap. She kept her eyes glued on his face so she could fully appreciate the look of surprise as his eyes flew open at the unexpected pressure of her tongue.

He tried to pull her shoulder up, whispering, "What are you doing?" as he strained to see whether anyone in the bus knew what was going on.

But if the old lady in row seventeen had stirred, it was only to sink lower into her seat as her breathing deepened in sleep.

"You don't have to do that, you know," he said as he caressed her cheek.

"I don't *have* to do anything," she said, mocking him for what he'd said to her the first time they met, when she'd tried to stop him from carrying her bags. He rolled his eyes at his own words thrown back at him. "I want to," she whispered, just as he'd said to her.

"Is this where I learn about your desires?" he asked, stroking her hair, reminding her how she'd called him strange that afternoon.

"Mmm, this has been a desire of mine for quite some time," she whispered, ignoring the fact that "quite some time" meant the two days they'd known each other—and half that time she'd been convinced she was never going to lay eyes on him again.

But in a way, it could also include all the years she'd longed to find someone she wanted to do this to, to lick and suck and nibble and stroke with the full enthusiasm of her hands and mouth, so eager to taste there was no way she could be stopped. She'd never, ever wanted it like this. Wanted it like it was for her own pleasure, not only his. Wanted it like she couldn't wait another second more.

"You and me both," he murmured, and a thrill coursed through her at the thought that he'd been wanting this, too. She lowered her mouth back to his cock, and he arranged the blanket over her. She lay down like she was his girlfriend sleeping with her head in his lap. A perfectly appropriate thing for a couple to do.

But they weren't a couple, and she wasn't asleep.

She tried to move slowly so as not to rustle their clothes or make any sucking noises from her saliva. The constraint made it all the more intoxicating as she had to hold them both back from full-on abandon, building him up as slowly as she could until she could feel his balls straining, pushing up in her palm, begging for the warm, enveloping touch of her tongue that would make all the pressure release.

But she wouldn't let him, not yet. She'd never enjoyed this so much and she wanted to savor her triumph. Up and down she worked her mouth, slippery and wet. He rested his hand on her head, playing with her hair, as she got into a slow, sensuous rhythm with her mouth. Danny would never have done that, thinking it degrading even if he wasn't pushing her head down. But the feel of Blake reaching to touch her made her want him even more, taking him as deep as she could while the wetness built again between her legs.

As his fingers dug in her hair, she knew he didn't have much time before he was done for. She wrapped her fist around the base of his shaft while her mouth moved over every inch of him, her tongue swirling over his swollen head each time she went up and back down. He held her tighter, pulling hard as she felt his thighs clench. He was close, he was so close, and she wanted to give it to him…

Outwardly he hardly moved, but his cock pressed against the back of her throat and under the blanket his hips bucked—once, twice, pushing in as she sucked him deep. When he pressed gently onto the back of her head, she knew he was telling her that he was about to come, so she could decide what she wanted to do. And yes, she swallowed. And no, she didn't care if that meant anything.

Finally he lifted her, still careful not to make any noise. The smell, the taste, the heat of him had filled her, thrilled her, and the sight of his satisfied face as he lay back in the seat smiling and totally spent was the icing on the cake. He squeezed her hand and she rested her head on his shoulder.

"Damn," he whispered, brushing the hair from her face and flexing his hand from where he'd been clutching the edge of the seat to keep himself from moving.

"This is when I ask if that was okay for you," she whispered.

His smile was a delight.

"I wasn't expecting that," he admitted.

"It doesn't have to be the last time," she reminded him as she zipped up her shorts—even as she'd already learned that there could be no planning with Blake, not even for a few days.

Now would be the time when, in some perfect dream she might have once had, he would turn and announce that he needed her, he loved her, and he was never letting her go.

But her dreams had never included blowjobs on buses, or Brazil, or men she barely knew. And she was actually comforted that he didn't say a word. It was a relief not to have to worry about the baggage and expectations that came when two people wondered how long they were going to last. If Blake was sex and Danny was love, there was no question she'd take Blake any day she could have him.

Blake buttoned his shorts and draped the blanket over them. This time, when she leaned against him, she had no trouble falling asleep to the rolling motion of the bus and the steady rise and fall of his breathing as he nodded off, too. Rio was coming at them closer and closer each silent minute that passed.

Julia had no idea what to expect, but she knew that whatever happened wasn't going to be anything like her long, lonely days in São Paulo, or her darker nights at home.

Chapter Eleven

Julia had dog-eared the page in her guidebook for budget lodgings in Rio, but Blake told her to put the book away. They were approached by a throng of drivers crowding around the bus station, and he went with the one who grabbed their bags first and ushered them toward his cab.

"Hotel Copacabana," he instructed, and did his best to haggle the rate down before they set off into the busy morning.

"Copacabana?" Julia said with eyes wide as she flipped through the guidebook. "Blake, I don't know quite how to say this but I—"

The car turned quickly and in the back seat Blake jostled against her. He took the opportunity to reach for the book and close it.

"Nonsense, this is on me."

He tried to use his most authoritative voice, the one he'd perfected on set for when he needed everyone to shut up and do their jobs so that he could do his. But naturally she wasn't falling for it.

"You can't do that," she said, striking back with what must have been her equivalent *listen here* tone, the one that doubtless made countless teenagers spit out their gum, crack open their textbooks, and sit cowering until she told them what to do.

"I can, I will, and I am."

"Your accent gets stronger when you argue," she laughed, and he'd have said she won the tiff by completely disarming him except for the fact that they were still heading for the stretch of hotels along the famous crescent-shaped beach and there was no way he was going to let her pay.

"Making fun of the opponent won't earn you any points," he said, and he tried to scowl but it was hard to look unhappy when she was so damn cute in the morning, her hair disheveled from the ride even though she'd tried to smooth it out, pillow creases still on her cheek.

"I wasn't making fun!" she exclaimed, and then leaned over and whispered in his ear even though the driver hardly spoke any English and probably couldn't hear them, "It's cute."

"The opponent will remember this when we're in our hotel room overlooking the ocean." He winked.

"I'm serious, Blake," she said, her tone changing once again. "I can't ask you to do that."

"You're not asking, I'm offering. And I've never stayed here, but what better excuse to stay in a nice hotel with a beautiful view on a world-famous beach than the two nights I have with you. Besides, after that hostel and a night on the bus, a comfortable bed sounds to die for."

Julia grinned. "Okay, I'll grant you that. But I want to go on the record that I didn't ask for the royal treatment and have no expectations for anything you have to do for me. A tiny hostel somewhere is totally fine."

Blake leaned over so that his hand was on hers and his breath in her ear. "There is one expectation you can have for something I'm going to do *to* you, but it's definitely something I very much want." He bit her ear gently and then slid away, looking out the window like he hadn't said a thing. When he snuck a glance back, she was blushing furiously, a devilish light in her eyes. God he couldn't wait to be in that hotel room, lying her back on the bed, spreading her legs...

He owed Jamie big time. The whole time he'd sat in the bus station, bags packed, waiting for his ride to Argentina, he hadn't been able to get his friend's words out of his mind. *She said she wasn't sure about me from the beginning...but she took the risk anyway.* Jamie had been trying to tell him something. Something important.

Chris hadn't been wearing a giant sign that read YOUR FUTURE IS HERE and neither had Jamie. But they didn't go running just because there were no guarantees.

It wasn't that Blake was looking for a relationship—far from it. He was just tired of things inevitably ending. A single night with someone forgetful couldn't be said to end when it had hardly even begun. A night and then another day and then the thought of more nights, more days to come... Well, that was a different story.

But like Jamie had said, *The only thing you can do is try.* He knew he had two days left. He wasn't going to let himself miss out because of what might happen down the road.

He was done worrying, done denying himself the things he eyed from afar but thought he shouldn't have. Which was why he knew exactly what hotel he wanted to stay in. Blake had been traveling simply, staying at clean but basic lodgings like the hostel in Foz do Iguaçu. He'd been raised by a single mother in a small town outside Melbourne. One of the things he was most proud of was being able to buy her a house and take care of her so she no longer had to work. That was the only part that felt good about the money the show had brought in.

Kelley was the one who'd been thrilled with their newfound fame and fortune, relishing the opportunity to buy clothes without considering the price tags, eating out all the time because they could. Moving in the elite circles of actors and TV personas, Blake had started to feel like the world around him was less real, less solid than he'd once supposed. Kelley's about-faced change proved that he didn't want his whole life to be like that.

But it was more than the desire to stay grounded that made his stomach constrict when he looked at the checks from the broadcasting company growing his bank account even while he was abroad. While he was able to take off from work to travel the world before his next season started, he didn't like knowing that he was only able to do it because of the success of *The Everlastings*. In other words, because of the appeal of Kelley and Liam together onscreen.

If he didn't spend the money, he could pretend it wasn't there. He could avoid thinking about why he was off traveling in the first place, or how his life had changed, or whether he deserved his success at all.

With Julia, though, he didn't want to think. He knew the first step to showing her a wickedly good time would be a room with an ocean view. He'd walked by the hotels on the beach the last time he was in Rio but hadn't gone in. Now he had a second chance. A chance to enjoy what he had.

They pulled up in front of a tastefully ornate building bordered by tall palm trees rustling in the ocean breeze. Blake was glad to see Julia's eyes widen, taking everything in. The hotel was part of a strip along the beach, amidst the bustle of the street, the crash of the waves, the colors and sounds of the busy morning getting underway. It was honeymoon suites and "May I take your bags, sir?" on one side of the street, and on the other, bathing suits, white sand, beach umbrellas, and a blue so bright and endless it stretched into sky.

He got them a room on the top floor, with broad windows that looked over the whole stretch of land. They could see the street below and then the crescent of sand that made up Copacabana Beach. To the right, where the tip of one crescent swept back into another curve, was Ipanema, and more beaches extending farther beyond. To the left they could just make out the distinct hump of the famous Sugar Loaf Mountain jutting straight out of the sea.

That was Rio, a city of contrasts. Mountains, oceans, skyscrapers, sprawling slums known as *favelas*, everything jammed together and not enough lifetimes to ever experience it all. He was torn between wanting to rush out and do everything and wanting to stay in and do everything to Julia before he lost the chance.

She solved his problem of what to do with one word: breakfast.

Blake tossed her the room service menu. She flopped down on the bed, kicking off her sandals, and rolled over onto her stomach. He rolled on top of her to see the menu over her shoulder and they laughed while the sun streamed through the windows, the city spread out below.

They ordered fresh guava juice, coffee, and tomato omelets that came with fruit and a basket of muffins on the side. They sat out on the balcony at a table set for two and dove in, famished from the long bus ride. Julia stretched her legs and rested her feet on the railing, looking out at the water and wiggling her toes.

"This is perfect," she sighed as she speared another piece of star fruit.

"See? I told you. I walked by here when I was in Rio before and thought to myself, *Damn. If only I could stay in that hotel eating breakfast with a beautiful woman.*"

"I'm so sorry your wish couldn't come true." Julia laughed, and he threw a napkin at her.

"Yeah, it's too bad I got stuck with a Julia instead," he teased, and she picked up the napkin and tossed it back. "More coffee?"

She held out her mug. "You're going to spoil me, treating me like this," she commented, gesturing at the view before them.

He lowered the coffee pot back on the table and looked at her intently. "Oh no," he said in his most serious voice. "I fully intend to ruin you."

"Be careful what you wish for. You're already well on your way." Julia smiled and sunk down in her chair, basking in the sun. She was all legs in those shorts, and Blake reminded himself that he was supposed to be eating his breakfast, not just looking at her.

But Jamie's talk had been a wake-up call. Blake didn't want to waste this time. Sure, as soon as he'd implied he wasn't coming, he'd wanted her to protest—to let down her guard and admit that it mattered whether he came to Rio or not. But even though she hadn't, he wasn't going to force himself away. He was here, and she was here, and nothing else was worth thinking about.

Finally, when they were so full they couldn't eat another bite, Julia made her way inside and Blake heard the sound of the shower coming on as he picked at the remaining crumbs on his plate. He stood and leaned against the railing, straining to take in the full view of the mountains and the endless beach.

He'd spent only four days here before moving on, and when he left, all he'd been able to think of was how much he wanted to return. But the open road had been calling him, and the falls, and Argentina, and he'd kept pressing on. That was when he'd had his itinerary laid out for himself, dividing up his months of travel to make sure he hit every spot on his list.

Now, though, that list was totally out the window. And instead of fearing that he might be missing out on something, thinking he should have been exploring a new city rather than back in one he'd already seen, he wondered if it might not be so important to keep moving on.

Blake yawned and headed back inside. The hotel room was spacious, with a king-sized bed in the middle, a dark sofa plush with pillows, and a long polished console with drawers, a minibar, and a flat-screen TV. He sat down on the bed and picked up the remote. It had been ages since he'd watched any television. He was familiar with the telenovelas that were popular in Brazil—loud, dramatic soap operas that played in every house and restaurant. He had no idea what was going on in any of them, except there was always a lot of sobbing. *The Everlastings* was often called a soap opera, but Blake knew his show didn't have anything on the real thing. There was drama, yes, but not even he could have come up with the plotline where a woman's maid came back from the dead to steal her husband. Or at least that's what Blake thought had happened, based on the snippets he'd seen.

But he didn't really want to know what was going on in the television world. Before he brought the mute screen to life, he had a better idea. Closing the thin curtains, he stripped off his T-shirt and cargo shorts and dropped them to the floor.

He opened the bathroom door to a waft of steam and her long, lean figure blurry behind the dimpled glass of the shower stall door. She was facing the water, standing under it as it poured over her. He stood in the doorway, transfixed, until she called out, "You planning on showering or just watching?"

Her skin was warm and soft from the water, and he was torn between how good it felt to touch her and how good it was to let the hot water pour over him. They spent far too long enjoying the luxury, Julia rubbing soap over his back, him slipping a hand between her legs as she passed the shampoo. But it was when she rested her hands on his shoulders, her forearms on his chest, and kissed him with such longing that he felt his cock press against her, desire come to life in the enveloping steam.

Julia went to drop to her knees but Blake had only one thing on his mind. He shut the water off and lifted her by her shoulders. She was pouting like he was spoiling the fun, but he didn't even bother getting a towel to dry them off. He lifted her up, her legs wrapping around his waist and his cock pressed up between them as he carried her laughing to the bed. He leaned her down and pulled the covers back.

Julia lying on the bed, dark hair spread over the pristine white sheets. Julia's molten eyes flashing as he kissed her from her forehead to her bellybutton and paused to look up, drinking in that smoldering look as he trailed his lips the rest of the way down. Julia arching her back, fingers gripping the sheets as he lowered his lips to kiss her thighs and then brought his tongue flat and firm across the small, eager nub of her clit.

He had been waiting all night to be alone with her like this, to lay her down and taste her, and she was just as firm and tight and wet and open and gasping and eager as he'd been imagining in his mind nonstop since she brought him all the pleasure in the world by going down on him. She was propped up by the pillows and he lay on his stomach, his feet hanging off the edge of the bed, his cock straining into the mattress as he turned to steel while she opened herself to his tongue. She was so sweet, so deliciously female, and so responsive that he had no trouble following what she liked. It felt like they fit together exactly, like he knew how to flick his tongue where she wanted, fast strokes and then deeper lashes that made her legs tremble as they clenched around his face.

He reached a hand up to stroke her delicate curls and she arched her back appreciatively. His fingers trailed over her hips, her stomach, her breasts, unable to get enough of her body as he kept furiously lapping at her. He tweaked her nipples, pulling hard and then harder as she whimpered and grabbed his hair, drawing him into her. He let himself be pushed as she bucked her hips against his mouth and coated his chin. There was no getting enough of how she tasted, how she moved, how she moaned, how she made everything feel so alive. He pressed his hips into the mattress, rubbing his cock against the sheets as the pleasure built for him alongside the decibel of her moans. Here in the hotel there was no need to be quiet anymore, and he wanted her to let it all out, panting, gasping, clawing at his hair.

She was so wet; he brought his hand from her breast and slid his middle finger inside her as he licked. Immediately her legs widened and she let out a cry followed by a series of whimpers as he worked his hand in rhythm with his tongue.

He slid in another finger, fucking her with his first two fingers while he sucked furiously on her swollen clit. He was sure that he'd enjoyed doing this before, but it was hard to imagine that he had ever experienced anything this good or gotten this much pleasure out of making someone completely fall apart in his hands. When Julia came, there was no question. Her legs clenched, her back arched, and she cried out loud enough to wake everyone on the hall if he gave a shit about them.

When she came down from her high, she raised her head to look at him, beautiful, flushed, wet hair disheveled, nipples bright and pink and hard. Positively fucking radiant. He slid his fingers out slowly, knowing how good his dick was going to feel inside. He kissed her clit gently and she twitched under him. He was massively, desperately hard, and he trailed his cock over her body as he brought himself to her lips, wiping his chin with his palm to take off some of her slickness before he kissed her.

Julia's hand around his cock while they kissed was heaven. Her legs intertwined with his as they rolled together in the bed, finally able to spread out and lie down together after their furtive, acrobatic endeavors. Who knew it could feel this exciting to be in a bed instead of somewhere wild? He kept kissing her, running his fingers through her hair, feeling her fingernails along his shoulder blades, tracing the ridges of his back.

She was still lying on her back when he threw one leg over her to straddle her, sitting up over her hips, his cock at full attention. He didn't try to disguise the hunger in his eyes.

"I think I need a minute to recover," she panted, even as she reached to stroke his cock and show she wasn't completely done.

"Take all the time you need." He smiled at her, watching her slowly run her hand along his shaft. Her slender fingers cupped his balls and his head rolled back, savoring the touch.

"I'll have to think of some way to keep you entertained until I'm ready for you," she murmured, and he looked down to meet her eye. Slowly, still maintaining eye contact, she licked her lips and then, as if that wasn't temptation enough, opened her mouth to touch her fingers to her tongue, beckoning him to her mouth. He sidled up, his legs on either side of her as she guided his hips forward, her arms extended up and running over his stomach, his ass, his hips, before grabbing his cock and bringing it to her mouth.

He moved the pillows behind her to prop up her head and then reached for the headboard to hold himself when his legs threatened to give way. She worked both hands over him, her tongue swirling over the head, and then she grabbed his hips and thrust him forward into her mouth, taking his full length all the way back to her throat. She ran her hands over his balls while she sucked and slowly he began moving his hips, working his cock in and out of her mouth, plunging deeper when it seemed she wanted it. Needed it. Had been thinking about it as much as he had.

He thought about her wetness, the smell of her still on his fingers, in his nose, the taste still on his tongue, the heady sweet scent driving him wild. Her mouth, open and wanting. Her hands were firm around his dick as she sucked him so deep he groaned, leaning against the headboard to press his hips in, feeling the hot, soft pressure of the flat of her tongue as she licked him up and down.

Christ, he was going to explode into that beautiful mouth if she kept doing that. He pulled his dick out, her mouth still open, and rubbed the wet tip over her glistening lips hungry for him.

"Better slow down there," he murmured as her lips kept trying to find him again. Her hunger made him ravenous. He hovered above her, trying to calm himself down enough to keep going, while she snaked a hand between her legs. When she brought her hand back, she lifted it to his lips for him to lick.

"I'm ready," she whispered, innocent and devilish and throaty from her swollen lips. As if he had any doubt about what she wanted. He slid on a condom.

"Are you sure?" he asked, rubbing his tip over her wetness until he thought he might scream from anticipation. She was breathing heavily and didn't answer. Instead, she used her hand to guide him in.

The feel of her was nothing less than a dream. She was more than ready and he built up quickly, feeling the pleasure of every thrust as he moved deep inside her body. He was panting, groaning into her ear, saying her name over and over again as she used her hands to press his hips into her harder, her legs lifting on either side of him so he could make his way deeper in.

It wasn't long before he had to slow down again, not wanting to climax and end it so soon. That was when they rolled over so she was on top, gasping when he pinched her nipples in his hands.

She rode him fast, skin slapping against skin, sweat pooling between their bodies. And then she rode him slow, leaning forward so her nipples grazed his chest, grinding her pelvis against him. She took her pleasure however she wanted until he was out of his mind with it. He'd never fucked anyone like this. No, he'd never *been* fucked like this. She was riding him so hard, moving up and down over the full length of his cock, that he didn't stand a chance. He came with a yell, holding onto her hips for dear life, bucking up to thrust deeper inside her as she drilled herself down onto him, raised her hips, and fucked him until he was spent.

When he subsided with a groan, she tilted her head back and took every ounce of pleasure that was hers, sliding over his still hard cock as she pressed into him. He could feel her orgasm spread in waves until she collapsed on top of him. They lay there together, not moving, as the sun worked its way through the thin closed curtains, lighting their bodies panting and sweaty across the giant white bed.

Forget his plans. Blake couldn't believe he'd been about to give this all up to be safe and alone.

Chapter Twelve

Julia couldn't remember the last time she'd been this excited. Not even her arrival in Brazil had caused this kind of giddiness to bubble through her like champagne. Then she'd been nervous, self-conscious about being alone, uncertain of what was to come. Stepping off the plane, she'd been afraid that getting too hopeful was bound to set her up for disappointment. And so when she'd walked out of the airport to a gray day as dark and uninspiring as the skyscrapers that cut against the sky, it was like the city had been giving her what she'd expected.

Now, though, everything was different. Some part of her knew she couldn't afford to get wrapped up in Blake. But it was too beautiful a day to give in to the warnings that she was leaving, he was leaving, so she'd better not get attached. There was so much to see as they ventured outside after their nap. The beach was directly across the street; all they had to do was step out of the hotel and they were transported to another world.

Families and couples and people lounging alone watched

the waves roll. Gaggles of teenage girls bronzed from the sun eyed shirtless boys running and shouting to get a kite airborne, the bright tail swooping along the shore. Julia didn't know what she wanted to do first—walk or swim or head downtown or stand and watch the life unfold around her.

But Blake seemed to know where to go. He walked purposefully down the sidewalk so strewn with sand it was more like an extension of the beach.

"Coconuts," he said as they stepped aside to let a throng of women in practically nonexistent bikinis pass by, chattering loudly in Portuguese as their laughter carried down the beach.

"What?"

"I want a coconut."

"Okay." Julia had never had a fresh coconut before, but she'd also never had guava juice on a hotel balcony or lain on her back to open her mouth to a beautiful man. And both of those things had been pretty darn enjoyable, so she figured a coconut probably was, too.

She wasn't disappointed. They approached a vendor camped out along the sidewalk, and Blake held up two fingers and rooted in his pockets for change. The vendor had a giant cart filled with enormous green globes, fibrous outsides streaked with brown from where they'd been torn from the trees. The man took a machete the size of his forearm and lopped a flap off the top of each coconut with one easy stroke, making an opening to slide in a bright plastic straw.

Julia hadn't realized how heavy they were, laden with cool water. It was sweet and slightly fruity and like nothing she'd tasted before.

They sat in the sand, watching the waves and the kids with the kite, and talked about the places Blake had traveled and Julia's other trips, up to the Wisconsin woods, east to New York City, long drives with Liz to Toronto and Omaha. She hadn't thought about them as really traveling—not like what Blake was doing—but he hung onto her every word, interested in how vast and varied North America was.

"Did you ever think you'd be sitting on a beach in Rio, sipping from a coconut, talking with an Aussie?" he asked, tipping the coconut to get the last drops of liquid inside.

Julia shook her head. "To be honest, as soon as I arrived in Brazil I thought I'd made a terrible mistake. Walking around São Paulo by myself wasn't exactly what I'd been hoping for."

"What were you hoping for?"

She thought for a minute, knowing she could brush him off but wanting to give a real answer. Wanting to remember what it was she'd dreamed of when she clicked to buy her tickets. She'd never thought about traveling to Brazil before she saw the sale on an advertisement in her inbox and decided that a trip was exactly what she needed for her Christmas, her birthday, and her life.

"I don't totally know. An adventure, maybe. Something different. Something I could do for myself, where I didn't have to take care of anyone or look after anyone or answer to anyone at all." She paused and winced. "I guess that sounds sort of selfish."

"No," Blake said slowly, mulling over her words. "That sounds like a very good idea."

"I guess sometimes you have to step back and think about yourself before you completely burn out—or explode."

She knew, though, that she'd never really explode in front of her friends or colleagues. She'd just keep plugging away like she always did, trying not to rock the boat, until she made herself so small she disappeared.

"You *should* be thinking about yourself. What you want, what you need. It seems strange that getting away helps bring us back to what we're really looking for. I guess it's like having a giant time-out from life."

"Where you can sit in the corner and think about what

you've done?"

"Something like that."

"And what is it you'd done that you needed to think about?" she asked, glancing at him out of the corner of her eye, keeping her voice light and playful but aware that she'd slid from joking around into more serious territory.

The waves surged in and out, the ocean a living, breathing thing. Julia wasn't surprised when Blake shrugged.

"Work, mostly," he said. "Things got really crazy on set, and I felt like the screenplay and production were completely taking over my life. Which is what I wanted, obviously—I'm definitely *not* complaining about creating a popular show."

Julia nodded. She suspected there was more he wasn't telling her, but she realized this was the first time he'd really mentioned anything about his job. Or the fact that, from what it had sounded like from Chris and Jamie, he was a pretty big deal. "Just because you're fulfilling your dreams doesn't mean you don't need to take care of the rest of your life," she said, waving her straw at him as she lifted the coconut and tilted it back to drink up the last bit inside.

A thin stream trickled down her chin and Blake brushed it up with his thumb, cupping her jaw for a moment in his hand. "Insightful."

"Normal," she corrected him.

"No, some people seem to think that when you're 'famous' or 'successful,'" he punctuated the words in air quotes like he didn't really mean them at all, "you have everything you could possibly want. Except for *more* fame and success, since, like money, one can never have enough."

Julia had a definite feeling that "some people" meant his ex-girlfriend, whoever she was. She must have liked Blake's popularity—maybe a little too much.

"And what is it that you still want?" Julia asked.

He looked over at her. Looked at her, looked past her,

looked through her. Maybe even looked into himself. Finally he answered. "To be happy. Is that too simple? Or too hard? Too impossible to even think about? I want to write—I've always wanted to write. So I just want to do it. I want to write and create and make things happen on screen. Make sure my mom is taken care of—don't laugh."

Julia didn't.

"And—" he looked away, gazing down the beach at the humpbacked dome of Sugar Loaf Mountain rising like a crooked finger where the line of sand curved away in the distance. "It'd be nice if there was someone else who shared that desire, who wanted something simple. Meaningful work, a close family, good friends you can count on, who like you when you're down as well as up."

"That doesn't seem like too much to ask for," Julia said, following his gaze down the beach.

He turned and looked back at her, squinting into the sun. "Doesn't seem like it, but I haven't had it so far. Maybe it's time to revise my expectations."

Julia shook her head. "Don't settle for anything less."

"See?" He smiled. "Insightful."

"No. Just trying like everyone else not to fuck up."

"Well, not everyone seems to be trying for that. So I'd say that, in and of itself, makes you a rare bird."

"Do what I say, not what I do. I'm the one who spends more time at work than at home, and I can assure you that I'm not bringing in any more pay. I'm too much of a sucker to say no."

Blake chuckled. "It sounds like you really care about your job, though."

"I care about the students," she corrected him.

"At least you always know why you're doing it."

Julia nodded. Sometime in the future, when she was grading tests on the weekends or trying to get through to a student who just didn't care, she was going to have to remember those words.

He reached for her coconut and she passed it over, watching him stand and brush the sand from his shorts. He moved with such grace, so easy in his body as he slid his sandals on and walked back to the vendor. When he returned, he was holding the coconuts balanced in both hands, each one split open with a stroke of the vendor's machete to expose the creamy white inside. He passed her a little piece of the coconut that the man had cut off, showing her how to use it like a spoon to scrape out the flesh.

It was smooth and slippery, firm yet soft, sweet with a distinctive flavor all its own. They sat for a while hacking at the pieces and slurping them up while Julia declared that she could never go home because now that she'd discovered eating coconuts on the beach, how could she return to a life without them?

Blake scooped up a piece with his little coconut-spoon. "Maybe you can start an import-export business."

"Then I'd *definitely* know why I was doing it."

"Yeah, purely selfish reasons. Making sure you have a constant supply of fresh coconuts."

"I was thinking more along the lines of bringing it to the cold, deprived masses in Chicago. I guess they're not as cold and deprived in Sydney." She paused. "Or wherever it is that you live."

"Sydney." He nodded. "There are coconut palms in Australia, but Sydney is definitely not the same as Rio. I'd say we're still just as deprived."

"I'm not going to tell you what the current temperature probably is in Chicago with the wind chill because I don't want to ruin my day by reminding myself of what's waiting for me."

"Good plan. All thoughts of home life officially banished

today."

"Deal," she nodded, picking at the last scraps of coconut clinging to the inside of the shell.

"Good. Now that that's decided, what's on the agenda next?"

Julia looked down the beach, hugged by the mountains and the buildings behind. "Anything? Everything? You know what's good here—I'm up for whatever you want."

Blake shook his head. "None of that. You have to decide what it is *you* want to do."

"I see." She leaned in close. "Is this another one of those times when I have to declare what I want, and then beg for you to give me exactly what I'm asking for?"

Given how little clothing most people on the beach were wearing, she felt no compunction about sliding her finger up his bare skin, raising the hairs on his forearm, before kissing him on the ear.

"I don't know which I like more, when you ask or when you take." His lips tasted like coconut, sweet and sticky, and he wrapped one arm around her neck and slid her hair out of her ponytail as he pulled her close.

"Is there anywhere with a good view?" she asked. "It seems like there's so much to see with the city nestled in the mountains like this."

Blake jumped up and extended a hand. "Your wish is my command," he said as he helped her up, planting a kiss on her temple. "I know just the thing."

It turned out that asking for a good view in Rio was like standing in the middle of the beach and asking to see sand. They started by taking the cable cars up to Sugar Loaf Mountain, *Pão de Açúcar* in Portuguese, a peak on the mouth of Guanabara Bay. First they went up a smaller hill that stretched beside the mountain. Then the cable car took them straight across from one peak to the other. It had glass windows all around and gave them a view of the whole city as it grew out of the mountains, the buildings a small attempt to mirror the peaks rising up to the sky. It was dizzying and terrifying and so beautiful it seemed unreal to float from one mountain to the other, water below them and the sky above.

When they finally reached the top, Julia was amazed to see rock climbers scaling the nearly vertical sides. Some people even climbed all the way up, sleeping on the ledges when they needed a break. The thought made her stomach clench.

"That is. So. Terrifying." She pointed to the small figures inching their way up the sides.

Blake laughed. "I guess we know the limits of your adventurous spirit."

She spun to face him. "You would do that?"

"Hell no! There are about a million other ways I'd rather die. Top of that list being quietly in my sleep when I'm old."

"Or at least with both feet on the ground." She shuddered, unable to pull her eyes away.

"But I like the *idea* of it," he clarified, "even if I wouldn't do it myself."

"You want to be that adventurous?"

"In my next life. Maybe."

"You keep working on that," she said. "I'm happy to spend all my lifetimes watching other people do crazy things."

"Always on the sidelines?"

"Sometimes you have to know who you're not," she said emphatically, even as another voice inside her wondered if that were really true.

"What if who you're not changes?" Blake asked as he grabbed her hand and led her around to the other side of the peak, and it was like he was reading her mind.

She didn't have an answer for that.

Later they crossed the city and climbed up to the famous Christ the Redeemer statue, one hundred feet of concrete and soapstone on a twenty-foot pedestal standing with outstretched arms. It topped the Corcovado Mountain in Rio's Tijuca Forest National Park, an enormous rainforest that Julia couldn't believe was in the middle of a city. Sugar Loaf and the Redeemer looked like they were facing each other, two points flanking the sprawl of buildings below them, endless blue water and mountainous green on either side. They were in the city, surrounded by concrete and throngs of tourists taking in the views. But they were also above it, surrounded by color and light, breathless and floating over everything on street level that hardly seemed to matter at all.

"Does this qualify as decent enough views?" Blake asked as he came up behind her and helped slide the strap of her patterned red sundress back up her shoulder from where it was starting to slip.

"I had no idea a city could even *be* like this," Julia said, not sure where to look first.

"I told you Rio was amazing."

"It's so close to São Paulo, yet so completely different."

"To be fair, I think São Paulo is a great city if you give it a chance. But you probably have to know where to go and what there is to do. It's not like this, where you can basically go anywhere and find something amazing."

"There's a rainforest *in the middle of the city*. The middle! How can that be?"

Blake laughed. "Sounds like you've been converted."

"I'm with Chris. Remind me why I'm not moving here?"

"Because you agree with Jamie that sometimes it's nice to go home."

"I thought we weren't talking about anything having to

do with the h-word," she reminded him with a grin.

"Right, you caught me. I have no reason whatsoever why you shouldn't move to Rio."

"Except I don't speak Portuguese."

"You can learn."

"And I probably couldn't get a job."

"Everyone needs math teachers."

"If I'm doing the same job somewhere else, isn't it just my same life transplanted?" she asked, gazing up at the impressive statue above them.

"I have no idea what the answer to that is. All I know is that it doesn't snow here."

"That's a good enough incentive for me. What about in Sydney?"

"Coldest temperatures we get are in July, where sometimes it's all the way down to eight. I don't know what that is in Fahrenheit, though."

"About forty-six," Julia said, doing the quick computation in her head. The thought made her laugh out loud. Forties in Chicago in the dead of winter would be considered downright balmy.

"What, that doesn't count as cold to you hearty Chicagoans?"

"Sorry, but you're a total wuss."

"Sometimes it even snows!"

"Yeah, like it snows in Florida and everyone freaks out from a dusting."

"In Brazil when it drops into the seventies, everyone reaches for a sweater."

"That's what I'm saying. Sounds like a good life to me."

"Okay, you teach math while Chris opens up an inn."

"What about poor Jamie?" she asked.

"He'll love being the house boy."

"And you?" she laughed before catching herself at her

presumption that he'd fit into their little foursome.

But it was a game, a silly fantasy to joke about as the bright sun and blue sky and endless ocean made her giddy with the thrill of so much to take in. Blake thought for a moment and then declared that he'd be the one writing the screenplay about their perfect existence. "Or else some reality show where we all move to paradise and then drive each other crazy."

Julia laughed. "That's probably more realistic." She paused, then decided to go for it. What did she have to lose? "You don't think there's something, I don't know, weird between Jamie and Chris?"

They were standing leaning over a railing under the statue, looking out over the view. Blake gave her a puzzled frown. "What do you mean, *weird*?"

Julia shrugged, not sure if she should have brought it up. She hardly knew them and it seemed like Blake and Jamie had become pretty good friends. She didn't want to say anything wrong or step on any toes. "I don't know, it's probably nothing," she backpedaled, trying to be conciliatory.

"No, no, I'm not offended. Tell me what you mean."

"It just seemed like… I mean, even with the way Chris was joking about moving to Brazil, or wanting to keep traveling forever. Like on some level, she really meant it."

Blake shook his head. "I don't think so. She and Jamie have been talking about how they're going back to Melbourne and getting married."

Somehow, the news that they were preparing to seal the deal made Julia all the more certain that something was up. Who joked about running away before getting married… unless some part of them was itching to go?

"And yet she's talking about opening an inn with Lukas, while Jamie is talking about how he's ready to go home. To me it seemed a little off."

"She's definitely joking. They have such a good thing going on."

"I guess," Julia said reluctantly. "I don't know if it's something I'd joke about, but I suppose everyone's different. Anyway, where do you want to go next?"

They let the conversation slide, moving on to more discussions about the city they were in and the cities they lived in as they walked down from the mountain, winding through the steaming rainforest before they emerged on the street below. It was a surprise to be back on concrete, like they'd passed through a portal from a completely different world. It wasn't long before they were swept up again in the surge and swell of the moving city, hopping a cab to a restaurant in Julia's guidebook for a late lunch.

But she couldn't stop thinking about their conversation. She wasn't as certain about Chris and Jamie as Blake seemed to be. Or at least as he *wanted* to be. Had he really believed what he'd said? Or did he want to believe that their relationship—or any relationship—could last?

She couldn't tell, but there was no way she'd ask. It wasn't like they were in the relationship business themselves. Besides, it was no use dwelling on things that didn't concern her when she had such a perfect travel companion. They rested when they wanted to rest, walked when they wanted to walk, and poked in and out of little stores along the avenues. They tried to guess all the different fruits for sale and bought roasted corn and grilled meats and cheese on the streets to try everything they could. When was the last time she'd laughed this hard? When was the last time she'd had this much fun? Not thinking about work, free of any obligations, not feeling like she had to worry about anyone else. She felt as liberated as the ocean, its one obligation to keep exploring the endless shore.

If only, she thought to herself as they strolled hand in hand along the avenues. *If only it didn't all have to end.*

Chapter Thirteen

It was late afternoon by the time they walked back in the direction of Copacabana Beach. When they passed a small internet café, Julia paused. "I know there's no talking about home," she said, "but it'd be nice to let some people know I'm still alive."

Blake reassured her that they were allowed to break the rules for good things—like rubbing it in everyone's faces that they were in eighty-five degree weather with a constant ocean breeze, alternating between the rainforest and the beach.

He didn't mind stopping by the café, either. It was probably a good idea to check in with Jed Anderson, the top writer working for him, about new material for the show and anything that might have come up in his absence. He was supposed to be shaping the arc of the next season, ramping up the dramatic tension between Celia and Reese. But thinking about them made him think about the actors that played them, and focusing on Kelley and Liam certainly wasn't how he wanted to spend his time away. Psychological torture was more like it. He'd been trying to limit his computer access as a result, checking in with his mom and a few friends when he had the chance but keeping his distance from work. With Julia now at the forefront at his thoughts, it seemed a little less awful to open up his email and see what was going on with the show.

The café was small, an entryway on the first floor of a larger building, and there was only one computer open in the line of units with dividers separating each cube. Blake paid for an hour and motioned for Julia to get started. He'd take whatever time was left. It didn't look like any of the boys engaged in a series of shoot 'em up computer games at the terminals were leaving anytime soon.

Julia settled into her kiosk, a frown of concentration stealing over her face as soon as the mouse was in her hand. Blake decided to wait outside to escape the dark confines of the café and watch the street life go by. He bought a *cafezinho*, a little cup of coffee from a street vendor so small it was just a few cents for even fewer sips, and strolled around the block admiring how even from the street, down in the belly of the city, he still felt nestled in the mountains as flashes of green peeked between the buildings every time he turned.

Would Julia tell her friends about him? He had no idea what to expect. Not that he'd ever know what she said in her emails, but he couldn't help feeling curious. Would she say that she was alone? Had met a friend? Was *with* someone?

That strange and ambiguous preposition could cover all the bases from thoughtless fuck to friend with benefits to actual relationship material.

So which one was he?

Blake sipped the scalding coffee, savoring the bitter bite on his tongue. It wasn't exactly pleasant to imagine Julia tossing him off to the side with a few quick strokes of the keyboard, either by gossiping about him with her friends or else neglecting to mention him altogether.

But she'd given no sign that this was anything more than the most casual of flings. It wasn't a one-night stand, but it wasn't much more than that, either. Just a few days in each other's company before the real world called and they went back to their regular lives. She was giving him exactly what he'd said he wanted: everything, and with no strings attached.

He'd already shown that his plans could be changed. If she wasn't going to reveal what she thought about what would happen on January first when she boarded that plane for Chicago, then he wouldn't get into it, either.

Wasn't that the whole point of the prohibition against speaking about home? Neither of them wanted to think about the weather, the work, the demands pressing on them. Right now they were supposed to be having fun.

And they were—the most Blake could remember having in ages. A few days with Julia had already sent his mind into overdrive. He wasn't thinking about *The Everlastings* like he should have been, but about new show ideas, new characters, new possibilities for the future and his career. The ideas were little wispy things, no more substantial than the clouds streaking over the bay. But if he watched them, worked on them, reached for them long enough, they would eventually turn solid in his mind. That's when he'd be able to grab hold.

Somehow he'd thought that *The Everlastings* was going to be his one show, the project he and Kelley and Liam would work on until…well, he hadn't been able to fathom a future that didn't have the three of them working together. His best friend and his girlfriend. His team.

Now, though, he was having the first inklings that there could be a different future for him. He could create a new series, and with more experience under his belt, it might even be better than the first. There was no reason to think he couldn't do it again, especially while he still had major network support. He crushed the paper coffee cup in his palm, feet tapping on the sidewalk like they did when he was excited about an idea and couldn't keep still. He'd write to Anderson and ask what was up with *The Everlastings*. He wouldn't talk about any other projects. But he'd keep his mind open, waiting for whatever new things might come.

He walked quickly, checking his watch. When he popped his head into the café Julia was still fixated on the computer, typing furiously and stopping every now and then to click through something on the screen. So he left, walked around the block in the other direction, and when he came back in, she finally looked up.

"I'm done," she said, closing out the browser and getting up so he could take her seat.

"Are you sure? I don't want to rush you."

"Nope, that was perfect. I got in an email to my parents letting them know I haven't been eaten by sharks and told Danny I was safe, and then Liz was online so we chatted for a little while she was at work."

Blake nodded like these names meant something to him. Who the hell was Danny? If she had a boyfriend back home, he'd be damned... There was nothing in their undiscussed arrangement that said they were available, but the thought that she might not be as free as she appeared sent daggers into his gut.

Julia seemed to read something on his face and laughed. "Sorry, you have no idea who I'm talking about. My best friend, Liz, her brother Danny. She constantly wants to have fun; he's the one worrying all the time. They're the ones who'll come peel my body off the floor of my apartment if I choke on a pretzel and die alone."

"That's a pleasant thought."

"What else are friends for? All right, I'll leave you to it. Do you want me to pay for some more time for you, since I took up so much of it?"

Blake shook his head, sure he wouldn't need more than a few minutes to bring himself up to date on the news from the other side of the globe and share some quick thoughts with Anderson. He watched her wave to the kid behind the counter and step out of the café. Then he brought his eyes back to the screen before him, trying to shake off the mental image of her long legs in her sundress as she strode out the door. Her best friend and her best friend's brother? That didn't sound like a boyfriend. He permitted himself one small exhale of relief and then berated himself for being so paranoid. She hadn't said she wanted anything from him. So he should stop acting like he had something to give.

Blake fired up his email, scrolled through a few messages from work, and sent back a quick note to a group of friends wondering where on earth he was since his last message, from before he'd arrived at the falls. He checked the news and looked up TV ratings in Sydney and any major headlines about his show. Then he scanned through a few articles with the expected smattering of fluff on Australia's new "it" couple, gorgeous co-stars in love on screen and then in real life—and quickly clicked back to his email before he could torture himself anymore. He wanted to let his mom know he was in Rio until the first, even if he wouldn't tell her why.

But when he started asking how the dogs were doing, it occurred to him that he hadn't finished reading one of the previous articles to make sure there was no mention of him. He knew it was narcissistic to check, but actually the thought that he might have faded into silence while Kelley and Liam took center stage in the tabloids came as a welcome relief. If he wasn't being talked about anymore as the jilted sidekick, then maybe he could get back to his life, get back to his work, and finally leave the whole mess behind.

He clicked on the history button to find the article. That was when his hand stopped cold.

Under his email and the websites he'd checked since logging on, there was a whole slew of websites about him. One after another: *Joshua Blake Williams. The Everlastings.* She'd even searched his full name.

His passport.

He'd taken hers and then she'd grabbed his in return. His name wasn't that unusual but if she put in the whole thing and then something about Sydney and TV, it wouldn't be hard for the search to reward her. J.B. Williams. His old life splashed across the screen.

He had no privacy on the net. Everything about him was known. She'd seen it all—the shit town where he'd grown up, the factory where his mom had worked until he could afford for her to quit. Jesus, there was even stuff about the writing scholarships he'd won. Why couldn't she have just asked?

No talking about home. He didn't even know the names of her best friends, and now she knew every single thing about him. He closed the browser quickly, his heart hammering in his chest, palms sweaty on the keyboard despite the AC. He sat there for a minute, watching the clock run down, and then he got up and left.

He stormed across the street, fists deep in his pockets, his mind churning. What the hell had she been looking for? Did she want to know what was wrong with him, why he'd left everything behind to go hang out in a hostel in the middle of nowhere for as long as he possibly could? Had she not believed him about the show? Did she want proof that he was famous? What must she have thought when she discovered everything he was famous *for*?

Because it wasn't only the show that had made him a household name in his homeland. It was the screw-up. And she had seen that, too. It was impossible to Google him and not find out. His name was permanently aligned with Kelley Fielding, for better or worse. Until the internet exploded.

Blake stopped suddenly in the middle of the street, heart racing, and realized he had no idea where he was going. She was probably back at the café waiting for him. A cab slammed on its horn, and he jumped out of the way, jogging to the other side of the street. *Think*. He had to think.

He'd gone into the café and seen her *after* she'd looked up that stuff about him, and she hadn't been weird. Or else he'd been missing the signs because he hadn't known to look.

He ran a hand through his hair. No, she hadn't been weird at all. He felt his breathing start to slow. He looked up at the buildings, at the mountains behind. Down the street. Out toward the water.

What was he afraid of—that she'd leave him? They weren't even together.

He bought a bottle of water, drank it quickly, and walked back to the café, his heart slowly returning to normal even though he still had no idea what to think.

She was standing outside, leaning against the side of the building, when he approached. All long limbs and flowing hair, red dress and dark sunglasses, her face lighting up as soon as she saw he was there.

"You do everything you needed to get done?" she asked, hooking her arm through his as they took off down the street.

"Yeah," he said. *And then some.* "I had a little extra time so I went to get some water."

"It was good to check in with everyone, but it's not like I want to spend all day in there. It's so beautiful outside, don't you think?"

He nodded, on autopilot, and let her slip her hand in his as they walked back toward their hotel. If she was thinking anything behind that smile and those dark eyes, he had no idea. If he hadn't unintentionally found out what she'd really been doing online, he'd have had no clue that she now knew so much more about him.

He didn't know if her pretend calm made him feel better, or worse. Not only did she not trust him, but she didn't even care about what she'd found.

Then again, maybe if you were having a run-of-the-mill fling, you didn't much care about the past. Or the future. There was no way he could confront her—not when they didn't owe each other a thing.

Blake tried to push his discomfort aside. Dinner. That was all he needed to worry about. That was all they could really expect from each other. No plans beyond the next meal. He exhaled, trying to make himself relax.

There were so many good restaurants in Rio, from French to Italian to traditional steaming black bean *feijoada* and elaborate *churrascarias* with enormous slabs of meat cut right at the table for diners to choose. When Blake asked Julia what she was in the mood for and she promptly answered seafood, he knew what to try.

They went back to the hotel to change and then hopped a cab to Ipanema, a long crescent of pale sand that ended in two tall peaks on its far end. The day was winding down and the light sent long shadows along the shore as the water turned a deeper blue. That wasn't stopping any of the beachgoers from enjoying the last rays of color and the ocean breeze, even as the bars and restaurants along the strip were starting to light up.

The place Blake had in mind was quiet and out of the main fray, but it had gotten rave reviews. They were early enough to get a seat outside on the terrace and ordered a bottle of Portuguese *vinho verde* recommended by the waiter. It arrived crisp and chilled, and Blake smiled at the intensity with which Julia held his eye as they clinked their glasses, taking seriously Chris's admonition not to tempt fate and risk bad sex.

Blake knew Julia didn't think the superstition was

anything but funny, but on the off chance that it was actually true, he hoped it only applied to the person you were locking eyes with. The thought of Julia having seven years of knock-out sex with somebody else left a bitter taste in his mouth that had nothing to do with the wine, which was fresh and acidic and slightly effervescent, ideal after a long day walking in the heat.

Still, he couldn't help feeling a heaviness steal over him as he watched her lean back in her seat, fingering the condensation on the sides of her glass. Was she even going to tell him what she'd done?

"This is perfect," she sighed, looking out at the water through the palm trees lining the walkway down to the beach.

Well, that answered his question, at least. It looked like avoidance was going to be the strategy of the evening. Blake was just going to have to learn to keep up.

They ordered a grilled hearts of palm salad as an appetizer and a chilled pumpkin soup with prawns and the hint of something spicy—cayenne, to balance the saffron threads?— that made the whole dish come alive.

"When I first came to Brazil, I was in the Amazon," Blake said between bites. "All I ate was the most basic fried fish and grilled meat from those ubiquitous food stalls."

"And pineapple juice?" Julia winked.

"And pineapples." He laughed. "And then I got to Manaus—that's the major city plunked down in the middle of the rainforest—and it was like I'd never seen food before. I had no idea Brazil was known for its cuisine, you know?"

Julia nodded as Blake remembered his first bite of the thick, smoky *feijoada* that was Brazil's national dish.

"I may have imagined that I'd be spending my vacation sipping cocktails on the beach, but I never thought it would be *quite* this nice." Julia swirled the light, straw-colored wine in her glass and took another sip before spearing one of the palm hearts with her fork, mopping up the cilantro and lime vinaigrette.

"I can assure you that my other travels have definitely not been like this."

"Tell me more about where else you've been."

"Tell me why you Googled me."

He had meant to keep quiet about it, but half a glass of wine later the words were out of his mouth before he even realized he was going to say them. A request to match her request. A challenge for more information to balance out the information she'd gained.

Her eyes grew wide and she paused mid-breath, suddenly at a loss for words. Then she smacked her forehead. "The search history?"

"Bingo."

"I'm not a very good sleuth."

"No."

The blush on her face was the deepest he'd seen. But there was no attempt to cover anything up or act like she'd done nothing wrong. Just embarrassment, pure and simple.

"I was chatting with my friend Liz and I told her about you. I'm sorry, should I not have? I didn't know. But," she laughed and gestured around her. "How could I not?"

"And then you said…?" he prodded, his stomach in knots.

"And then I admitted to her that I didn't really know that much about you." Julia put her glass down. "That I *don't* know that much about you." She changed her tense emphatically, stressing all that still remained unsaid between them.

He put his glass down on the table louder than he'd planned. "And you couldn't, for instance, *ask* whatever it was that you were so desperate to find out?"

Julia jumped, looking startled at his tone. "It wasn't like I set about to go snooping on you."

"But that's exactly what you did," he pressed, aware of

his voice rising in the restaurant. How could she not see what she'd done?

She bit her lip. "Look, you're making too big deal out of this. I honestly wasn't even going to say anything."

His fork clattered on the table. "Well then I'm glad my whole life isn't a big deal to you."

Julia looked stunned and for a moment Blake regretted his words. But the flash of all those cameras on him still stung. How could he be on the front page of the tabloids and at the same time not matter at all?

"You know that's not what I meant," she said quietly, clutching her glass and looking away.

Blake sighed. Suddenly he felt exhausted. What did it matter? They barely even had two more days. "Look, let's forget it. Forget I found out, it doesn't matter anyway."

"I didn't think it was a problem," she said. "But obviously it was, and I'm sorry."

"I just wish you would've asked me directly, instead."

"Ask you what?" She threw her hands up on the air. "I barely know anything about you. You're completely vague on whatever you do say about your life, and I'm sorry but it didn't occur to me to check in with you beforehand about whether you were a famous TV writer who'd gotten completely screwed. I didn't think it was my business." She paused, then added, "I still don't."

Blake opened his mouth, then closed it again. That was what she thought—that he had been screwed? Not that he had it coming to him? In the scandal and gossip of Australia's celebrity world, public opinion had determined there was something wrong with him for not holding on to his star. But here it was like Julia cared but also didn't, and Blake didn't know whether it made them closer or further apart to know that she'd seen this side of his life and basically shrugged.

"So what did you tell Liz?" He wasn't sure he really

wanted to know, but he still had to ask.

He was surprised to see Julia laugh. "I mentioned that I'd met someone, and Liz said—okay, first you have to understand that she's Liz. She's been my best friend since kindergarten and we've been through everything together. It made her life to know that I was having a good time."

No, Blake had to revise his earlier assessment. *Now* she was sporting the deepest blush he'd ever seen on her. It made something bubble through his insides, cutting through his anger. She was having a good time?

"And then she was all, *Oh my god who is he, Google him, look him up*, blah blah blah." Julia imitated a frenetic, high-pitched voice and Blake got an instant picture of who Liz was. "Sooooo." She took a gulp of wine far more sizeable than the sips she'd been enjoying. "I did."

For a second Blake couldn't speak. "Wait—you were just like, I don't really know this guy, and it was your *friend* who told you to stalk me?"

"I wasn't stalking you! It's the internet! *Everybody* uses it."

"I didn't Google you," he pointed out.

"Maybe you should have. What if everything about me is totally made up? What if I'm actually...I don't know. A wanted fugitive in the States."

"Julia." He reached across the table and grabbed her hand. "Nobody makes up being a high school math teacher."

"That's why it's the perfect disguise!"

He shook his head. "Nobody."

She frowned. "So that's why I never go on any dates?"

"I find it utterly impossible that you don't go on any dates."

"You think I'm lying to you?"

"I don't know. You're the one with the built in lie detector."

"Not lying. Math teacher, no dates." She paused. "Are you

still upset?"

Blake took a deep breath and looked out across the terrace to the endless ocean outside. Was he? "I thought you—"

"Didn't trust you?"

He shook his head. "It's not just that. Well, yeah, it is, but also I thought you wanted to find out if I'm really..." he trailed off, not sure how to finish the thought.

"I'll admit that when Chris and Jamie were talking about your TV show, I didn't quite realize that when you said famous, you meant *famous*. But, uh, I don't care, if that's what you're thinking about. I mean, wait!" she said quickly, choosing her words. "I don't mean I don't care, like I don't care about your life. I mean that the objective state of your fame or lack thereof is of no interest to me, or has no bearing on my interest in you." She exhaled warily. "Is that better?"

Blake tried to separate out the different strands of thoughts tangled inside him. He was surprised to find that it was nice knowing she'd mentioned him to her friend. It wasn't like he was a secret, after all, and it meant that even as a fling it had enough significance to warrant a conversation. If she was telling the truth, which she'd given him no reason to doubt, then it had just been curiosity and appeasing a friend's prurient appetite for detail.

"I felt like it was snooping and told Liz that it was weird," Julia said softly, lowering her eyes. "But it's a good thing I looked at your passport that one time because I would have been totally mortified to have been gushing to Liz about you and then been forced to admit I didn't even know your last name."

Two pink spots darkened on her cheeks from where her previous flush hadn't gone down. Blake leaned forward, intrigued.

"Gushing? Do tell."

Julia rolled her eyes. "Whatever, *Josh*." But she stuck out her tongue when she said it.

"I was always Blake growing up, but then when I started writing professionally it was J.B. Williams, so I became known by my first name instead." Blake shrugged like it had just happened, but actually he'd made a conscious choice to create his public persona as Joshua, the first name he never used. When he became Josh Williams, it felt like the real him, the one who had always been and would always be Blake, was still the same inside, no matter where his career went.

It had wound up being a blessing to have that extra layer separating who he was inside from the man he was to everyone else. When the acclaim started rolling in, it was weird to read about this Josh guy who was sort of like him, but also sort of not. And when everything in the tabloids was about the Josh who'd been cheated on and dumped, turned against by Australia's favorite celebrity couple both on and off the screen, the one thing that kept him sane was that at least all that was happening to Josh and not him.

It wasn't really true, of course, but it was also a way to test how well people knew him. If they saw only the celebrity side, they knew Josh. But to his family, his friends, and the people he loved, he was Blake.

To Julia, he would always be Blake.

Their waiter came by and for a minute they were quiet as he refilled their glasses, taking away the empty plate and leaving them the soup to polish off. Julia soaked up the creamy bisque with a slice of bread and Blake followed her lead, splitting the last prawn with his knife for them to share.

"I'm sorry about Liam," Julia said so quietly Blake thought he'd misheard. It was so not what other people had said to him when they heard about the scandal. He must have looked completely confused because Julia repeated it again. "Your friend, Liam. I'm sorry, that sucks."

"Yeah," Blake said slowly, chewing on the last bite of bread. "It did suck."

He sighed then, deeply. A sigh that, as soon as he let it out, he realized he'd been holding in for months.

"God this wine is good," Julia mused, taking another sip, and Blake couldn't help it. It was so ridiculous, he laughed as she put the glass down.

"What?" she asked, looking over her shoulder like maybe she'd missed something funny.

"I just—" Blake shook his head.

"It sucked? This wine is good? What's so funny?"

"I've spent *months* dealing with the fallout from this, so much so that if I had to hear one more word of fake pity, or commentary on how I must have had it coming, I probably would have done something that would not have reflected favorably upon Australia's largest TV network. Which was why it was definitely time for me to flee the coop for a while, so to speak. "

"And?"

"And then you come along, and I don't want to tell you this stuff because God, who wants to talk about it? I nearly had a heart attack when Chris and Jamie started talking that day in the van, like what if they said something incriminating… But you *Google* me and you find probably the worst, most salacious websites on the planet and all you can say is, *Sorry about your friend*?" He exhaled again.

"Wrong thing to say?" She furrowed her brow.

"Perfect thing to say." He smiled warmly, meaning it.

"Friends should be your friends. Otherwise, what's the point?"

"It sounds so simple when you say it."

"It is," she said, and the look in her eyes was fierce and protective. She'd said that she'd been friends with Liz since they were kids; he had a feeling that when she was close to someone, she didn't let them go.

He'd sensed that what they were doing was new to her. But now he felt a warning, too. She'd acted fine with their fling and fine when he said he was leaving for Argentina. This was different, though—whatever it was. He didn't want her to be hurt when January first came and they were inevitably done.

But he didn't want to remind her of that. All he said was how lucky Liz was to have Julia in her corner.

Julia made some kind of half-laughing, half-huffing noise that could only be described as a snort, something so out of character for her normally composed features that it made him laugh. "At least the girl knows it," she said. Blake raised an eyebrow but she didn't elaborate.

Their main courses arrived, grilled flounder with coconut rice and fried plantains and a spicy fish stew with coconut milk, tomatoes, cilantro, and lime. The fish was fresh and flaked off the bone, the stew rich but still light, balancing sweetness with a spicy kick.

"Remind me again why I live somewhere landlocked," Julia commented as she pulled apart pieces of fish in the stew to soak up the broth.

"I have no idea," Blake said, spearing a plantain and passing it to her to try. "I'm a coastal boy, remember?"

She imitated the way he said "remember," slow and particular and then garbling the consonant on the end. "You've got that accent and don't appear to know what a sunburn is. How could I forget?"

He teased her about American Midwestern accents, cracking up until they realized people at the other tables were looking and they'd better pipe down. By the time they finished eating and had polished off the wine, the sky was a brilliant orange lighting up the palm trees. It made the mountains look like they were on fire over the sea.

"Dessert?" Blake asked when their plates were cleared.

Julia shook her head. "I'm stuffed."

"Too stuffed for chocolate soufflé? I'm sorry, I'm not familiar with that sensation."

"Oh, if there's going to be *chocolate* involved…" Julia conceded that she might have a little extra room.

It was dark and drizzled in raspberry sauce, with a dollop of homemade brown sugar and rum whipped cream dusted with pistachio bits. Blake groaned in delight.

When they left the terrace, the beach was empty but the streets were starting to fill, the pulse of the Brazilian nightlife singing its siren song. Blake wondered what he'd be doing right now if he were in Buenos Aires. Would he have found a group to latch on to? Would he be in a bar, with tourists or locals or grizzled gauchos swapping stories before parting ways the next day?

Would he be thinking about Julia? And if so, would he be congratulating or kicking himself for letting go?

But there was no way to know. It was impossible to picture what he might be doing if he weren't in Ipanema, like it was impossible to imagine what he'd be doing with his life if *The Everlastings* hadn't broken through.

If he'd grown up with a father. If he hadn't scrapped an old script that was giving him endless agony and started furiously sketching out new ideas fast as he could, the wisps of ideas turning real as bricks the faster the words poured forth.

If he hadn't met the right people who saw the idea and helped bring it to life. If he hadn't known the perfect aspiring actor and actress to play the leads.

And then, if he hadn't come back early from a run and walked in on that actor and actress, his best friend and his girlfriend, in his trailer. If he hadn't seen the man he'd come to think of as a brother going down on the woman he'd been sure would become his wife.

For all her Googling, Julia didn't know that part of it.

No one did. Not even the tabloids got that detail right. All anyone knew was Kelley and Josh, and then Kelley and Liam, the transition so seamless it was like something out of a screenplay, with no real people involved. *No live animals were harmed in the making of this feature.* But Blake didn't have to bleed to feel pain.

Somehow Kelley's newly hired publicist had known how to give it the right spin. Josh could be pitied and perhaps a little bit scorned, for what had he done to drive her away? But it was orchestrated in a way that created intrigue and boosted ratings instead of turning people off. Meanwhile Kelley got to be everyone's darling, living the fantasy of true love with her dear friend and co-star, recounting in interviews the moment when everything "clicked" and she realized that when she looked deep into Liam's eyes, she wasn't acting when she proclaimed her love.

Yeah, Kelley, he'd wanted to ask her. *When exactly did this all "click"?*

But there was no way to know. Blake still wondered how much of her feelings for him had ever been real.

But maybe they had all three been acting, and he'd been pretending as much as she and Liam were. *J.B. Williams.* Just who did he think he was?

"Penny for your thoughts," Julia said, and Blake was startled out of the downward spiral his mind was on. She slipped her hand in his as they walked down the winding side streets where the beach turned and the mountains began.

It wasn't a question, though. Or a request to know more. Just a comment, a murmur, like the waves that kept on nudging the shore. Just a reminder that they were still there.

"I was thinking about Liam," Blake admitted, steering them back toward the water. It was nice to stroll around like this, light with wine and heavy with food, admiring the way the breeze rustled through Julia's loose hair and the hem of her skirt.

"I'm sorry, I shouldn't have brought it up."

"It's weird," Blake said like he hadn't heard her. "I would've assumed that I'd miss him, you know? But then I think about it, and it's hard to even remember anymore why we were friends."

Julia nodded, letting him talk. Now that the dam had been broken and the big secret out, it was easier, somehow. And easy to talk about with someone who didn't know the parties, didn't know the history, and didn't particularly care. Someone he was, in all likelihood, never going to see again.

Maybe it was because they weren't close that he could talk to her like this. Jamie had become a friend, but even they didn't talk about details. It was better to pretend he didn't know anything, so that Blake could be just a regular guy.

"I guess I miss the idea of him more than the actual person. I miss having these people who were always my people, you know?" He paused, considering. "But I don't need them the way that I thought I did."

When they got to the beach, she kicked off her sandals and he followed suit, holding them in one hand while they walked across the sand and down to the shoreline. The water came up to their ankles, still warm. When the waves retreated, the breeze on their toes was a sudden surprise in the dark.

"Maybe it was good to let go of them," Julia said after a pause. "Maybe they aren't what you need anymore. Not that it was good that they made that decision for you. But, you know. In the end."

Blake thought about that. Everyone had tiptoed around the issue, knowing but not knowing what happened, unsure how to respond. Calling Kelley a bitch or Liam an ass wasn't helpful, because who wanted to feel like the fool who'd sunk time and energy into such awful people? But trying to rationalize what they'd been thinking when they got together was even worse. Blake's mother had pursed her lips and avoided the subject, only telling him when he came home after his whole world was shattered that she thought the camera lights had gone to Kelley's head and he'd find someone better suited to him.

Which may have been true, but at the time it felt, again, like he was the one with the problem and she the shining star absolved by the brightness she cast.

If he hadn't scrapped his failed project. If he hadn't started *The Everlastings*. If he hadn't thrown Kelley and Liam together in front of the camera. If he hadn't walked in on them. If his whole life hadn't changed.

Then he wouldn't be walking down the beach in Rio on this night, full of chocolate soufflé, the mountains behind him and the ocean lapping at his feet.

And he wouldn't have met Julia.

Chapter Fourteen

Down where Ipanema curved into Copacabana beach, Julia sat and brushed her skirt over her knees, burying her toes in the sand. To either side of her were Rio's distinctive mountains stamped against the blue-black sky. Behind her the city was coming alive in the night, but Julia hardly seemed to notice. From somewhere down the beach they heard laughter, the swish of a car up the street, and then silence again.

They'd been walking along the beach since they finished dinner, and it was nice now to sit and let the night wash over them like a wave. It was hard to see any stars from the moon and the city lights, but far out over the ocean, where the black of the sea became the black of the sky, she could make out a twinkling where the earth curved and dropped away forever.

Blake sat with his legs bent up, arms around his knees, and looked out over the water. He'd seemed agitated that evening, and Julia couldn't figure out why until he'd confronted her out of the blue about why she'd been looking for more information about him. She'd been surprised—and embarrassed. And then angry that he'd gotten so mad over something that wasn't a big deal.

But she also liked discovering that he wasn't particularly good at keeping secrets, or even keeping things to himself. He was easy to talk to. There was no sitting there silently seething, stewing over things for days or weeks or months, building up an army of resentments until the whole legion attacked.

Once they'd talked about it, Julia had at least been able to clear up what she'd been looking for, which really wasn't much.

She sat in the sand and thought about her chat with Liz. She hadn't meant to say anything about Blake, but it hadn't taken Liz long to figure it out. Like Blake, Julia was a terrible liar. She could practically hear Liz's ear-splitting shrieks through the computer screen as she typed into the chat, "Tell me EVERYTHING."

Williams. At least Julia knew his last name was Williams.

That wound up not being that useful, but Joshua Blake Williams—now that was another story.

She hadn't known what she'd been expecting to find, but a whole lot of gossip about someone named Kelley Fielding wasn't it. She didn't know every single detail, but she certainly knew enough. Your best friend winding up with your girlfriend… No wonder Blake had wanted to flee the country, the continent—everything he knew of the world.

No wonder he didn't want to get too close.

"Penny for your thoughts," Blake smiled, and she sighed and brushed her cheek against his shoulder, resting it there while she twirled a strand of her hair.

"I was thinking about how much my friends would like it here," she said wistfully.

"Liar." Blake smiled.

She grinned back at him. "Okay, you're right. I was thinking about how nice it is to have a break."

"From them?"

"From everything."

"Now that sounds more like the truth." He leaned back, propping himself up on his forearms. "Tell me about them. What was it—Danny and…"

"Liz. Liz's my age, Danny's three years older."

"And this guy spent his whole childhood hanging out with his little sister and her pals?" Blake raised an eyebrow skeptically, and Julia gently shoved him for teasing.

"No, he didn't know I existed until later."

"Yeah, until you got smoking hot and he realized he'd better stick around if he knew what was good for him."

"No, before that." She stuck out her tongue, glad her face was bathed in shadow because the blood was rushing to her cheeks…and elsewhere. Hot? Really?

"Wait." Blake held up a hand. "You said you never dated this guy, and yet you have patently *not* denied that he knows you're a fox."

"I never said we didn't date," Julia said carefully. Lying and selectively omitting were two totally different things when it came to avoiding the whole tangled history of her best friend and her ex.

"You did! You told me—"

"I told you he wasn't my boyfriend. As in, present tense. As in, I am plenty single and available."

Am I single? A voice in her head wondered. *Am I available, if I'm sitting here with you?* But he hadn't given any sign that their relationship—that their *thing*—was anything more than these few days. In fact, he'd already shown that he had no trouble packing up and heading out of town when the time came. Clearly she was single. So was Blake. They were just having fun.

She tried to focus on the task at hand, which was getting the subject off of Danny. But Blake was persistent.

"Explain," he commanded in that voice he used for sex,

for telling her what to do with a throaty bite that seemed to always bring her to her knees. Literally, in fact.

Explain? How could she explain? They were friends, and then they dated, and now they were friends again.

But Blake wasn't buying that at all.

"Tell me," he said, softer now. "Tell me about you."

That was his other voice, the one so tender it made her feel like they were the only two people in the world, and everything was finally safe to say.

Julia swallowed hard and fixated on the pale white foam where the surf broke and broke and broke. She had nothing to tell. She was like the ocean. She was just there, that was all.

"There's nothing to it," she tried to say, but her voice cracked and that, she knew, was her tell. Like Blake's frown, it was the way anyone who knew her well enough could see that she was withholding.

Liz could sniff it out of her before she ever opened her mouth. It was like she sensed it—even when they were chatting online, thousands of miles between them.

It was one of the things Danny had never figured out, because he was so sure he knew her and so sure that he always got it right.

But then he had asked her, begged her, honestly, to let him know if he should stay. And she had said *yes, stay*, but he had packed and left her anyway.

So maybe he did know. Because she never would have said she wanted him to go. Until he did, and it felt like she'd known that was the right thing all along. Known ever since they started that the only thing they both knew how to do together was end.

Blake gave her the silence between them, letting the stillness stretch and grow. But it wasn't stretching thin. It was a fullness that gathered and swelled. In their own private world on the beach, their faces were veiled and all they knew for certain was the feeling of skin against skin. At night, under the great dark bowl of the sky, two people could talk freely, knowing they never had to see one another again.

Blake touched her hand and lay back in the sand, one arm bent to hold his head in the crook of his elbow, the other hand reaching for hers.

She brushed the sand out of her skirt and lay down with him, resting her head on his chest, feeling his heartbeat somewhere inside her own chest and the steady swell of his breathing alongside hers. A finger twirled absently in her hair. A reassuring touch that he was there.

It was, she thought with a thud in her heart that ricocheted up to her throat, perhaps the most intimate she had ever been with another being. Not having sex. Not even lying naked with him. It was like their clothes didn't matter, because they were naked in another way. In the night, on the beach, she looked up at the black, heard the waves, knew that elsewhere there was a city. There were worlds upon worlds upon worlds. But the only world she was in right now had Blake in it. And the touch of his hand and the rise of his chest and the catch in her throat as she tried to think of what to say.

"Don't plan it in advance," he whispered. "Just tell it from the beginning. Tell me about your friends."

Julia took a deep breath and found herself sort of smiling, thinking back. "I guess like most stories, it started with a boy."

"Danny?"

She shook her head against his chest. "His name was Mark. He was a dick."

"Okay."

"And Liz was in love with him all through high school."

"Even though he was a dick?"

"Are you going to let me tell my story?"

"All quiet from the editor."

"Yes, she was dating Mark, and yes, he was a dick, and

yes—everyone knew it but her."

They had fought about it, actually. Their first real fight in all the years they'd been friends. Julia wasn't being "supportive enough." Julia didn't know what she was supposed to be supporting. Liz had cried. Julia had stood there, stunned. Liz had called her heartless. Said she didn't know what it felt like to be in love.

Julia, of course, had nodded. She had absolutely no clue. That she acquiesced to Liz's superior authority on the matter at least helped smooth things over. Julia didn't know about love. Therefore her opinions were not to be trusted.

So she kept her opinions to herself. A safe move, one that had always worked successfully and continued to come through for her then.

Mark was a year older and Julia was relieved when he graduated high school and went off to college. But their break up was worse than their dating. The tears, the fights, Liz sobbing hysterically curled up on Julia's bed. How could she lose her virginity to this guy who just *left*, like college meant he no longer knew how to drive or operate a phone? Secretly, Julia was relieved that he was out of their lives. But she was wrong about that.

It happened the night of the bonfire. Julia tried to describe it to Blake. It was tradition for the graduating seniors and the college kids back for the beginning of summer to throw an enormous party out in the woods, where they wouldn't attract any cops. Maybe some people knew. Maybe they thought it was campers, or hunters getting an early start. Nobody worried. It was just the bonfire, and once they had joined the ranks of Easterbrook High Alumni, they were officially allowed in.

"Drinking?" Blake asked.

"Hammered. Everyone."

"You? I'm shocked!"

Julia twisted to face him as much as she could while lying down. "Absolutely not! I was way too good for that. Liz dragged me along because she wanted to find Mark. And so I was officially on Liz duty. Making sure she didn't get so drunk she'd puke in my parents' car. I still had to drive her home."

"And then?"

"And then somehow I lost her."

And then there was screaming, and she'd found her again.

"Mark tried to pull something out in the woods and I got Danny, because I knew he was there at the party. I knew he could help. We took Liz home and that was when we all started hanging out. Liz swore off men for—for a long time. And we stuck pretty tight together, the three of us, that summer. Danny and I started dating the following winter. It lasted eight years."

Blake let out a low whistle.

"In the end, mostly what we had was our friendship and looking out for Liz. But Liz is all grown up, and she doesn't need us to take care of her anymore."

Blake spun a lock of hair tight around his finger. "I get the feeling there are some major gaps in this story."

Julia lay still, wanting to curl up beside him and bury herself in his skin. Wanting to turn away and run down the beach until her legs couldn't keep going. Until she never had to see him again. It felt like an enormous weight was crushing down on her, paralyzing her with pain. There was no way the words could squeeze through all that pressure. No way they could come out without ripping her to shreds if she spoke.

But this was her one chance to tell someone who wasn't Danny or Liz, who wasn't in it from the start. And if she could say the words, the relief might crush her as much as all those years of accumulating silences, keeping Liz's secret safe. And so keeping Mark safe as well.

"In the woods, that night. She went to find him and he

wanted to take a walk, said he wanted to see her again."

She could feel Blake's stomach tighten as he stopped breathing.

"It was like he thought that because they'd had sex before, they could always have sex again. So hey, you know, in the woods after almost a year of not talking? Sure!"

She barked out a bitter laugh. He had kept slurring out obscenities as she and Danny had pulled Liz away, trying to patch together her torn dress, carrying her instead of bothering to look around for the sandal she lost. *You wanted it before, so what the fuck?*

"She was lucky to have you as a friend looking out for her that night." Blake's voice was soft, and deeply sad. She wondered if he was thinking about his own friend, the one who would have stood by his side but was now lost to him for good.

But Julia shook her head against his chest. She always felt like it was somehow her fault. Like she shouldn't have let Liz go to the party, knowing Mark would be there. Like she should have been able to *do* something besides tie the strap of Liz's dress up and drive, stone cold sober, knuckles white on the steering wheel, shaking with rage.

She hadn't said anything to Mark. Not one single thing. Hadn't yelled. Didn't raise her voice. Didn't use her voice at all. How many kinds of useless was she? Who couldn't even defend her own friend? Who brought her into the lion's den and wandered around making inane conversation while she was mauled?

"It wasn't your fault," Blake said slowly, as if reading her mind.

"I know," Julia said, but her voice cracked as she lied.

They had stayed up all night. Well, she and Danny had. Liz had fallen asleep, bruised and bloodied from where branches had whacked her shins. But Julia had been shaking too hard to sleep and Danny was ashen, gripping a coffee mug in the kitchen so hard she thought it might crack.

Liz's parents had been away, and Liz refused to tell anyone what had happened. She was afraid no one would believe her. She didn't know what she would say. She thought because she hadn't been "raped," it didn't count. Maybe she really believed what Mark had said, that somehow she owed it to him. Mostly, she felt ashamed.

Julia and Danny stayed up all night drinking coffee because they didn't know what else to do, until they were wired and strung out on nerves and no sleep and caffeine. After that, they were united in taking care of Liz, helping her through the aftermath, spreading her burden across three backs instead of one.

"I think that's the only all-nighter I've ever pulled," she said with a forced laugh, rolling onto her stomach so that she could see Blake.

He was incredulous. "Only? Ever? Not even for something *fun*?"

Julia shook her head. "That's the part of the story you find shocking?"

"Jesus, *no*." Blake exhaled through his teeth. "That's the only part of the story I can wrap my head around without exploding." His arm was around her and his grip tightened protectively. "I don't know how you three got through that."

"I feel like I spent so much of my twenties under water. Sometimes I wonder what college would have been like if I wasn't—" She stopped abruptly, biting her tongue. The last thing she wanted was to say anything bad about Liz. So why was she talking like this, so free with someone she'd known for a matter of days when these were things she'd been holding onto for over a decade, alone?

"If you weren't what?" he asked, and she knew then why she was talking. Because he would listen and cared what the answer might be. He didn't know it in advance or have his own version to tell. He wanted to know her story, because it was hers.

She thought about the things she could say. About the time she and Danny spent looking after Liz, who retreated so deeply into herself that sometimes Julia wondered if the girl who dressed up in sequins and bossed her dolls around at tea parties would ever come back. Or how vast and terrifying her world became, and she so small and alone, that long night listening to Liz cry herself to sleep only to wake up still crying, and keep crying for years before she was finally able to stop.

But instead she said simply, "It wasn't a great introduction to sex." And in that one wry line, her lips pursed and frowning, she felt like she'd summed up pretty much all there was to say.

"You were…?" Blake trailed off.

"A virgin," Julia finished his question. "Danny, too."

"And did you…?"

"It took us a long time to work up to it," Julia admitted. "Longer than it probably otherwise would have, in normal circumstances."

"You were afraid." It wasn't a question.

It wasn't something she normally talked about with people. There were so few men besides Danny that she would have had a reason to share anything about her sexual history with, and she always felt it was something she would have been judged for. For taking her time, for thinking sex was something that wounded more than it salved, for needing to know from whomever she was with that it didn't have to be violent.

"It took so long for us to finally do anything. We were around each other nonstop and yet for him to first kiss me was epic. But I knew it had to be him. It was like it could only ever be with him. Because I always felt like…like he was the only one I knew I could trust. What if everyone harbored a secret Mark inside, and I'd think I knew who I was with but then one day I'd turn around and see this whole other person come out?"

"But you already said you didn't like Mark," Blake pointed out. "I mean, not like you can tell that about someone. But you knew there was something about him that was bad news."

"I know, and it's not like I can go around assuming that everyone is a Mark until they prove they're not, or assume that even if I *think* I trust them, there might still be this dark side lurking around. But it was hard not to feel that way for a long time. Danny was a good big brother. Yeah, he mostly ignored us when I was over, but I knew what he was like in the family. He was protective, the kind of guy who looked out for his kid sister. He was devastated by what happened, not just that it happened to Liz but also that people were capable of these things at all. Some people who knew or found out later tried to rationalize—oh, Mark was drunk. Oh, he thought Liz still wanted to go out with him. But Danny knew that was bullshit, and he couldn't understand."

She paused for a minute. "He's a nice guy, Danny. He really is. But it was like we were afraid of each other. Afraid of what sex might do."

Blake stroked his hand down her cheek and rested his forefinger lightly on her lips. She bit the pad of his finger lightly. It was nice to see him smile, after she'd made the evening so heavy instead.

"And now?" he asked quietly.

Julia swung one leg over him so she was lying on top of him, her hips straddling his, her dress cinching up toward her waist as she felt the front of his shorts press between her legs. "There are good thing about growing up." She kissed him like she'd been wanting to all night, as though they were alone in the world, the only two souls on the beach.

"Is Liz okay?" Blake's voice was pained.

Julia thought for a minute. "Liz is busy getting back the years she lost. She calls it her 'second adolescence.' Really it's her new college years. I think she's making up for the fun she didn't have, the sex she never experimented with, the dates she didn't go on when she was young." Julia laughed. "She's having more fun than anyone else I know, that's for sure."

Blake's hands were sliding down her back now, getting progressively lower as she spoke. "When did you start making up for lost time?"

"I think I just started this week."

"I hope you're having fun."

She inhaled the scent of him, the salt on his skin. "Maybe this is what you do all the time, but I guess it's okay to admit to you that it's a little new for me."

"Mmm, which part?" he asked, teasing the fabric up her skirt to expose her thighs to the moonlight.

"Let's see…fucking a stranger, fucking a stranger in Brazil, no wait—fucking an *Australian* stranger in Brazil. Fucking in a pool. Fucking under a waterfall. Hopping a bus to an incredible city and wandering around with no set itinerary and—oh yes—fucking some more." She lowered her voice, loving how delicious it sounded to say everything they'd been doing. Loving even more how much Blake seemed to obviously delight in her saying it.

"Are we about to fuck some more?" he whispered, sliding his hand under her skirt to feel—yes, she'd put on thin lace panties, black this time, and it made her pulse quicken to feel his fingers pause at the fabric and then hook under the band, groaning and pulling her toward him.

"God, I hope so," she whimpered, not sure how she could go from pouring her heart out to unspeakably horny in a matter of minutes. Was that, too, what intimacy was? Not just being without clothes but being without boundaries, moving fluidly from one state of openness to another, following the conversation wherever it turned?

"I'm not sure this counts as new anymore—I'm not a stranger, am I?"

"Not since I Googled you," she teased, and he yanked on her panties in response.

"I still want to be a little new," he breathed. "I still want to excite you."

"Let's admit that fucking is new, and so everything you do to me is exciting."

In one swift motion he flipped her over so she was on her back in the sand and he was pressing his weight into her, making sure she could feel his cock through his shorts.

"You didn't fuck Danny?" he said, his face in the shadows but his eyes alight.

"Danny didn't fuck." She looped her fingers through Blake's empty belt loops and pulled his hips to her. "Poor Danny."

"What did Poor Danny do?"

Julia bit her lip. "Poor Danny made love. He was always so sweet. He would never, ever fuck me." She pressed her lips to his ear and whispered, "No matter how badly I begged him to."

"You begged for it?" he asked, his voice catching, his cock rock hard against her hip.

She shook her head. "You're the only one I beg to fuck me."

That did it. His hand was up her skirt in a matter of seconds, his thumb pressing against the crotch of her panties to feel her wetness seeping through.

"Inside," he said. "Now."

When they were back in their hotel room, their clothes were off so fast Julia couldn't believe nothing ripped. Blake paused for a moment to enjoy her in her panties, but even those were off before she knew it as she lay back to take him in, feeling his mouth hot and searching where his cock soon followed.

He fucked her like she'd always wanted, hard and fast and slow and sweet and dangerous all at once. He fucked her until the sweat poured off their bodies. He fucked her until she was completely gone, her body a fire that knew nothing but how to consume.

When it was done, she slept as though she'd forgotten everything—who she was, where she'd been, even her own name.

She slept like she was ready to wake up new.

Chapter Fifteen

Blake felt Julia stirring and rolled over to see her sleepy eyes blinking at the sun streaming through the thin curtain covering the window.

"Sleep okay?" he asked.

"God yes." Her smile was heaven, everything glowing. He could tell how much she'd enjoyed last night. He'd hardly been able to keep his hands off her in the elevator. As soon as they'd reached the hotel room he'd slammed the door behind her and thrown her up against the wall, lifting her up so her legs wrapped around him. Lifting her up so he could get at that tiny, lacy nothing under her skirt.

Her hair tousled and streaming, sand everywhere from where they had lain on the beach. Her neck arched back, her lips parted, her mouth whimpering as he fumbled with his belt. Her nipples so hard between his teeth.

Just the thought of how hot he'd been for her last night was getting him aroused again. Julia noted it appreciatively as she turned in the tangle of sheets to reach for him.

"What do you want to do today?" he asked. It was December thirty-first. They had a long night ahead of them ringing in the new year on the beach. But it was hard to stay sleeping when the whole city was beckoning them.

Hard to stay in bed but for the fact that Julia, instead of answering him, was wrapping those sweet, swollen lips around the head of his cock once again.

"Mmm," she groaned as he slid farther in. Her pleasure and the eagerness with which she sucked him drove him insane. Last night when he'd carried her from the doorway and dropped her back on the bed, she'd taken over yanking off his shorts so fast he was powerless to stop her. She'd slid to her knees with her shirt half off, letting him pull her hair up to feel it cascading through his fingers while she took him deep down her throat.

He had understood at last what she was giving to him: all of herself. That was what existed beneath the mask she wore. That was what she'd withheld from other men. Her passion, her pleasure, her joy. What made him so special he couldn't say, but she seemed to have decided she could trust him. Whether it was despite the fact that they wouldn't see each other again or because of it, he didn't know and didn't ask. All he could tell was that her frenzy made him want her more and more. He turned her around on the bed so he could lick her wetness while she worked his cock.

She ground her pelvis over his mouth, working her clit against his tongue while his fingers found the places she wanted to be touched. At the same time, she swirled her tongue over his tip and then plunged her mouth over his shaft, up and down, up and down, as he felt the orgasm build.

"I can't believe I still have anything left in me," he groaned as she cupped his balls. He could feel her smiling with her mouth around his dick.

"What? You only came twice last night. I'm trying to even the score."

Blake laughed as she locked her lips around him once again. It was true. He couldn't believe how much she'd come. In his mouth, on his fingers, clenched around his dick, and then again as his tongue lapped her up. He had felt every single one and the force with which they shook her. When he finally lost control himself, he was sure it was the hardest he'd ever come, first in her mouth and then, when she'd worked him back up with her tongue, deep inside her, holding her legs up while she grasped the headboard with both hands, hips bucking up to meet him, everything begging him to give it to her deeper, harder, faster until he was gone.

She wasn't working on him too hard right now but he could feel himself approaching the edge. The ground was hurtling toward him faster and faster, the moment of impact closer and closer. Gently he drew her off him. Her lips were swollen, eyes glassy with pleasure, skin radiating heat.

"Too close," he panted, and she grinned with a look that he knew poor Danny had never seen. That pure, unadulterated desire that said there was no thinking, no judging, no rationalizing, no doubt. Just desire and need, and no chance for walking away.

"Come for me," she urged, stroking his cock.

"I want you to feel it, too," he said, not wanting to hog all the morning's delight.

She shook her head. "You have to give me a rest."

Again the memories of her shattering orgasms last night, one after another. Her teeth on his shoulder when he held himself up on top of her. Her hands digging into his hair.

"I can't believe there isn't some part of you still ready to go."

He saw her blush and knew he was right. He lifted her up and flipped her so she was lying on her back in a sea of pillows, naked legs spread before him. She hooked her heels around his thighs and pulled him toward her, wrapping her arms around his shoulders as he smothered her with his weight. He was rock hard and the taste of her lips only made him feel further out to sea, rolling about in a tangle of sheets, completely unmoored.

He worked his lips down her body, over her neck and to each breast, tickling down her side, across her belly, into the divots of each hip. Between her thighs, over her knees, down to the tips of each toe. Had he ever adored a woman like this? Slowly, taking his time, knowing he had all day. All night. As long as he wanted—until four p.m. the next day, when a bus and then a plane would take her away.

He had to get in as much of her as he could. There could be no chance for regrets.

When he kissed his way back up her thighs, her legs parted, trembling in anticipation of his tongue. He ran his mouth over her and started sucking her delicate clit. A moan escaped from her lips.

"Tell me what you want," he panted. The view when he looked up at her was stunning, especially when she raised her head to look down at him, locking his gaze over her breasts.

"I want to come," she said breathlessly, her words and the sureness with which she said them making his cock strain against the mattress where his hips were pressed. She had been so shy before, as though it was wrong to take what she wanted. He hoped he had given her a gift she could always use.

But would she be this way with another man? The thought made him cringe, and then a ferociousness rose in him.

She might, but it would always have been the first with him.

She seemed to be awaiting his instructions, forward yet obedient all at once. And so he gave her what she wanted, which was to be his.

"Touch yourself," he said, reaching for her hand to draw it between her legs. "Touch yourself for me."

Her eyes widened, then narrowed playfully. "That's what you want?"

"I want to see you make yourself come."

He thought she'd protest, but a shy smile curled across her lips. She began circling her clit with two fingers, moving right where she liked it. She saw him looking and spread her legs wider so that he could see the pink of her lips where her fingers slipped in.

Two red spots blossomed in her cheeks, her breath quickening with every touch. Her hips shifted beneath him, rolling to the rhythm she had made. He grabbed his cock in his fist.

"I'm going to come when you come," he whispered, pumping harder now, his hand keeping time with hers, the two of them trying to come and yet trying to hold off, too.

She let out a whimper, caught her breath, and then another moan escaped her lips. "I'm getting closer," she said as though it pained her, a wincing sort of pleasure searing through her the more she touched.

He leaned forward on his left arm so his body was arched over her, his right arm pulling furiously as he brushed the tip of his cock to her stomach.

"Let go," he whispered soothingly. "Let it go."

She pinched her eyes shut as the first waves tore through her. He knew she was coming by the way her breathing deepened, her panting turned to wails, her cheeks bloomed, and her hand jerked furiously across her clit drawing out the sensation. When he knew she was at the height of her pleasure, he released. Cum spurted across her stomach, over her nipples, between her breasts. He worked his shaft, drawing it out, shuddering over her body as she gasped with her own aftershocks and the warmth on her skin. The way it felt when he looked at her, really *looked* at her… He leaned down and kissed her forehead, her ear, her cheek.

"Shower?" he finally whispered.

"That was hot," she whispered back.

"Now what do you want to do today?" He pretended to bite her nose.

"Something fun."

"I'm sorry but there's really no way I can go another round right now."

She laughed. "I meant something *else* fun."

"Such as?"

She grabbed his wrist and dragged him out of bed, heading straight to the bathroom.

"I want to do something I've never done before," she called from behind the shower curtain, through the steam and spray of water as Blake hung the towels by the bathtub for when they got out.

When he stepped in, the water was blissfully hot and her hair thick and wet down her back.

"Something new?" he verified as he reached for the soap and lathered it over her body.

"Something I haven't done before. Something I might never do again. You know, something that says last day in Rio!" She laughed and rested her cheek between his shoulder blades as she washed his back. "Something I'll remember when I'm home."

Home. That one little word. How could it hit him so hard?

She sounded like she'd be ready to go back. But despite all he had planned, the itinerary he'd pieced together to account for every minute, every mile, every piece of his once-shattered heart, he suddenly had no idea what he would do when he said good-bye and put her on that plane.

But she was looking up at him expectantly, holding her

palm out for the shampoo, and he knew this wasn't the time to ask about what "home" meant for the two of them.

"I think I know just the thing," he said, trying to sound happy despite the heaviness that had settled in his chest.

"What is it?" she asked, eyes wide, but he shook his head. "It's a secret."

"Damn," she pouted, and turned to rinse her hair. "I hope it involves breakfast, I'm starving."

"Find a café, and then coconuts?"

"Perfect," she agreed.

He rushed out of the bathroom to check the address in her guidebook before she had a chance to come out, naked with her hair wrapped up in a towel, wheedling him for hints.

"Secrets," he whispered in her ear as he pulled the towel from her hair and wrapped it around her body, holding them close.

It seemed impossible to leave the hotel room when every step she took toward putting her clothes on made him want to take them off again. But the sun was bright through the curtain, and Blake couldn't wait to execute the new plan that he had up his sleeve.

Chapter Sixteen

They had finished a breakfast of pancakes with fresh berries, coffee, and a sweet, tart pink juice from the small *acerola* fruit, and the promised coconut while strolling along the beach, when Blake hailed a cab and gave directions to a part of the city Julia had never heard of.

"Oh, are you going to—" the driver said excitedly, but Blake cut him off before he could finish.

"Shhh," Blake silenced him, pointing toward Julia. "It's a secret."

The driver roared with laughter, and Julia suddenly found herself feeling apprehensive. Maybe it wasn't such a good idea to put so much trust in Blake. He hadn't steered her wrong so far, but the driver obviously found something funny in where he was taking her. She was always so in control—in Chicago, at her job, in her personal life. It was freeing to be reckless this week, like it wasn't just a vacation from Chicago but a break from her whole life. A new way of being thirty, for the brand new decade to come.

She hoped she wouldn't regret it after today.

Blake squeezed her hand as they looked out the window at the city rolling by, the northern hills along the coast getting closer with every block.

"Something new," he reminded her.

"I guess all of this is," she laughed, trying to keep her nervousness in check.

They pulled up at a nondescript street corner, and Blake ushered her out if the cab. Julia looked around, unsure where they were. But as the cab pulled away, Blake set off resolutely toward a cluster of green where the road ended and the hills began.

She followed him into a park and then along a wide path that climbed steadily up. Julia matched her stride to his as they headed deeper into the lush green foliage. She figured they were climbing the hill and imagined the view they'd get at the top. They'd be able to see the whole city, both Christ the Redeemer and the Sugar Loaf Mountain they'd seen yesterday and the ocean curving around the whole city as it jutted out from land.

A different view—not exactly a wild deviation from their day yesterday, but the short hike was a nice way to get moving after lounging all morning in bed, and it was sure to be beautiful to stand up on such a cliff and look out over the sea.

The thought of their morning made Julia's pulse leap. How was it that no matter what they did together, she still wanted more of him? More of his smooth chest, his sweet smile, that look on his face when he rolled his eyes back as she sank down on her knees. As he plunged inside her. As her own orgasm made him come so hard, it was like he was memorizing her body and not just capturing it. She slid her hand in his, heart beating from more than the climb.

But along with the thrill of touching him came the fear of that thrill, a voice of warning in the back of her mind. This wasn't allowed to be more than it was. She couldn't afford to let herself forget that.

As the path began leveling off, Julia realized there was starting to be something of a crowd. More people were hiking on the path, alone or in couples and groups, and it was louder than she usually associated with hikes. Everyone seemed to be chatting animatedly as they breathed hard through the climb. Julia shot Blake a questioning look. She knew why the tourist sites they'd gone to yesterday had been so crowded, but there were plenty of hills right here along the coast. What was so special about this one?

"Almost there," he said, flashing a smile and squeezing her hand. "Come on, let's try to get ahead of this group."

They sped up to pass a cluster of middle-aged men and women with thick New York accidents who screamed *tourist!* with every bounce of their neon fanny packs. They were talking loudly, marveling at the heat and the climb, gulping at water bottles as they stopped to point out the different flowers along the path.

"I can't believe we're really going to do this!" one of the women squealed to her friend as Julia walked past.

"I don't think I can," the friend said.

"You have to! You promised!"

"I'm too old to die," the woman gasped, and her friends erupted into laughter.

Julia clutched Blake's arm. "Where the hell are you taking me?" she demanded, but Blake leaned around to cover her ears.

"Don't listen to them, it's going to be amazing."

"*It?*"

But she didn't have to wait for an explanation. At the top of the hill the path opened into a clearing. And at the far end of the clearing was a van.

"Oh shit," Julia said, and stopped in her tracks.

CONRADO HANG GLIDING COMPANY, it said on the side of the van, next to stacks of colorful harnesses laid out on tall racks. Everywhere people were milling about, duck-walking with harnesses cinched around their legs and waists, helmets perched awkwardly on their heads.

"No." Julia shook her head. "No, no, no, no, no."

Blake flashed his most charming grin, and she practically growled.

"Hang gliding? Are you *kidding* me?"

"You said something you'd never done before!" Blake paused for a second and frowned. "You haven't done this before, have you?"

"God no!"

"Good, me neither," he said, at the same time that she added, "Because I *like* my life!"

Laughing, he dragged her toward a tall Brazilian man with a dark ponytail and a company T-shirt who was signing people up.

"Come on," Blake urged her. "Do something with me you'll never forget."

She almost said, *I couldn't forget you even if I wanted to*, but she bit her tongue. If Blake wanted to have one last hurrah before they went their separate ways, then she wasn't going to ruin things by getting maudlin about it.

"Okay," she said, taking a deep breath to steady her nerves, and gave the man her information. The next thing she knew, she'd signed away her life and was being outfitted in a tight harness, bobbing around in her own round blue helmet, alternately laughing and, to put it mildly, totally freaking out.

"I can't believe we're doing this," Julia said, watching the other groups anxiously waiting to jump. The atmosphere atop the mountain was jittery and frenetic as the anticipation grew.

Blake kissed her nose, their helmets bonking as he leaned forward. "You look adorable in a harness," he whispered, and then laughed as Julia's cheeks colored.

"You weren't sure where to find one in a hotel room so you took me here instead?" she teased, trying to keep cool and act like harnesses and sex was totally a combination she was familiar with.

"Trust me, if this place weren't crawling with people…" He trailed off with a low moan, a shining look in his eye.

"Are you this insatiable with everyone?"

Blake stepped back as though considering her question. "I haven't been with everyone," he said, "so I really can't say."

Julia stuck out her tongue. "You know what I mean." But she also knew that his refusal to answer her teasing meant that what to her was unusual—an appetite that seemed to click, that grew the more they had each other—was just another lay for him. The fact that she thought it meant something both inside and outside the bedroom didn't mean he was thinking the same thing. She had to stop herself from going down that path before she inevitably wound up hurt. It was time to stop thinking about Blake and start thinking about the fact that she was about to jump off a giant cliff with nothing but fabric wings holding her up.

Because even that was less terrifying than facing the truth she had realized that morning when she opened her eyes and saw his body practically glowing from the sun diffused through the curtains: how hard she had already fallen, and the crash that she knew was to come.

She must have been frowning because Blake cupped her chin in his hand and raised her eyes to meet his. "Not this insatiable with anyone," he whispered, and she felt something inside her trip and stumble before her heart could resume its beat. "You said before that you wanted to feel what it would be like to fall."

"I wasn't *serious*," she said. "I was talking about jumping off a waterfall. You know, hypothetical. Poetic. That sort of thing."

"And I'm here to tell you that you can really do the things you want."

"I don't even know how," she protested weakly.

"You don't need to. They'll take care of everything for us—the only thing you have to do is enjoy the moment."

"I'm not very good at that," she grumbled, well aware that she was stalling so she wouldn't have to peer over the edge and think about what Blake was asking her to do. The leap he wanted her to take.

"Aren't you ready to go flying?"

"More like falling," she said, and shook her head. She couldn't tell him that she already had. Not through the sky, of course. But in the ways that mattered. Whether she wanted to or not.

The giant contraptions lay in wait, folded before they would take to the air. They looked small and frighteningly simple. Julia swallowed hard and looked away, her legs starting to shake.

But when she looked at Blake, he was beaming, excitement radiating off him in waves. Seeing his face, she knew that she couldn't say no. If she was getting off this mountain, it was going to be by jumping.

And not for Blake—not really. If she was being honest, she knew it was for herself, too. That was why he was doing this, for him but also for her. How could she live with herself if she walked down the same way they'd come, passing all the people on their way up for the flight? They would know that she was the one who'd chickened out, who'd gone all the way to the edge but been unable to throw herself off. The one who looked and watched and waited but never *did*, taking notes while other people lived.

She was in Brazil. In Rio, the most beautiful city she'd ever been in, with the most beautiful man she'd ever been with, who never failed to surprise her. If she wanted something new, something to shake up her life, some way to prove to herself that she was more than the quiet, passive single girl who did her work and then went home—well then, this was it, wasn't it? This was completely insane, so out of character she barely recognized herself.

And then their names were being called and it really was it. There was no turning back. She followed Blake and the man with the ponytail to the edge of a clearing, the peak of the mountain where the ground dropped off and all that surrounded them was sky.

"Julia?" the man asked, elongating the vowels so that suddenly her name sounded beautiful, alive, like some kind of bird already in flight. She nodded tentatively, as though waiting for someone else to rush up and say there had been a mistake, she was somebody else, there was some reason why she couldn't go through with this. She was lying, she was an imposter, she was a high school math teacher from Chicago and not this bold and surprising woman about to do something so unthinkable she felt like her brain had completely stopped working the minute he said her name.

But he was off on a series of safety instructions she could barely keep track of. They were each going to be strapped in with an instructor who would be flying the glider; all they had to do was enjoy the ride.

Julia tried to laugh along with him, but all that came out was a nervous titter. Blake rested his palm on the small of her back, a simple, calming touch to let her know he was there.

But then he wasn't, because they were being divided up and introduced to the instructors they were going to jump with. Julia wanted to protest that this wasn't part of the arrangement—Blake never said they wouldn't be jumping together! How could she do this without him?

But she had to, she realized. This wasn't about them

doing something together. It was also about her—alone, solo, independent—and who she wanted to be when she went home. Blake may have gotten her up the mountain, but she was determined to get off it without his help.

She took a deep breath and slid his hand off her back. She was going to be fine.

Blake was paired with a tall man whose name she didn't catch but who seemed to be Blake's new best friend, giving him high fives and laughing loudly. Julia's instructor was a petite woman with a mass of curly hair named Suzi whom she didn't believe could possibly navigate such a giant and unruly bird. Suzi was all business, cool as could be, like this was the ten thousandth jump she'd done. She had her own harness with carabineers that hooked onto Julia's so that the two were lined up unbearably close, the puff of her ponytail hitting Julia's chin whenever she moved.

"It'll be more comfortable when we're in the air, don't worry," Suzi said, as though she knew what Julia was feeling because every other person she'd taken out had felt the same exact thing. It made her feel almost silly for her nerves. She reminded herself again to stop freaking out and start enjoying herself, like Blake was. He was asking all sorts of questions about how the harnesses worked, where they strapped in, and how his guide was going to steer.

"You've done this a few times before?" Julia laughed nervously, trying to make light of her question even as she sought reassurances from this tanned and perfectly toned woman who now held her life in her hands.

"Eight times already this morning." Suzi stopped what she was doing with the harness and looked at Julia, her sunglasses resting on her forehead. "Don't worry, honey, once you get in the air it's going to be the most amazing thing you've ever done."

The most amazing thing you've ever done. Julia repeated

the words in her head like a mantra. Then they stepped together, one body with four legs, toward the edge of the mountain, and the words became a frenzied pitch in her mind, just so she didn't keel over and take this woman with her.

"You go first!" Blake called behind her, flashing her a giant thumbs up.

She flipped him the finger instead.

His guide roared with laughter.

"He's making you do this?" Suzi asked, probably having seen the same dynamic dozens of times before.

"No, I want to," Julia said emphatically, as though if she said the words they would come true. *Nobody makes me do anything.* The newfound resolve gave her legs the strength to keep standing as she and Suzi practiced moving together for the run they would have to take to lift off.

"We're going to start at the edge of the ramp," Suzi explained, gesturing toward a wooden platform extending beyond the rocky mountaintop. "We'll run seven steps together, starting with your right foot forward. It's important that we keep our strides together. Okay?"

Julia nodded. The ramp was 1,700 feet above sea level, on the edge of the São Conrado Mountain. *1,700 feet.* She was about to jump from a 1,700-foot drop with nothing but a strange contraption of fabric wrapped around a metal frame to hold her up.

"How many steps?" Suzi asked.

"Seven," Julia repeated automatically, like one of her students saying what the teacher wanted to hear.

"When we get to the edge of the platform, keep running. No stopping, no stalling, no slowing down."

"Keep running," Julia echoed diligently. If she said it, she could do it.

"At the edge, you're going to pretend that you're taking another step right into the air. Don't jump, because jumping will jerk the glider. You're going to run and then let yourself fall forward. I'll be right there with you, so follow my lead."

Don't jump, Julia repeated in her mind. But what if she did? What if she forgot? What if she couldn't stop herself? Would they go tumbling if she messed everything up? She looked around for Blake but he was off with his own guide, going through the same routine.

No Blake, she reminded herself. All she had to do was fall.

And fall, and fall—was she seriously going to willingly run off the edge of a platform nearly two thousand feet up and *keep running into the air*?

She tried not to cry, because crying while both feet were still firmly planted on land would not bode well for the actual flight. Suzi gave her arm a gentle squeeze. "You see the ocean?"

The platform faced the sea, and before them the vast blue inhaled and exhaled below.

"It's the most beautiful moment, when you're running straight into the ocean and let yourself drop into the sky."

Suzi really loved what she did, Julia realized. She stood atop this mountain countless times each day because she couldn't get enough. There was beauty all around them, in the rich green foliage and the curve of the mountains and the bend of the beaches and the rise of the tall city spires. But looking wasn't enough. Blake hadn't wanted to take her to another view like the ones they had yesterday. This time, they were going to be a part of it all. It was his gift to her, not to witness but to experience everything herself.

She took a deep breath. "I can do this."

"I know you can." Suzi smiled back. Then she dropped her sunglasses down over her eyes. "Ready?"

After Suzi strapped them into the hang glider wings, Blake made his instructor crabwalk over with him to give her a quick kiss before they took off. The four of them were crammed together, the two guides helplessly strapped into their charges, the glider wings bulky and awkward behind them, while Blake gave her one last peck for good luck.

"Your boyfriend is very sweet," Suzi said right before they lined up at the edge of the ramp.

He's not my boyfriend, Julia almost said, but caught herself. "Yes," she said emphatically. "When he's not trying to kill me, that is."

"Remember, seven steps, keep running, and don't jump!" Suzi called, ignoring Julia's comment about impending death. It would have been nice to hear one more round of encouraging words about how they were definitely *not* going to die, but it was too late, there was no time, Suzi was running and so Julia was running too, following in her footsteps directly behind her, the woman's strong, petite body propelling them forward, the wings rising up behind. The edge of the platform was getting closer, there was nothing beyond but nothingness itself, and there was something she was supposed to do, something she was supposed to remember…

But it was too late, they were nearing the edge, and the platform was ending. She was going to fall. Everything tightened in her chest—

And then the next thing she knew she wasn't running, she wasn't jumping, but she wasn't falling, either. Her toes hit the edge of the ramp one second after Suzi's and her next step brushed through the air and for one terrifying second Julia braced herself for a sickening lurch and the spiral down— their glider wouldn't work, the harnesses would be strapped in wrong, she didn't run correctly, she jumped when she shouldn't have jumped, or maybe she was *supposed* to jump and she'd misunderstood… But nothing happened.

Or rather, nothing happened and then everything happened at once.

It was so smooth she suddenly knew why it was called

gliding. They ran off the edge of the platform, toward the water, into the sky, and when the ground stopped holding them the wings took over seamlessly.

Together in the harness their bodies rocked forward so they were lying on their stomachs, Suzi gripping the bar that helped her steer and Julia hovering above her. Their feet were connected to a strap that had hung loose when they were running but was now pulled taut, holding them up. Julia had thought it would be awkward, but it was okay hanging there, floating, supported by the straps and the air that buoyed them up as gently as if they'd been on land.

They started off facing the ocean, Suzi letting the air lift them up until they were even higher than when they started. And then the glider slowly started to turn, so smoothly Julia hardly noticed they were moving until she realized they were flying over land now, the whole expanse of the city laid out at their feet.

"Everything good so far?" Suzi called, and Julia gave a breathless shout, her heart hammering in her chest, so giddy she wanted to scream and whoop and pour out her lungs to the rolling hills so small below her.

"Let go!" Suzy shouted up to her as she shifted to keep the glider from giving in to the wind.

"What?" Julia asked.

"Let go! You don't have to hold on!"

Julia realized she had been gripping the handles behind Suzi so tightly her knuckles were white.

I can't, she wanted to say, but the wind was in her face, wisps of hair from her messy bun whipping behind her, and she couldn't make the words come.

Gingerly she released one hand and let it hover over the handles, testing out the feeling. Her upper body rocked a little, but the harness was secure and Suzi's capable arms kept the glider steady. In one rushed move, before she could change her mind, Julia let go of both hands and spread them out to either side like she was flying.

"*Aiiiiiieeeeeeeeeeee!*" she called, a deep shout that came from her toes and up through her belly and out her lungs with the force of the sun and the wind and the forest and the sea, something long dormant inside her snaking out and stretching, breathing, testing its new legs and then running, leaping, flying deep within her, soaring through her mouth and her heart until she was breathless, laughing, so exhilarated that she couldn't stop. She heard Suzi laugh along with her, encouraging her to keep her arms out and soar, and she knew, too, that this was also why Suzi did this. Not just for her own jump, but because no matter how many times she did it, it would always be the first time for somebody else.

It was the same reason Julia taught, going through identical problems year after year after year, because every time she did it there was someone new who was seeing it for the first time, getting it for the first time, finishing it for the first time in their lives. Watching it click for somebody else never, ever got old.

"We're currently flying over the Tijuca National Park, which is the green you see here." Suzi lifted one arm off the steering bar to point below them, and Julia's breath caught, but the glider held steady and she made herself keep from grabbing back onto the handles. They were useless, of course, except for giving her the illusion of safety.

And maybe she didn't need to cling to that illusion anymore. Maybe nothing was as safe as she wanted it to be. But maybe the things she saw as risky weren't as bad as she thought.

Or maybe they were still worth doing, despite the risk. Because of it.

"It's beautiful," Julia said, marveling at how the forest stretched for as far as the eye could see, wrapping around the city that glinted in the sun, clusters of towering buildings nestled in among the rolling green.

"It's the largest urban forest in the world. That mountain over there, with that pointy peak, is called Pedra da Gávea. *Pedra* means stone and *gávea* is like a kind of sail. Topsail, I think you call it?"

"The sail above the gaff sail," Julia said.

"Gaff?"

"On a large sailboat, the gaff is the square sail, and then the topsail is the smaller, triangular sail on top." Julia remembered how she'd lied about getting seasick so she could run off with Blake and laughed to herself.

"That's what it looks like, you see? It's 842 meters high and the largest monolith along a coastline in the world—that means it's made out of a single rock, in this case granite."

Even from this high above Julia could see how the elements had eroded the granite into a dramatic, smooth face that jutted up and out and then swooped down. It really did look like a sail stretched full in the wind.

"You know a lot about the area," Julia observed.

"I'm a geology student when I'm not jumping. I'm a *Carioca*—someone from Rio. This city is in my blood." Suzi shifted her shoulders so the glider swung right, closer toward the ocean, giving them another view of the face of the Topsail Rock, and Julia understood how being here could make someone so much more aware of the land and the water. Millennia of shifts had created this landscape. Julia felt impossibly small in comparison, and yet somehow a part of it all.

The more they hung in the air, the more the city unfolded to them. There were more sites to point out, more mountains and forests and tall granite peaks. Built up the sides of a hill was one of the country's largest *favelas*, a slum that Suzi explained was being bought up by wealthy landowners. The corrugated tin roofs sparkled in the sunlight, and Julia wondered about all the lives being lived below her, the different heartbeats drumming around.

As she took huge gulps of the cool air rushing by, she felt her own heart begin to normalize and her breathing slow until the *panic, panic, panic* alarm ringing inside her was replaced with an exhilarated hum. The wing dipped and Suzi steered them toward the ocean. The white foam where the waves crashed looked like a thin broken line snaking along the shore.

The water came closer, the white sand beaches extending until the city ended in the point of the peninsula and curved around on the other side of the hills. It was a different feeling to be over the sea. Even though Julia knew the land wouldn't protect her, it was scarier to have nothing below them but endless, unforgiving blue so bright it almost hurt, a light clear turquoise in the shallow parts toward land.

They circled over the water, slowly losing altitude, until after what felt like an eternity but also way too soon Suzi was telling her it was time to prepare to land. Julia had forgotten everything she was supposed to do, but suddenly there was no time. The glider was pointed out over the beach and heading straight down like it was coming in to a landing strip. The lazy circles were gone; every movement was purposeful as Suzi steered them in. The beach rushed up faster and faster until Julia could see the peaks and crests in the sand and the waves were no longer snakes of white but large breathing things that swelled and crashed beside them.

They were coming in fast, so fast, something had to be wrong—

"Lift up and run," Suzi instructed, and before Julia knew it her body was swinging forward, pulled upright once again. When they touched the ground, she felt a little kickback from the glider but then she was running behind Suzi, and it only took a few steps for the whole thing to slow, brought in to such a smooth landing it seemed impossible that they'd been flying so fast.

Suzi unhooked her harness, asking how she felt. Julia was breathless and giddy and relieved and amazed, and all she could do was laugh and keep saying how great everything was. She had jumped, she had fallen, but instead of crashing and breaking into a million pieces, she felt more whole than ever before.

They moved out the landing area and Julia watched Blake's glider circle overhead, so high she couldn't tell it was him. She wondered if she had looked like that, a small dot suspended effortlessly in the sky. Then they circled down for their landing, and she spotted the sun-kissed curls and those tanned, strong arms she would recognize anywhere now.

They landed like she had done, coming in fast and then suddenly standing up, Blake shouting and cheering as soon as he caught sight of her on the beach. When he was unhooked he ran up and enveloped her in a giant bear hug, rocking from side to side and refusing to let go.

"How was it?" he exclaimed, brushing the loose strands of hair from her face.

"My legs are shaking," she said, and it was true. She was trembling like she was even more terrified now that it was over because she couldn't believe that she'd actually *done* that, jumped off the tall, sheer peak towering above them.

But she was laughing, too, and kissing him and so exhilarated she thought she might burst. From the beach they couldn't see the rest of the city anymore. It was mind-boggling how much she might have missed if she'd stayed with her feet planted firmly on land.

They thanked their guides whole-heartedly, leaving generous tips and wishing Suzi good luck on her studies. Blake kept his arm wrapped tight around her shoulder as they walked along the beach away from the peak they'd jumped from, São Conrado, and the landing strip. Every so often they looked back to see the cliff as it faded from view and the gliders circling like birds in the sky.

"Are you mad that I took you there?" Blake asked.

"Mad?" she said, surprised. "I was pretty shocked, but definitely not mad."

"You seemed really terrified."

"I *was* really terrified!"

"I'd thought you weren't afraid of heights."

"I have a healthy fear of the insane, Blake!" she cried.

"But it was worth it?"

She linked her arms through his. The ground still felt wobbly and strange after being in the air. "Some day my legs will start working again."

"You could have said no and that would have totally been okay," he reassured her.

She stopped walking and faced him, taking both of his hands in hers. She could feel the sand solid yet shifting beneath them, the steady *swish swish* of the ocean all around.

She grazed his lips. "Sometimes don't you have to take a risk and fall?"

Chapter Seventeen

Blake's knees were still knocking as he and Julia made their way down the beach, splashing their toes through the water, marveling at what they'd just done. They were north of the more crowded city beaches. Here on the outskirts of the wealthy Barra de Tijuca neighborhood the sand was fine, the color of pale straw, and there was hardly anyone around. They walked hand in hand, laughing and breathless, hearts beating a mile a minute after such soaring sights.

"How on earth did you think of doing that?" Julia asked, still shaking her head from the rush.

"I'd heard of people doing it when I was here before, but it seemed, uh, a little crazy."

"A little?"

"I was going to do it. Really. I was halfway down the street and trying to make myself hail a cab when I just…oof, I was chickenshit."

"You?" Julia raised an eyebrow incredulously.

"Maybe if I'd had some peer pressure, but it was only me and I…I couldn't." Blake shrugged. He might not have wanted to admit to just anyone that his nerves had gotten the better of him, but Julia wasn't just anyone. Seeing how scared she'd been made it easier to admit that it had felt like a risk for him, too.

"So you got your second chance," she smiled.

"It's your fault really."

"*Me*?"

"If you hadn't been talking about how badly you wanted to do something new and different and exciting, something you'd always remember—that is an exact quote, is it not?—then I might have let the whole thing go."

"No way, you had this planned from the start. You knew you'd get your second chance in Rio, and this time you'd make me do it so that you didn't chicken out."

Blake lifted his palms to the sky. "Guilty?"

"It's okay. I won't tell anyone about failed attempt number one if you don't tell them how loudly I screamed as we were taking off."

"Deal," he said.

They shook on it.

Julia was right, of course. As soon as she'd said she wanted to try something new and put the day's plan in his hands, he'd known what to do. The whole thing had felt like a sign. Deciding to return to Rio meant he had the opportunity to do it over again, only this time better, deeper, without holding anything back.

Sometimes it's good to get second chances, he reasoned, and then wondered if he was talking about hang gliding, or Rio, or perhaps something else altogether.

"Second chances, birthdays, the new year…" Julia mused. "Sounds like a time for a lot of new beginnings."

"I was hoping that when you said you wanted to try something new, you weren't talking about fresh pineapple juice or something."

"Already tried it, so it's not on the list anymore."

"So what, now things have to keep getting bigger and better? Do I have to take you skydiving next?"

Julia planted her feet firmly on the ground and looked him square in the eye. "You have to let me catch my breath first."

He laughed. "All right, I promise I'll try to stick with smaller firsts."

She started walking again and pulled her hair from its elastic. It tumbled over her shoulders, lifting in the breeze. He trailed his fingers over her back to feel the soft strands.

"I think I've made it clear that everything we've done together qualifies as new," she said. "You could say we were going to sit and watch paint dry, and I'd think it was perfectly fine, as long as I was with you."

"Well good, because I don't know how you managed to guess what we're doing this afternoon, but..."

She laughed and he did too, but inside his heart was pounding like he was standing back on the cliff, preparing to run. Was it Brazil or the beauty all around them or just her hair in the breeze that made this, this *thing* they were doing feel so right?

Or was Julia trying to say something else, that it was the two of them together? Would it be like this no matter where they were?

But she didn't say anything else. Part of him thought it was the perfect opportunity to insert something about watching paint dry in Chicago for a little while — after all, he had the money and the time.

But he couldn't. It was like the cliff was there but he couldn't make himself run off it. Like he couldn't make himself get in the cab and drive to the mountain the first time he'd thought about jumping.

And then the moment was gone, they were on a tangent

about how to build so many houses right into the hills, and Blake was glad he hadn't said anything. It would have been easy for her to broach the subject but she obviously hadn't, and he intended to follow her lead. They had one more night together and it was the biggest night of the year, New Year's Eve in Rio. He didn't intend to ruin it by making things awkward for her.

He knew the problem with Kelley wasn't that he'd let her go but that he'd pushed too hard, asked too much. Offered a life she didn't want. Somehow he'd been completely unable to read the signs she'd so obviously given to him. He wasn't going to make the same mistake twice. He swore he was going to give Julia what she wanted, even if it wasn't him. He would let her ask for her desires, and then step back when what he had given was enough.

They walked a long time on the beach until the mountain they'd jumped from was lost in the distance and the more familiar sights of the city came into view. Then they cut away from the water to find a café for sandwiches. They were strolling through the streets of Ipanema, window shopping, when something suddenly occurred to him.

"Are you ready for tonight?"

"If it doesn't involve jumping, falling, or in any other way endangering life or limb."

"How about drinking, dancing, swimming in the ocean, hanging out on the beach with two million of our closest friends, and heavy bouts of making out, if I'm lucky?"

"Sold," she said, and leaned over to kiss him on the cheek.

"One thing Jamie was telling me about before we left, though, is that apparently everyone wears white. Do you have anything?"

Julia thought for a minute. "I have a white tank top. Maybe that's okay with denim shorts?"

Blake remembered the outfit she'd been wearing when he

first saw her standing by the front desk, waiting to be checked in. If she was wearing that flimsy shirt, there was no way he'd be able to keep his hands off her all night.

"Way too sexy, but I suppose it'll have to do."

Julia made a face. "What about you?"

"I have a white T-shirt, I've been wearing it to sleep in sometimes."

"I didn't know that."

"That's because pajamas are entirely unnecessary when it comes to you," he said with a straight face, watching her blush.

"I know what you should wear," Julia said, pointing across the street to a display window where a headless model wore white pants low on his hips. "No white shirt, just that." She gave him an obvious once-over with her eyes.

"Well if I'm wearing that, you know what you'll be in."

"What?"

Blake jogged across the street, holding her hand and guiding her over to the display window.

"Oh very funny," she scoffed, wrinkling her nose at the display. Next to her headless man in white pants was a female mannequin in a white shirt that could only be described as tiny.

"Come on, you'd look great," Blake said, entirely serious about how well she could pull it off even though they were both joking. But Julia shook her head, horrified at the thought, and suddenly Blake felt like there was no reason for their impulsive adventure to be over just because they were back on land. "Yes, oh my God you should, you really should wear it."

"You're crazy," she said, trying to pull him away from the window. But she was laughing, too, and Blake could see in the reflection of the window how they were both still flushed and giddy from the adrenaline rush of the jump.

"I'm serious! You have to get into the spirit of things."

"I am in the spirit. The spirit of *sane*."

"It's not bungee jumping."

"That's no argument—that because it's not an extreme sport it's totally a good idea?"

"I don't see a problem with that reasoning."

"But I *can't*."

He folded his arms. "Why not?"

"Because!" she sputtered, then paused, clearly trying to think. "Because I can't, that's all. Because I don't wear stuff like—" she gestured at the bare midriff of the mannequin, "that."

"Mmm, why not?" he asked, this time genuinely curious. Why did she see herself that way, like there were things she "could" and "couldn't" do? Like someone would come along and correct her if she stepped out of line?

Was she afraid?

"I just can't," she sighed, and Blake thought of what she'd told him about Liz and Mark, about what men did to women they thought they had a right to.

"You can with me," he whispered, nuzzling her ear.

Her smile came back, even as she shook her head no.

The shopkeeper came out, a young, fashionable woman who must have seen them in front of the window.

"Can I help you?" she asked, looking at the display. "Are you looking for an outfit for tonight?"

"Why does everyone wear white?" Julia asked.

"It's for peace and luck. Don't forget to make an offering to *Yemanjá*, goddess of the sea."

"See?" Blake said. "You don't want to upset the goddess."

Julia raised an eyebrow at Blake.

"Try something new?" It wasn't so much about the outfit as about her fear. He wanted her to say yes to running, yes to jumping, yes to diving, yes to falling. He couldn't bear the thought of her standing on the side.

"Only if you do it," Julia said emphatically, but Blake didn't have to think very hard about that. Experience was how he learned.

"Deal," he said, and for the second time that day they shook hands while the shopkeeper laughed and went to get them their clothes for the night.

It was a costume, really, and hardly expensive since the stores wanted people to buy new clothes for the holiday. They walked away with a small bag containing the shirt and a white skirt for Julia and the long, silky pants for him.

"The goddess had better love us," Julia commented.

"I'd say she already does," Blake said with a wink.

New things. Blake had left Australia thinking that what he wanted was for things to go back to the way they'd been when Kelley was his girlfriend and Liam was his best friend and *The Everlastings* was just beginning and everything seemed possible and assured.

But maybe it had never really been like that, and he'd been so focused on what he wanted to see that he hadn't paid attention to all the cracks in the surface he'd constructed. Kelley's long silences; the clothes she started buying him after the show took off, saying "the creator" needed to look like one; the way Liam always seemed to be hanging around, so he could never just be with his friend or with his girlfriend because they were three, always three.

Until they were two, but it was the two under the camera lights, the two sneaking away to be alone. How had he missed so much that was right in front of his eyes?

Maybe things had never been as he'd imagined, and what he didn't want was the old but something new, too, like Julia—the possibilities he'd never imagined, the dreams he'd stopped allowing himself to dream. In the warm sun and the rush of the jump still in his limbs, anything seemed possible. Anything at all.

What would he decide to do tomorrow, the start of the new year and the day that Julia left? He had no plans, no sense of which way the winds would turn. He could simply head to Buenos Aires and push his whole itinerary back a few days.

But the need to follow a schedule didn't seem so important anymore. He would figure it out. For the moment, not knowing seemed okay. Because he had the rest of the day and the night and the following day with Julia. And if that was all he had before she took a plane back to Chicago and out of his life, then so be it.

"What's your New Year's resolution this year?" he asked as they headed back toward the hotel.

"Leave school no more than an hour after my students do," Julia said immediately.

"I can tell you've been thinking about this."

"It's one Liz's been trying to get me to do for years, but my heart wasn't in it enough for the idea to stick."

"And you think this year?"

"Consider it reflective of a larger change." She grinned, her eyes alight and flecked with gold. "What about you?"

"Start my next project. Use the upcoming season of *The Everlastings* to transition the writing reigns to Anderson and then get a pilot up for this untitled thing I've been brewing."

He hadn't thought of it in such final terms, but now that he was saying it aloud he knew that was exactly what his plan was—and that he could do it. He didn't need Kelley or Liam to make a show. People watched *The Everlastings* for the actors, sure, but everything started with the script, and it came to life through the producer. There was no reason he had to keep himself tethered to them when his whole imagination was wide open to new ideas.

"You'll have to get a U.S. distributor, or however that stuff works, so that I can watch," Julia said. "Are you on Netflix? Or Hulu?"

"I'll send you links," he promised. "I can usually get stuff before it airs."

So that was it, then. He didn't even need to ask what was next for them, because it was clear. Like Blake's initial decision not to go to Rio, everything was decided without them saying a word. Their resolutions for the next year revolved around their jobs—meaning they'd be back to their regular lives, in Chicago and Sydney, moving forward and moving on, presumably trying to find someone who fit into the lives they'd already constructed in their respective homes. The real world was waiting, and while Blake had a few more months to be on the road, time was ticking down until Julia would be gone.

But he wasn't going to dwell on it. Not now. They swung back to the hotel room to drop off the bag of clothes and changed into their bathing suits, a flashback to the first time they'd met and swum together. This time they would actually be swimming, since the beach was full of energetic crowds eager for the night's celebrations to begin. They brought only a towel and enough money to buy coconuts and snacks on the beach from the vendors who came around with small portable grills, cooking skewers of meat and soft cheese. They talked with the vendors about the best places to go on the beach that night, but everyone said the same thing. They should just get out and cover the whole beach.

"Don't forget to wear white," one boy said as he pocketed Blake's change.

"We will," Julia said seriously, and then flashed Blake a grin. They were definitely getting into the spirit of things.

They spent the afternoon swimming and lounging on the beach. There was barely enough time to collapse in the hotel room for a nap with the windows open and an ocean breeze streaming through, and then they woke up and showered off the sunscreen and salt water and got ready for the night.

With a towel around his waist and water dripping off his hair, Blake pulled out their brand new, bright white clothes and tossed Julia her skirt and shirt.

"No peeking," she admonished as she took the clothes and closed the bathroom door in his face.

Blake pulled on a pair of boxer-briefs and then the white pants, leaving a thin line of the band showing around the low waist where the pants hugged his hips. They were like dressy pajama pants, trim around his hips but with a loose, wide cut through the legs. He could easily get behind a New Year's Eve party that involved being comfortable.

He debated whether he should wear his V-neck white shirt, but it wasn't as new and bright as the pants. He decided to hang out shirtless and wait to see what Julia thought. What was taking her so long? It wasn't like she had a lot of clothes to put on, what with how little fabric there was to that shirt...

He rapped gently on the door. "Everything going okay in there?"

"It's a good thing it's going to be dark when we're outside," she called back.

Finally she opened the door and Blake realized a major downside of his outfit: the fabric of his pants was so thin, there was no way to conceal the bulge that grew as she stood in the doorway.

She could see it and she pressed her lips together, trying—and failing—not to smile. "This will officially be the most naked I've ever been in public," she said, running her fingers through her hair as Blake raked his eyes over her, trying—and also failing—to keep his hands and cock at bay.

"Hopefully it will also be your first officially fun all-nighter," he said as he came toward her, brushing his hand down her side.

"To add to all the other new firsts."

"Such as?" he asked, wanting to hear the list.

"Sex in a pool."

"How about under a waterfall?"

"And don't forget about hang gliding."

"Maybe we'll get lucky and there'll be sex on the beach, too," he murmured, gathering her hands in his and pressing his body to her.

"With two million people around?" she giggled, rubbing a hand over the head of his cock where it strained up against his fly.

"We'll have to find a quiet spot." He was breathing harder now, his lips brushing hers, bringing his hands to her breasts to run his fingers across the thin white fabric doing nothing to keep her nipples at bay.

The fabric was cut low into a V that showed off her cleavage but then stopped, leaving the rest of her midriff bare. There were small capped sleeves over her shoulders and a full back as though it were a normal shirt with the bottom half cut off, so it covered her more than if she were wearing a white bikini top or something similar.

But it was still cut so low that the top of her bra showed through, and she must have been saving it because it was one that he hadn't seen before. A pale peach, lacy thing that he hoped matched her panties, just enough of the delicate fabric peeking over the top to make him want to tear the whole thing off.

The skirt was short and hugged her hips, the bright white drawing out the glow in her skin, her stomach and hips, her long, long legs. He bent down before her and pressed his lips to the skin below her belly button, running his hands over her hips and the gorgeous crest of her ass.

She tugged at him to get him to stand and he took the opportunity to run his lips up her bare skin, skipping over the small clasp of fabric between her breasts and then kissing the exposed line of her chest where her bra and the fitted shirt pushed her soft curves out.

She put her arms around him and ran her fingers under the waist of his boxer-briefs. He was getting way, way too excited, but the sun was going down and they could hear the music coming up from the beach, a low bass drowning out the whispers of the ocean and the high-pitched swell of the gathering crowds. It was definitely time for them to get out there. He tried to make his cock behave as he kissed her warmly on the lips.

"All ready?" he murmured, unable to keep his hands off her ass as he leaned in to smell the soft, clean scent of her shampoo and the lotion on her skin.

"I want you to know that I'm only doing this because when else am I going to be on Copacabana Beach for New Years."

Her stern resolve made him laugh. "So you don't walk around Chicago dressed like this all the time?"

She shot him a withering look. "Very funny, hot stuff."

"Should I wear this shirt?" he asked, motioning to pull on the V-neck to see if she thought it went with the pants, but she snatched it out of his hands.

"If I'm naked, so are you."

"Fair is fair," he grinned, and together they slid on their sandals and stepped out into the warm, electric night.

Chapter Eighteen

Everything had seemed fine in their hotel room. But once she was under the harsh lights of the hotel lobby, Julia felt herself shrink. As she and Blake strode outside, she desperately wanted to tear her hand out of his, race upstairs, and change back into her familiar cut offs and tank top.

Or hide under the bed and not come out at all.

It wasn't that she was uncomfortable with the outfit itself, but it was so far outside how she normally dressed that it felt like it wasn't even her. She was afraid everyone was going to stare at her accusingly, like they knew she was doing something wrong.

But no one batted an eye. The concierge at the hotel was dressed in a crisp white suit and flashed them a smile and a wave as they crossed the lobby, wishing them a *Feliz Ano Novo*, a phrase Julia knew she was going to be hearing a lot of in the coming night. No sirens wailed, no Good Girl Police came to take her in for breaking the contract that said she was supposed to stay home, be practical, and take care of everyone else while they had a good time.

If only Liz could see me now, she thought, and grinned as she and Blake stepped out into the night.

"What's got you so happy?" Blake asked, his eyes dancing in the soft light that spilled out into the street from the buildings along the strip of sand.

"Thinking about how low Liz's jaw would drop if she saw me," Julia said truthfully.

"Something tells me Liz would have a blast tonight," he laughed.

"Yeah, and normally I'd be the one telling her to be careful and don't get back too late and drink another glass of water before taking more shots."

Blake squeezed her hand. "No babysitting tonight."

"Not like she really needs it," Julia admitted, and Blake nodded like maybe that's what he'd been thinking, too. It was starting to dawn on her that Liz had never really needed a babysitter—just a friend. She and Danny had been so focused on taking care of her, they'd forgotten that it was still okay to have a good time. Anything that had happened was Mark's fault. Liz didn't need to punish herself anymore.

Julia understood it now. Of course Liz wanted her to go off and have fun on her own. Julia could be a good friend and still have the time of her life. She might even be a *better* friend for letting herself experience all that the world had in store.

As the crowd on the beach swallowed them in, Julia felt a strange weight lifting from her shoulders. It was like something she hadn't even realized she was carrying around had jumped off and was now circling far above them in the night sky, never to return.

The beach was crowded but even with all the people pouring steadily onto the sand it didn't feel stifling. Julia had spent other New Year's Eves crammed next to strangers to watch fireworks, her fingers and toes so frozen she just wanted the ball to drop so she could go home. More recently she'd taken to staying in with a small group of friends so they could drink champagne and eat hors d'oeuvres and fall asleep in a heap on somebody's couch, waking up to stuff themselves with French toast in the morning.

It was always fun, but not like this. This was the pulse of music in her veins, the smell of salt and charred, grilled foods, the cold tartness of a *caipirinha* in her hands as Blake passed her a drink from a stall under a beach umbrella. This was warm and alive and exhilarating as she pressed the cup against her to keep it from being jostled and a cold drip of condensation snaked down her stomach with a thrill.

There were all sorts of platforms with bands and performers set up along the stretch of beach, as well as trucks and vans with sound systems on top and people setting up right on the sidewalk along the sand. One sound merged into the next as they walked from stage to stage, carried by the surge of the crowd and the driving, rhythmic beat.

And everywhere the sea of sweaty, gyrating bodies illuminating the ocean and the sand, millions of bright, breathing things swaying and churning with one pulse.

One *caipirinha* was replaced with another, and more food from the stalls, and soon she and Blake were dancing on the beach, bodies pressed together, his bare chest glistening with sweat as he guided her hips to move with his to the frenzied beat. *If only the clubs in Chicago were like this*, Julia thought— Liz might actually succeed in getting her to go more often.

They danced barefoot in a throng of people, and then a circle spread, and they were clapping along with everyone else as one by one dancers entered the center of the circle and performed the fluid, powerful motions of *capoeira*, a martial-arts based dance that took Julia's breath away. The dancers were incredible, something between hip-hop and break dancing and karate. They flipped from their feet onto their hands and back again, moving low and circling each other, building up a competition between each dancer who took to the center of the circle. They clapped and cheered and egged the dancers on, sweaty and breathless, and when that circle broke up, another formed, and then another, so that the whole beach was one surging group of dancers finding their own ways to move.

It was impossible to feel self-conscious anymore. Everywhere she turned, people were laughing and smiling and having a good time. It wasn't like being in a crowded club, where there were too many bodies pushing against each other and everyone was eyeing each other in judgment. Here there was such a mix of bodies and ages and people and outfits so that in the dark it was impossible to make out who was who or what they were doing. And besides, why would anyone care? The woman at the clothing store had been right—they fit in perfectly. It was nice to feel the ocean breeze on her stomach and to touch Blake's chest, knowing he was right by her side. She needn't have worried so much about what people would think; they were too busy having a good time to care about anything other than the fact that she was out there dancing and having fun, too.

"This is incredible!" she gasped when Blake pulled her out of the crowd so they could take a breather and buy some water from a woman selling bottles out of a cooler.

"I knew this was supposed to be a party, but I still had no idea it would be this fun," Blake said, downing the water and then pouring some of it over his head and on Julia to cool them off. She laughed and took another swig.

"What would you be doing if you weren't here?" she asked, imagining the celebrations in Sydney.

"I'd probably be by myself somewhere in Argentina, moping and thinking of you," he said, flashing a grin.

"Not if you hadn't met me."

"I'd still be moping and thinking of you. It'd just be the

you I'd wish I had met."

"Yeah right, you'd be out dancing with some other girl." She stuck out her tongue.

Blake pretended to shudder. "Perish the thought."

"Come on, let's walk down the beach," she urged, skirting up the road that ran along the beach and trying to keep to the outside of the crowds.

"Something tells me you don't spend New Year's on the beach in Chicago," Blake said.

"Polar bear swim!"

"You Yanks are insane."

"I didn't say *I* did it. I happen to like not freezing my ass off."

"You also don't jump off of cliffs," he reminded her, and she had to acknowledge that he had a point.

"There are some things it turns out that I will, in fact, do. But swimming in Lake Michigan in the middle of winter still isn't one of them. I think I'll reserve the whole trying new things out for when I'm somewhere tropical, thanks."

He laughed. "So you're just going to go home and be boring?"

"I like boring!"

"You do not," he smirked, and Julia had to laugh. Okay, maybe he was right about that. Did she really have to go home and be the same old Julia again, layered in sweaters in the middle of winter, staying in the classroom until nine at night because, let's face it, there was nothing much calling her home and there was always more work to be done?

Could she be the person who jumped into pools, rushed down paths to waterfalls, hopped overnight busses, jumped off cliffs, danced in next to nothing with a crowd of strangers with the sand between her toes…even when she was far from here?

She tugged on Blake's hand and pulled him through the

crowd, this time leading the way instead of waiting for him to decide what they were going to do. Farther up the beach, they could look out and get a view of the crowds stretching all the way down the long crescent of sand, miles of revelers of every age and walk of life, the ocean bobbing with flowers and little wooden boats laden with wishes and prayers, offerings to the goddess of the sea.

Blake bought a bottle of champagne from a cooler for the equivalent of about three bucks, laughing that when in Rio, they'd better do as the locals did. Which, judging from the group they were watching along the shore, meant shaking the bottle and spraying everyone when they uncorked it with a pop as though it were a blessing to be shared.

Julia couldn't stop laughing as Blake shook up the champagne. Whatever he said, she couldn't hear it over a sudden roar of cheering from a nearby platform as a band took the stage. To a swinging beat that everyone started singing along to, she splashed her feet in the warm embrace of the ocean, letting the goddess Yemanjá take all her worries away.

Blake waded out to join her, pointing the bottle away so that when it popped the cork went somewhere into the water, their offering to the sea. It bubbled forth explosively and Blake covered the lip with his thumb, still managing to completely douse them both.

They splashed in the shallow waves as he poured the bubbles into her mouth. The bright fizz danced on her tongue. It wasn't terrible, although most of it went down her shirt. Blake laughed and took a swallow himself, spilling more on his chin. A couple splashed by them and sprayed some champagne on them with shouts of *Feliz Ano Novo*, so Blake sprayed them back, and they cheered.

Everything buzzed, their skin soaked with sweat and salt and champagne. Swimming in their clothes under the darkened sky, watching the pulse of bodies writhe and sway in a dancing mass along the shore, the ocean felt like a vast, endless embrace. They swam parallel to the shore, keeping close to the beach but moving away from the crowds until an unexpected quiet filled them, so much more noticeable compared to the far-off thump of music and cheers from the beach.

Julia stopped swimming and stood up to her hips in the water. Blake grabbed her around the waist and softly bit the side of her neck as he pressed his warm, wet body against hers. Her hair was everywhere and she tried to knot it back but it was too wet to obey, so she let it go. She knew her white clothes were practically see-through now that they were soaked, but it was hard to care when she was in Blake's arms.

A roar went up from the crowd as the first bursts of color exploded over the ocean. Neither of them had a watch, and Julia had lost all sense of time on the beach, but it must have been midnight because the cheering intensified along with the crackle and boom of the fireworks exploding overhead.

It seemed like the colors were raining down directly over them, spirals of orange and red and green and silver spreading wide, willowy arms across the sky. They burst and fizzled into darkness as the next round shot up. Julia dunked her head under the water and heard the boom reverberate in her ears. When she lay floating on her back in the waves, it felt like the colors were raining right on top of her.

There was so much cheering going on but in their own tiny bubble of the world they were quiet and awed. "Happy New Year," Blake whispered, his wet lips against her ear, his breath making the hairs on the back of her neck stand up.

"Happy New Year." She kissed him, tasting the salt on his lips and the champagne on his tongue, and that indescribable *Blakeness* that only ever seemed to make her want more.

And then his arms were around her, crushing her, holding

her tighter, and they were kissing and kissing as the fireworks exploded and the ocean heaved and sighed. Somewhere there were other people on the beach, there was an enormous party going on, but all of that was distant when she closed her eyes and slid into his kiss. Then it was only the darkness of the night and the dark behind her eyes and his body strong and alive against hers.

They sank lower in the water, unable to stop kissing, legs intertwined, Blake's knee pushing apart her thighs where the tight fabric of her skirt wouldn't budge. His body responded instantly to her touch. She bit his lip harder than she meant to and opened her eyes to apologize, but the look in his eyes was so insistent that the words died in her mouth. There was no way she could speak, no way she could do anything except move with him in the water away from the crowds, until they were somewhere farther up the beach where rocks jutted into the water and they were alone.

They weren't out too deep and it must have been low tide because the waves were round and calm. Julia leaned back against one of the rocks, trying to get a handhold as Blake held her face in his palms and continued to kiss her furiously with his tongue. She was dimly aware that they were still in public, but the lights were concentrated farther down the beach and there were no major hotels or landmarks behind them, which meant this wasn't where people were spilling out on the beach.

A stronger voice in her head told her that she didn't even care. Her nipples pressed through the thin fabric, scratching against the lace so that every movement sent a shot of pleasure coursing down between her legs. Blake's hand on the curve of her breast made her arch her back to him, begging for his touch. His thumb pressed against her nipple through that tiny white shirt, so thin and wet as to be meaningless now. She reached for his pants, his hips in the water so that his cock bobbed above the waves. She was already so turned on she didn't think she could take much more of his fingers pulling on her nipples without taking him inside her. Right here, right now, on the beach in Rio as the fireworks exploded overhead.

They shifted together as she slid down, and he pulled the bottom of her skirt up. She spread her legs, her knees bent up, knowing that she didn't even have to tell Blake to fuck her because everything about her body position and her eyes and the quickness of her breath told him what she needed right now.

He held his cock in his fist and she wanted to take him in her mouth but she knew this would have to be a quick one, hard and fast with all their need, and so she pulled him closer, bracing herself against the rocks. He didn't bother pulling off her panties, just pushed the cloth aside, slid on a condom, and plunged his cock in. She was slick with wanting and he slid in easily up to the hilt, pausing for both of them to savor the feeling of him filling her before he started to move.

He fucked her how she wanted it, how she begged him for it, the words no longer sounding strange and wrong in her mouth. "Harder," she urged him breathlessly, her breasts bouncing in the lacy bra and the flimsy white shirt as he grabbed her thighs and plowed into her.

"That's it," he gasped, burying himself in and then drawing back to nail her again as she pressed her hips forward, taking him as deep as he'd go.

It was fast and rough and there was nothing held back, just the slap of skin against skin and her ass on the water as he worked her hips up and down. The fireworks boomed and the sea hissed and the distant crowd cheered as they danced the new year in, and Julia and Blake kept on fucking as the night unfolded around them.

Julia was feeling the low prickle of an orgasm building deep within when headlights flashed from the road. Immediately she and Blake dipped down into the water, just two people swimming exceptionally close… But the car didn't stop and the headlights carried on. They heard the sound of car doors slamming as some group was dropped off, probably from a cab, and headed down to the main party on the beach while the car turned around and drove away.

Blake was still hard inside her as the waves splashed gently against them and he picked up their momentum as the darkness fell on them once again. The side of her panties chafed where he'd pushed them over but the rubbing added to her excitement and the illicitness of their whole affair. Her skirt pushed up over her hips, reminiscent of how he had taken her in her sundress under the waterfall. It was thrilling and filthy and wonderful, and she felt like she could hardly breathe.

"I'm going to come inside you," he whispered in her ear as he wrapped her wet hair around one hand. It wasn't a question; it wasn't even a demand. He was just telling her, knowing that the words and the way he claimed her body would send a shudder through her thighs and bring her that much closer to coming with him.

Blake turned her around so he was entering her from behind and then found her clit with his fingers. "Come with me," he whispered as his cock continued to press inside her, and then again: "Come when I come."

His steady breathing, his insistence, the way he ground his hands and his hips into her, the splash of the water on her nipples, the feel of her feet trying to hold steady in the sand as he took her and took her and took her. The final, breathless finale of the fireworks overhead turning the sky into an explosion of color and light, and the cries from everyone who had gathered on the beach and in the water and lined the streets and the hotel balconies to see. Everything seemed to bombard her so that when he said "Now," she couldn't help it.

She shattered.

The orgasm racked through her as she felt him release, and in the noise of the fireworks and the crowds and the sea she cried out while his hot, gasping breath filled her ears. She cried out for her orgasm and his, for the night and the new year, for her thirties and what had turned into an unimaginable gift: the chance to remember herself.

"Yes," she cried out as he thrust one more time inside her, drawing out each wave of their pleasure together. "Yes," she sighed as he rested his cheek against her back and buried his face in her salt-water hair.

"Yes," he groaned back as he slowly withdrew and guided her panties back where they belonged, her skirt around her hips, her breasts tucked in her bra and her small white shirt covering everything just enough that nothing looked covered at all.

She turned in his arms so she could face him again and kissed him. "Happy New Year," she whispered, pushing back his wet hair from his forehead.

"Somehow I have a good feeling about this year," he said back, and together they swam slowly back to shore to rejoin the rest of the party, soaking wet and thoroughly sated and ready to dance the rest of the night away.

Blake was right. It turned out to be the first time she stayed up all night except for that one awful time with Danny. That had been a gray dawn, cooler than June should have been, everything misty and sharp. This was the first time she had seen the sunrise without having fallen asleep first, a lightening so subtle she didn't even realize it was happening until somehow the sky had gone pink.

Brilliant streaks of orange seemed to rise straight out of

the ocean, slowly and then more insistent, demanding that the revelers notice that the night was over and the new day ready to begin. The beach had thinned but it was a long time before the music stopped thumping. Julia and Blake made their way back along the sand littered with cups and bottles and flowers and discarded clothes, broken flip flops and sequined boas and all the detritus of the night that would soon be picked up by crews before it could be swept out to sea.

They walked back to the hotel room, ran a quick hot shower, and practically fell asleep in the steam. Julia collapsed on the bed, her wet clothes stripped off and discarded in a pile on the bathroom floor, too exhausted to toss and turn as Blake's arm draped over her, holding her close as his steady breathing told the sunlight through the curtains to hold off until they were ready for the day to begin.

If she'd ever be ready.

The last thing Julia thought about as she fell asleep was that there was no more pushing this day from her mind. She snuggled closer to Blake and fell asleep wishing the sun would stop rising and the afternoon never come, so her plane never had to take off.

Chapter Nineteen

Blake was surprised at how early he rose, considering they'd stayed up until late became early and the morning sun burned from bright orange to white. But his mind was too busy to sleep.

This was it. Today was the day.

Quietly he slipped on a pair of shorts and a T-shirt while Julia slept. On his way out, he stopped at the front desk to get them a later checkout time so they could stay as long as they wanted until the bus.

Then he went to procure them some breakfast. Who wouldn't like waking up naked in bed, wrapped in soft sheets, to a delivery of hot coffee, fresh tropical fruit juice, and pastries? He lingered for too long over the counter, picking the ones he thought she'd like best. An apricot puff with vanilla pastry cream. A chocolate croissant marbled with cherries inside. He could practically taste the sugar on her lips.

It was still early, though, so on his jaunt back he stopped

at the computers in the hotel business room for a quick check. He figured he should pop in and wish everyone a happy new year, see how his mom was, and find out whether Anderson had responded to his previous emails—even though Blake wasn't expecting much to be happening over the holidays. Really he wanted to give Julia a little more time to sleep, knowing that if he hung around the hotel room, he'd be too impatient about spending his last hours with her to let her rest.

If he was honest with himself, he needed the time, too. He hadn't given any thought to what he was going to do next. He could barely wrap his head around the bus ride to São Paulo. And after she got on that plane?

He logged into his email. After was after. He'd deal with it then.

He had a few general happy new year emails from friends, a quick note from his mom saying everything was fine, no reply from Anderson, an update from the assistant director he set aside to read more carefully later, and an email from Jamie with the subject line, *Ahoy there, mate*. Blake clicked it open, hoping to hear that his friends were doing well in Chile and getting ready for their final flight home.

What he saw made his chest squeeze and his heart thud. Something thick and sour rose in the back of his throat and he wanted to log out, shut down the computer, get up and keep walking like he'd never stopped. If only he could pretend that he hadn't seen what was on the screen, everything would be fine.

But instead he sat there, frozen, rereading the email as though he didn't trust the words. When he couldn't take it anymore, he ended the session and sat there until a German man in a loud floral shirt asked if he was done. Blake apologized quickly and left.

All the way back up to the hotel room, something

hammered away in the pit of his stomach. He opened the hotel room door and got straight to work. He had to pack. He had to get his stuff together.

And then he had to leave.

Julia awoke to a sudden banging and groaned. Not daylight—it wasn't fair! She wanted to sleep forever. What was that noise?

She gathered the sheets up across her chest and sat up sleepily. *Bang.* Blake slammed a drawer shut.

"Too early for noise." She yawned. "Mmm, do I smell coffee?"

"On the dresser," he said without looking up.

She sat up straighter. "What's going on, Blake? The bus isn't until four—we have plenty of time."

"Yeah, I gotta go sooner than that." He balled up a pile of T-shirts and stuffed them in a bag.

It felt like someone was lining up to punch her in the gut. But the hit hadn't connected yet, because Julia didn't understand what he meant.

She just knew that for some reason, in a matter of moments, there was going to be pain.

"Blake?" she asked.

He straightened his back. "Have you seen my trainers?"

"Blake, what are you doing?"

"Shit, can you see if they're under the bed?"

"Blake!" she practically shouted, trying to make him snap out of it. She reached for one of the hotel robes and wrapped it around her, suddenly aware of how naked—how vulnerable—she was. "I thought you were coming with me to São Paulo."

For a moment he stopped, one sneaker hanging out of his

bag, the other still in his hand. "And do what? Spend all that time stuck on a bus to wind up in a city where I don't want to go?

"We were just talking about this last night. You said you wanted to take me to the airport. You said you didn't have any plans."

"Yeah, well, something's changed."

"Apparently it has." She stared at him in disbelief.

"What does it matter? You're going home anyway."

"Is that what this is about? Me going home? Talk to me, Blake," she pleaded as he hastily crammed clothes into his bag. "Where are you going?" Her voice sounded small in her ears.

"Santiago. No point going to São Paulo when I can get a flight from here."

"Well aren't we Mister Practical." She swung her legs around so she was sitting on the edge of the bed. "Blake, will you slow down a minute? Why Santiago? Why are you so upset?"

"I'm not upset!"

"Like hell you're not!" Julia gestured at the room, which looked like a tornado had torn through it. In all his packing, he'd made the place a mess.

"Something's come up," he said with exaggerated patience, as though talking to a child. "Believe it or not, there are things I have to do that aren't about you."

"That's not fair, Blake."

"No, not fair is waking up to a note and half your bank account gone."

"What are you talking about?" Suddenly she realized. "Oh my god—Santiago. Did something happen to Jamie and Chris?"

Blake shoved the contents of the bathroom counter into his bag. She didn't bother pointing out that he'd taken her toothpaste, too.

"She left," he said.

"What do you mean, *she left*?"

He shrugged like it was no big deal, but he was a terrible liar. "I got an email from Jamie this morning. They were going to Chile and then flying out later this month and she just…up and left. With Lukas," he added like an afterthought, and Julia felt her heart stop. *Shit*. So that's what this was about.

"I thought Lukas was going to the Pantanal," she said carefully, still trying to put the pieces together.

"He is. With Chris."

"So what, Chris is traveling with Lukas and then meeting up with Jamie for their flight?"

"Don't you get it, Julia?" He turned on her in exasperation. "Chris is gone. She isn't going back to Australia. And she isn't going back to Jamie." Blake leaned against the bathroom counter, his back to her. "I thought they were joking," he said quietly. "When they said that in the bar by the river that night, I thought they were joking."

Julia stood, but she didn't reach for him. She felt herself poised taut on the narrow tight rope line that connected them. She had to walk carefully, but she didn't know how.

"Jamie's in Santiago now?" she asked.

"He got on the plane to Chile like they were going to, an empty seat beside him the whole time. His flight to Australia isn't for another two weeks, and it's expensive to change it."

"So you're going."

"Yeah." He locked eyes with her through the mirror. "I'm going."

"I guess this is good-bye, then."

"I guess it is."

The silence between them dragged on, Julia standing behind him, both of them looking at each other through the bathroom mirror. She took a deep breath. This was going to be okay, because it had to be. That was all there was to it.

"You're a good friend," she sighed, feeling suddenly exhausted. "I'm surprised he asked you to come, but I understand needing to help. It's good of you to be there for him."

Blake frowned in the mirror and his eyes darted away.

"Wait." Julia took a step back, wrapping the bathrobe tighter around her. "He did ask you, didn't he?"

"What does it matter?" Blake said quickly, turning around to face her. "Obviously I need to go."

"Blake, you know I'm the last person who'd ever say ditch your friends. But no, there's nothing obvious about it."

"What were you expecting? It's not like I wasn't going to go anywhere after you left."

"But you're not just leaving, Blake. You're making your big dramatic exit so that you can be the one to leave before I do."

"I didn't plan to get this email from Jamie," he started.

"The email that doesn't ask you to come to Santiago."

"What do you want me to do, Julia? Ditch Jamie? Come to Chicago? As if you'd ever ask."

"You didn't even give me the chance!" she cried.

He shook his head. "If you wanted it, you would have said something."

She couldn't believe what she was hearing.

"Do you want to come?"

He looked her right in the eye. "Of course not," he said coldly, without even the smallest trace of a frown.

He was telling the truth.

Julia staggered back and sank onto the edge of the bed. The punch had finally come, knocking her down. It felt like everything within her had stopped working—her legs, her brain, her heart.

"You stormed in here determined to be mad at me," she

said. The tears were streaming down her face, but she wasn't crying. Her voice was remarkably calm. "Congratulations. Now you'll never be left, since you get to leave first. I hope you have a nice life, Blake. I hope you have fun *traveling*."

She said the last word with as much venom as she could muster, trying not to hiccup through her tears.

Blake grabbed the last of his clothes and zipped up his bag, heaving it onto his back. "You'd never ask—not for real. You didn't ask me to Rio. You didn't bring up anything about Chicago earlier. Of course you wouldn't ask without me first paving the way."

"How dare you—" Now she really was crying, but her hands were balled into fists and she was too angry to wipe her cheeks. "How dare you pretend your leaving is my fault."

"I'm just speaking the truth. You've got this vault, and sometimes I think I've gotten through but then your guard is right back up again, telling me *you're a good friend* like you're not upset. Pretending that everything's fine."

Careful. She'd tried to be so careful. Until, before she knew what was happening, it was too late.

"Leave," she whispered, everything watery through her eyes. When he didn't move, she said it again, stronger this time. "Leave." She didn't have to take this from him.

"Don't worry, I've got the bill covered. Turn in your key when you go."

"Fuck you, Blake."

There, she said it. She'd thought it the night that he made it clear he wasn't going to Rio with her, and now she had finally said it out loud.

She should have seen it coming. He'd already shown her he wasn't going to stick around when he said he wasn't coming to Rio with her. Of course he would drop her when it was convenient. It was when things got a little too real that she could count on him to bounce.

She knew that Jamie was hurting now, and that having Blake there would make a difference. But she also knew that it was an awfully convenient excuse.

"Nice knowing you, too," Blake said.

And then he was gone. Just like that, her days with him were over without so much as a proper good-bye.

She'd once envisioned him holding her at the airport, the last feel of his lips, the hope that finally, in their last moments, there might be a chance for something more. Suddenly she couldn't imagine anything more foolish.

When the door clicked shut, Julia cried so hard her shoulders hurt from shaking. She stood under the shower and the water mixed with her tears until everything felt like drowning and she knew that this was it. She had finally crashed.

Blake waited in line for a cab. He waited in line for a flight. He waited in line through security. He waited in line to board. When the plane took off, he felt like he was still waiting. Waiting for something to happen.

But of course it already had.

It hadn't been definite. Not even when he'd said it out loud. There had still been time for anything to happen. For Julia to shake her head and tell him that if he really could go anywhere and do anything, he should come to Chicago with her.

Not an invitation that he backed her into, said in anger and tears, but a real one. One that she meant with every part of her.

But she didn't.

Blake reminded himself again that he was doing the right thing. Maybe not the right thing by Julia, but the right thing by Jamie. He was determined to show the loyalty that Liam hadn't. Relationships didn't work out—people cheated, they left, they said they loved you until it turned out they no longer did. But Jamie had shown that friendship still meant something. And right now, his friend needed someone to supply the coffee and the booze and to make sure he wasn't alone on his ass in Santiago waiting for his flight.

Blake knew the reasons he had to go to Jamie. Yet when he'd told Julia he was leaving, some small part of him had hoped she'd be able to talk him out of it, to point out everything wrong with his so-called reasoning. For one wild, crazy second he'd even hoped that she was going to say she'd leave her job for the rest of the year and travel to Chile with him.

But that was preposterous. There was no way she could do that and no reason she would. And so he wasn't surprised but it still hurt like hell when she told him he was a good friend.

Like she wanted him to go. Like she was okay with him walking away.

Like this was a fling, nothing more.

But of course it was. What they'd had would never work in the real world, in their real lives, where they were completely different people who lived thousands of miles away. It wasn't his fault for being the first to slam them back to reality. The one relationship he had believed in, that had given him hope after Kelley that some people really did find each other and work together and stay through all the ups and downs, finding joy in each other's company even after so much time... The relationship he'd admired in the friends he'd met was over. Just like his.

Julia had said she thought there was something up between Jamie and Chris, but Blake hadn't wanted to see it. Why was it that he never wanted to see it? Jamie had advised him to go after Julia, and yet he'd failed to realize what was happening to his friend before it was too late.

He leaned back in his seat and closed his eyes. How much had he ignored when it should have been obvious that Kelley's heart wasn't in it anymore? He wasn't going to let that happen again. He wasn't going to go out on a limb just to watch it disappear once she'd had her fun.

And he wasn't going to let someone suffer through the shock of heartbreak alone. Not the way he'd had to, with no friend to support him because it was precisely that friend who'd caused such pain.

Blake's stomach rumbled, reminding him he hadn't eaten breakfast. The bag was probably still sitting on the hotel dresser, vanilla cream oozing out the sides, the pastries partially crushed from where he'd knocked them swinging his bag around.

He wondered if she'd bother to eat any of it. It was hard to imagine her ever standing up from that spot on the edge of the bed where she'd sat, frozen at his words. She'd been oblivious to the bathrobe sliding off her shoulder, the knot coming undone. He'd almost reached out to slide it back up. But then she'd cursed and told him to leave.

He'd thought her voice sounded funny, higher pitched or something, but his mind was swimming so he couldn't really tell. He'd stood outside the hotel room until he heard the spray of water come on. He knew then that she wasn't frozen. She was fine without him.

So he left.

Chapter Twenty

Julia was disappointed when the bus pulled into São Paulo and she had to uncurl from the fetal position she'd wrapped herself into in the very last seat. *Stop crying,* she scolded herself again and again as her final hours in Brazil ticked down. Did she expect Blake was going to drop everything and—what? Come back to Chicago with her on the spot, like some trinket she happened to pick up? Blake had his friends. He had his plans. He had his life. What had started as a fling could never be anything more.

She'd known the rules when she got into that pool their first night in Foz do Iguaçu. Somewhere over the week she'd forgotten them. But the rules didn't change just because now she had feelings involved.

But didn't he feel something, too? She couldn't believe that things like this happened to him all the time—meeting someone and clicking with them so well, having this good a time over so many days and nights, moving from quiet to laughter to serious conversation with such incredible ease.

And the sex. Oh God, the sex. Would she ever experience

anything like that again? There was no way that it was always so good. It wasn't just that she had let herself go in a way she'd never been able to with Danny. It was that she felt something with him she'd never had with anyone else, period. At first she'd assumed that was just Blake and the way he rolled with everyone he was with. But the more time they'd spent together—the more they'd *needed* each other—the more she'd been convinced that this was something special, something different, for him, too. She wasn't sure she'd ever find anything like it again.

So then why was he getting on a plane to Santiago while she was boarding for Chicago? Why had their last words been so mean? She didn't want to remember Blake with that icy stare, looking so disgusted by her tears. She didn't want to remember what she'd said. If he had come to her, put his arms around her, she knew everything would have turned out okay.

But instead he'd blamed her. After all the things they'd done together and all the ways she'd opened up to him, he turned around and told her it wasn't enough. Maybe he was right and she should have been the one to take the leap and beg him to turn their week into something more. But why was that *her* responsibility? What if she hadn't been sure until he left that a relationship was what she wanted from him? It was complicated, their lives were complicated, and yet he'd ended it all without giving them any kind of chance.

She didn't understand. It wasn't like they needed carrier pigeons to communicate. She had his address and cell number in Sydney scribbled on a piece of paper in her bag, along with his email address. He was the one with the open schedule and money to spend. He could have taken the time to come with her or suggest they meet somewhere in another few months, or—Julia didn't even know what she wanted, just that she'd hoped for *something*. She'd let herself go when she knew that she shouldn't, and all she wanted in return was some indication that it had meant something. That there was more to Blake than the man who'd stormed into the hotel room and then stormed out.

She knew why, though. It was easier to be angry than sad.

When she finally boarded, she sat down in her window seat and set her jaw, keeping her face blank, refusing to cry as the plane took off and carried her away from the best time of her life.

It was only when she landed in Chicago, freezing, the snow piled so high for so long it had long since crusted over into gritty gray ice, that she lost the strength to keep the mask on. Liz picked her up from the airport early in the morning and threw her arms around her, gushing about her tan and eager to hear all about it.

But when Julia collapsed in the front seat, exhausted from two nights of not sleeping, all she could do was cry.

Chapter Twenty-One

It was surprising how easy it was to slide back into her old life. As easy as pulling on her snow boots: one foot at a time. Step by step, day by day, and there she was. A few innocuous details bandied around the faculty room during breaks—*the waterfalls were gorgeous! Rio is such a lively city!*—and by the end of the first week, it was as though she'd never left.

Except that buried in her heart was a deep, pulsing throb that still remembered the taste of fresh coconuts on the beach, and the sand between her toes, the feel of Blake's soft lips on hers. The last word that she'd said to him. *Leave.*

She hung out with Liz and Danny and showed them all her pictures that didn't involve Blake. Liz wanted to see the evidence: Blake in front of the waterfalls, Blake with his arms stretched out in front of the giant statue of Christ the Redeemer, Blake making goofy faces under his round blue helmet before they made their jump. But Julia didn't want to keep living in a past that could never be her future.

Danny had a new girlfriend, Amy, whom Julia liked well enough. She was hard to get to know, but the four of them went out together, sometimes accompanied by Liz's new beau of the moment, and Julia tried not to feel like there was someone missing.

Amy was a great match for Danny, no question. She was shy and accommodating and incredibly kind. She would never say *fuck me* or jump off a cliff with wings on her back. Would never stay up all night wearing next to nothing, dancing and laughing too hard to care.

Danny didn't know these sides of Julia. But now Julia knew they were there. They were a part of her and not some fluke or a thing she could try on for a few nights and then discard, like cheap clothes or a bottle of wine to enjoy until it was done. But the knowledge made the long, dark nights of winter even harder to get through alone. The loneliness was a palpable ache, so strong it seemed like another body taking up space in her bed.

Because what could she do? Dates were unimaginative and dull when they weren't with Blake. The usual things she did in Chicago—restaurants, bars, a few museums—seemed pitifully small now that it no longer felt like she had the whole world at her feet.

What was he doing? Who was he with?

Would he ever write to her?

Chapter Twenty-Two

Winter, still.

"Come on, Rob and I got tickets to this comedy show. Danny and Amy are coming and we're taking you with us."

Liz had swung by Julia's apartment and was rooting in her cabinets for something to eat.

"Who's Rob?" Julia asked, closing her laptop. She'd been diligent about her resolution to come home from work on time, especially on Fridays. But that didn't mean she didn't bring work home with her instead.

"New guy, you met him last week at Trina's party, remember?"

Julia didn't, but she nodded anyway. What had happened to Greg? She decided it was best not to ask.

"Come on, I thought you were going to stop working all the time. Those kids can teach themselves algebra for all I care—that's what the internet's for."

"It's new student evaluations to conform to state standards for the federal funding we got last year."

"I'm telling you, just look up whatever other schools have done."

"I know, but I like these kids. I want them to do well."

"You don't have to reinvent the wheel." Liz plunked a glass of wine next to Julia and turned the laptop toward her, opening up a new browser and typing in a search. Julia tried to stop her, angling the computer back, but it was too late.

"Whoa-ho, what do we have here?" Liz asked, lifting up the laptop to get it out of Julia's reach and depositing herself on the sofa beside Julia's desk.

"It's nothing; close the screen."

"Oh my god, J. You're not still watching his show, are you?" Liz clicked through something on the screen and Julia heard the *pip-pip-pip* of the volume rising on the computer, followed by the swell of violins from the opening credits she could now hum from heart.

"He sent me a few back episodes," she groaned, sinking down into her chair, wanting to disappear.

Liz looked up sharply from the screen. "So you're in contact?"

"I don't know." Julia threw up her hands. "A little?"

"You didn't tell me there was potential here." Liz narrowed her eyes like she'd been lied to.

"There isn't. He's God knows where right now—Patagonia and about to go to South Africa? And then who knows where, and in the end, he'll wind up back in Australia. Last time I checked, none of those places were anywhere near Chicago."

"So? What have I been telling you?"

Liz lifted up the laptop to make her point.

"Yeah, I know. The internet. But I don't want some kind of weird long-distance online sexcapade."

Liz laughed. "I don't know who this guy is, but he was definitely good for you. Leaving school before it gets dark out, remembering to stay stocked in good wine, using un-

Juliaesque words like *sexcapade*. What have I told you? Don't give up so fast."

"I didn't give up," Julia protested. "He knew I had a return ticket back and on the day I was leaving, he was all, *Hey I'm going to Santiago!*"

"Yeah, but to see his friend who got jilted, right?"

"Jamie. But he made that plan totally last minute, like he was looking for anywhere in the world he could go that *wasn't* Chicago or the U.S."

"But did you talk to him about it at all beforehand? Did you say *anything* about what would happen at the end of your stay?"

Julia shook her head, feeling worse by the second. "I asked him to come here," she said weakly, but Liz wasn't buying it.

"At, like, the very last second, when he was on his *you can't tie me down* kick."

"So? He wanted me to ask him so that he could say no."

"How do you know he wasn't waiting to see if you'd bring anything up sooner, and then when you *didn't*," she wagged a finger accusingly, "and this other thing came up, he went with that because it was something for him to do?"

"Because he could have said something if he wanted to see more of me!" Julia cried, exasperated.

"So could you!"

"He told me it was just a fling," she said defensively.

Liz rolled her eyes. "One night is a fling. Two nights. A week of nothing but fucking and no talking whatsoever. But you guys? Please tell me he wasn't dumb enough to really say that, and that you're not dumb enough to believe it. You guys needed to talk about this, not have some stupid fight that neither of you meant just to make it easier to leave."

"It wasn't just some stupid fight," Julia said defensively, even though she'd thought the same thing a million times before. "He acted like I have, I don't know, intimacy issues."

She wrinkled her noise. "That's hitting below the belt."

"You do have intimacy issues, sweetheart," Liz said matter-of-factly. "Obviously he does, too. That's why you *talk about it*." She over-annunciated the last part, as though explaining to a child not quite able to grasp the concept.

"I can't believe I'm getting lectured on communication by *you*," Julia grumbled.

"I know," Liz agreed. "It may be the strangest thing that's ever happened in the whole history of our friendship."

Julia couldn't help it. She cracked a smile.

"Almost as strange as the fact that I saw Rob last night and *still* want to see him again tonight," she added, and Julia raised an eyebrow.

"That *is* surprising," she said, grateful as usual for Liz's ability to turn any conversation back to herself.

"Which is why you have to come to the show tonight to check him out again. I need to know what you think."

"Yeah, fine, of course I'm going," Julia sighed.

"I think Blake went to see Jamie because he was scared," Liz said as they got their coats and headed to the door. "He didn't know what to do, and he didn't want to look like he was hanging around waiting for you to invite him."

"I think he went to see Jamie because he wanted to," Julia said crossly. "After all, he made it quite clear that we had come to the end. And anyway, Jamie's his friend."

"So? You can have friends and still have a life. You're acting like this was inevitable."

"Wasn't it? He's some hotshot TV writer and producer in Sydney. I'm a math teacher in Chicago. We only met because we were both completely out of our elements, but we can't live outside our real lives forever. Sooner or later, things would have to get practical anyway."

"Why?" Liz asked. And it was in the way she cocked her head at Julia, with that puzzled expression as she unlocked the car door, that Julia knew the question was a serious one.

Why did they have to get practical? Because that was what life was. Someone had to be there to take care of the everyday issues, the day in day out, the problems as they inevitably arose. Someone had to live in Chicago and trudge through the snow and smile at the other couples and laugh even when the jokes weren't funny.

Didn't they?

More to the point, didn't she?

Chapter Twenty-Three

Months passed. The snow melted and the spring came too slow, like it always did. A painful unfolding full of fits and false starts. Flowers pushed up the first sunny weekend only to crumple in the next frost. The restaurants put out their sidewalk seating and found the chairs dusted in snow.

But eventually the sun came, the afternoons warmed, and then it was June, another school year over. On the last day of teaching Julia went out for drinks with her co-workers after class like she always did. Dutifully she clinked glasses around the table, congratulating everyone on a job well done. But every time a cry of "Cheers!" went up, she cringed. She'd held Blake's eyes every time they said it and what did it matter? She was alone.

She made her excuses and headed home, but it was only to change out of her work clothes before going out again. Julia had been roped into dinner with Danny and Amy, and with Liz and Rob, who were still going strong. It was Liz's longest relationship in forever, and while Julia was happy for her friend, she couldn't help feeling like the third—or really fifth—wheel sometimes. Rob was supposed to be bringing a friend of his to dinner in some kind of awkward set-up for Julia. She wasn't exactly interested, but she still didn't know what to wear.

"The floral number with the low neck," Liz said over the phone as Julia stood in front of her closet, frowning.

"Too much cleavage for a stranger. I don't even know the guy." Julia tucked the phone against her shoulder and rifled through the hangers.

"All the more reason to show off, silly. What about one of those cute sundresses you have? With a little shawl for later, it'll be perfect for the garden bar."

But Julia knew which sundresses Liz was talking about. The blue dress Blake had hitched up over her hips as he took her under the waterfall. The red one she'd worn in Rio, feeling his hand idly slide up the straps when they started to slip.

She'd tried to forget about "her Brazilian thing," as Liz called it. But months later everything still reminded her of Blake. Something she read, a thing someone said, something she wanted to do...

On the nights when she let her resolution slide and stayed late working, assuring everyone else that they could go home to be with their families while she finished up the work that needed to be done, she wished she had Blake there to remind her that she didn't have to be the one taking care of everyone else.

She wished she had Blake there to take care of *her* sometimes.

"I take it that's a no." Liz's voice cut in. "So I guess we're stuck with the usual, dark jeans and something cute on top. At least go for flimsy cute, not teacher cute—okay?"

"Sure," Julia said. But she'd stopped paying attention. Automatically her hand had strayed to the soft fabric folded in the back of her closet. She hadn't been able to get rid of the white skirt and shirt. She'd never wear them again, obviously, so they sat hidden. But even though she'd washed them, she swore they still smelled like salt water and champagne.

"You're moping," Liz said into the silence.

Julia drew her hand back quickly, as though caught. "I'm not. I'm just…tired. Everything was nuts wrapping up at school."

"Aren't you supposed to be celebrating? It's summer, the only time I'm jealous of your job."

Julia laughed, making herself pull away from the outfit she couldn't believe she'd actually worn.

"I'm serious," Liz said. "Tonight is to make sure you start your break right. You have these months off and you should take advantage of it. Sleep until noon. Go swimming every day. Have an affair or three."

Julia snorted over the phone.

"Or if that doesn't work, you could finally buy that goddamn plane ticket to Australia I know you keep thinking about."

Julia groaned. "I am *not* going to Australia."

"Why not?" Liz said, and Julia wished they could go back to her wardrobe crisis instead of rehashing this whole conversation again. Ever since the postcard arrived, Liz hadn't been able to let go of the ridiculous idea that Julia had an actual future with Blake. One in which they weren't running around for a week, but were together. All the time.

A couple, even though Julia couldn't wrap her mind around what that would look like for them.

Whenever she brought up that minor detail, Liz would conveniently fall silent. *I don't know, you'll figure it out*, she'd scold, like that was the easy part. Like Chicago to Sydney was a distance that could be easily bridged.

But it couldn't. And so when the postcard came, into the closet it went, alongside the clothes from New Year's Eve.

It wasn't even much of a card. On the front was a picture of an enormous waterfall. On the back he'd written simply: *Thinking of you.* Not much from someone who was—she knew from re-watching *The Everlastings* more times than she'd care to admit—extremely capable with words.

And yet as much as Julia complained to Liz that Blake hadn't said a thing, she'd known what he'd been trying to tell her.

Because it wasn't just any postcard. The picture showed Victoria Falls seen from the Zimbabwean side. Massive, churning, the spray misting across a chasm flanked by green. Julia wasn't sure whether to feel good that something had made him think of her, or whether it hurt all the more knowing that he could gallivant anywhere, seeing whatever he wanted, and there was nothing special about the fact that for a few days, he'd done so with her.

She hadn't written him back. What was she supposed to say? *I love you, don't fuck anyone else under the waterfalls?*

Liz was wrong. A postcard didn't mean anything. The only option was to move on.

"I'm not going to Australia," Julia repeated emphatically. "There's nothing there for me. All we did was have a good time for a week and everybody knows that's not what a relationship is."

Liz groaned. "I hate to break it to you, Julia, but relationships don't have to be suffering. It's supposed to make your life better, not hold you back."

But Julia already knew there was no use wondering about something more with Blake. Besides, there were plenty of men who didn't live 9,238 miles away—she'd Googled it—and who would actually say they wanted to be with her instead of bail without warning, send a cryptic postcard, and leave it at that.

She just hadn't met any of them yet.

She was about to remind Liz that she was supposed to be

rooting for what's-his-name, the guy Rob was setting her up with that night, when the buzzer to her apartment rang.

"Hang on," she said, dropping the shirt she'd pulled from her closet and going to the intercom. "The door buzzed."

"Package?" Liz asked.

"I didn't order anything."

"Ooh, end of school year present?"

"I hope you got me something good," Julia said with a laugh. She pressed the button on the intercom.

"Hey," came the voice from the sidewalk, and for the split-second before Julia registered what was happening she had the strangest sensation that everything was tingling from her fingertips down to her toes, so that she was more worried about what was wrong with her than about what was to come.

Her "Hello?" came out barely a whisper, so that he had to buzz again and ask who it was.

But Julia didn't have the same question. Even with the static from the intercom there was no mistaking that voice, the accent light and buoyant, so distinct she could practically hear him running his hand through his curls.

"Julia?" he said. "This is —"

"Oh my God." Julia squeezed her eyes shut, the phone still pressed to her ear.

"What is it?" Liz asked, at the same instant the intercom buzzed again.

"Oh my God," Julia repeated.

"Jules," Liz said urgently. "Are you there? Is everything okay?"

"It's him," she whispered, staring at the intercom.

"It's who?"

Julia could barely form the word. "Blake."

Liz gasped over the phone. "*What?*"

The intercom trilled again.

"It's him. Liz, what do I do? It's *him!*"

Julia turned away from the intercom, taking in her apartment strewn with papers, the morning's dishes left in the sink, the clothes she'd just now dumped all over the floor. How many nights had she lain awake fantasizing that she hadn't heard from him because he was on his way over right that second, so desperate to see her that he couldn't settle for the phone or email or any way in which his true intentions might be misconstrued?

But now that it was happening—or something was happening, she couldn't say what—she had no idea what she wanted. How could she run to him after all the silence and distance between them?

On the other hand, how could she not?

Liz's voice cut through her panic, so loud Julia had to pull the phone away from her ear. "What do you mean, *it's him*? Downstairs? Now?" Liz inhaled sharply. "Are you going to tell me what the hell is going on?"

"The door buzzed, I said hello, he said hello…" Julia couldn't remember what came next.

"And?" Liz prodded.

"And now I'm freaking out talking to you!"

"He just said, *This is Blake*?"

"No. He just said, *Hello.*"

"But you know that it's him?"

Julia didn't want to say that she'd know his voice anywhere. That she heard it at night in her dreams, whispering to her. That she imagined him mouthing the words as he wrote *The Everlastings*. That no matter what she said about moving on, she would have given anything—everything—for the chance to hear him say her name again.

"And now he's downstairs?" Liz asked.

"Uh huh."

"Okay." Liz paused. "So explain why you're still talking to me?"

"Because I don't know what to do!" Julia cried.

"Inviting him in would be a good start."

Julia gripped the phone. "I can't."

"I'm hanging up now."

"No! Don't go."

"You have things to do."

"I know—what time are we meeting for dinner?"

Liz barked out a laugh. "You, my dear, are not coming to dinner tonight. I'll tell Rob's friend you had to cancel. And suggest he not get too hopeful about rescheduling."

"There's no way this is happening. I don't even know what to say."

"Julia. You're not marrying him. You're just telling him he doesn't have to wait on the sidewalk. Did you know he was in the States?"

"No."

"That's a long way to come to say hello to you through an intercom and turn around again."

Julia didn't move.

"Do it," Liz said.

Julia still didn't move.

"Do it before he thinks you don't want to see him and leaves."

Julia's breath caught. The thought of him buzzing up to her, knowing she was there, knowing she knew who it was, and then waiting for an invitation that never came…

Chapter Twenty-Four

Blake kicked his toe against the front stoop, waiting. She'd heard him, right? It was possible she hadn't known who it was, but he doubted it. He'd heard her inhale as soon as he'd said her name.

And then nothing. No hello, no buzz of the door letting him in. Did he have the wrong apartment number, scratched on a piece of paper she'd given him with her email and mobile before things went sour for them? Or was this her way of saying, *Go away*?

But he could wait for her to be ready to see him. He could wait however long it took.

He'd already waited for the months he'd been traveling, for the time he'd been back home, for the end of the school year so he wouldn't be interrupting when he knew she'd be at her busiest. He'd waited for the more than twenty-four hours it took to get from Sydney to Chicago, the image of her dark hair spurring him on. He'd even waited once he arrived, spending the night in a hotel so he wouldn't show up completely bedraggled on her doorstep, despite the fact that it was torture to be in the same city and not rush over in the middle of the night.

And then he'd waited all day while she was at work, giving her what he hoped was enough time to come home.

Hoping she'd come home and wasn't out with friends or colleagues or—an unimaginable thought, he pushed it aside right away—a boyfriend, someone she'd met since her return.

It didn't matter. He was here. And this time he wasn't going anywhere.

He was done making mistakes, done running away, done stopping himself from going after what he wanted no matter the difficulties that stood in the way. She might not want him, but that didn't mean he was going to slink off without giving it a try.

He buzzed again, squinting up at the building to see if he could tell which window was hers. *Let me in*, he willed from afar. He stamped his feet against the pavement and looked down the street. Chicago was massive, sprawling, and colder than he was used to—he should have brought a jacket now that evening was settling in. He tried the door again, thinking maybe he hadn't heard it buzz. But it banged uselessly, locked.

It occurred to him then that she really wasn't going to see him. It had been too long, he'd done nothing but send one lousy postcard and a few brief emails that could never stand to capture all that he'd wanted to say. She had every right to turn him away. He raised his hand to the intercom one more time and then dropped it. He'd known it was a possibility as soon as he'd booked his ticket. It could be a trip for nothing. She could be done with him.

But it wasn't nothing, he reminded himself. Trying wasn't nothing. Nothing only happened if he walked away, waiting for life to happen to him, waiting for love to knock him out cold like he didn't have to put in any effort when the right person came.

Nothing was how he'd felt when he was alone in Australia, going through the motions, missing the fullness he'd once held inside. Realizing how much he'd lost when pride and fear kept him from taking that trip to São Paulo and telling her he wanted to give them a try—not for a week while they were traveling, but for however long they could make their lives intertwine. No matter how many plane rides it took.

Blake knew the opportunities he'd had as a writer had come because he'd made them happen, pursuing what he wanted even when it seemed the whole world was telling him no. He'd had to make hard decisions and be persistent to make his dreams come true. Why did he think the rest of life, and love, would be any different? Why did he think he shouldn't have to work for any of it?

Standing outside Julia's apartment, though, he worried that he'd come to his senses too late. He had no right to assume she'd open her door after so much time had passed. He had no right to her heart anymore.

He took a sip of the fresh coconut water he'd gotten from one of those overpriced health food stores he'd gone to way on the other side of town. The sweetness reminded him of her lips and the way her eyes had lit up the first time she tasted coconut on the beach.

But the taste wasn't the same. It was an imitation of the thing they'd once had, the kind of thing he knew now could never be recaptured. He was going to have to go back to his hotel, email Jamie to let him know he'd failed, and book the next flight home.

He was turning away when the noise he'd been waiting for suddenly came.

He leaped for the door, pushing it open before she could change her mind and stop buzzing him in. There wasn't an elevator and he raced up the stairs, heart pounding in his throat. He tried to slow down but he couldn't hold himself back.

This had to work. There was no other way.

He'd imagined this moment countless times since he'd left Rio in a rush. Long before he fully understood that he had to go to Chicago and see her he'd imagined her apartment, where she lived, what her life was like. Now he was here, standing in front of her door, and he couldn't believe it was real. He raised his hand to knock but before it came down the door swung open, and he was face to face with Julia, her eyes wide and an almost frantic look on her face, and she was so beautiful, she was so goddamn beautiful, he didn't so much step into her apartment as fall into her arms.

But he didn't fall into her, not really, because she pulled away immediately, as though she'd been reaching out for him and then stopped herself short.

It hurt, but he understood.

For so long he'd been thinking about this moment and now that it was here, he almost didn't know what to do.

"Hey," he said gently, eyeing her up and down. She looked tired, softened, and he wanted to run his fingers through her hair, press his cheek to hers, tell her it was going to be okay.

But he couldn't. He hadn't earned that yet.

"What are you doing here?" Her voice was quiet, flat, nothing he could read except that he knew her well enough to know what it meant when she was hiding, putting on that calm exterior, keeping everything else in check.

But no, he thought suddenly, that wasn't quite right. The smallness in her voice was different than anything he'd heard from her before. She wasn't pretending, acting tough and in control. She was showing her uncertainty, her fear. She was showing herself to him.

He extended the large plastic cup. "I brought something."

Julia eyed him uncertainly. "What is it?"

He grinned. "Taste."

Gingerly she took the cup, looking at him like he was a wild animal who'd stepped out of his cage. Safe for the moment but ready to bite.

Still, she didn't toss the liquid in his face and kick him down the stairs. Slowly, watching him, she brought the straw to her lips.

Realization dawned over her face as she drank. "Where did you find this?" she asked breathlessly, staring at him not with the same caution but with something else now, as though he were a creature she'd never seen before.

He couldn't stop the smile. "It's not the same as the real thing, but it's as close as I could get. Better than the packaged stuff, that's for sure."

She took another sip. So far, so good.

But then she turned and put the cup on the kitchen counter, and when she faced him again her arms were folded, eyes narrowed with the same suspicion they'd held when he walked in.

"Blake," she started, and he took a step forward, holding up his hand.

"Don't say anything," he pleaded before she could give him the piece of her mind he so deserved. "I'm here because I have to explain."

He'd thought about it the whole flight over. But in the end there was no planning. He didn't have the perfect thing to say, because there was no perfect thing. There was only the truth, and the force of his feelings for her. He stood in the doorway to her adorable apartment, filled with so much Julia and messier than he'd expected—books, clothes, an empty bottle of red wine—and spoke.

"I fucked up," he said. "I fucked up as soon as I got on that plane to Santiago. No, even earlier—as soon as I walked out that door. Don't think I didn't realize I'd made a mistake."

Julia sank into a kitchen chair. She didn't invite him to sit with her so he leaned against the counter, taking her in.

He went on.

"I was afraid of what I had with you, what I felt for you. I thought that if I ran away from it I could keep going with my life as though nothing had ever happened. That way I wouldn't lose anything. I wouldn't have to risk being hurt."

Julia looked away, the pain of what he'd done clearly etched on her face.

"You could have come back," she said quietly. "You could have met me at the airport. You could have called me from Chile. You could have emailed at any point during your trip." But even though her voice was small, she wasn't backing down. Her eyes locked into his and held him there. "You could have done any number of things to give me some kind of sign that you cared. That the week we spent together was more than some random fling."

A million protests came into his mind. That it wasn't his fault, he hadn't known what to do, she hadn't come after him either, and anyway what did it matter—he was here now. But he pushed them aside. That was the old Blake, making excuses and running away. Instead he said simply, "I know."

She seemed surprised by his admission. "Then why are you here?" she asked, confused.

Blake sighed. "I went out to dinner."

"What are you talking about?"

"I went out to dinner with Jamie and his new girlfriend, Laura."

Julia's eyebrows shot up. "So Chris is still with Lukas?"

"Shocking, isn't it? I haven't been in touch with her, out of loyalty to Jamie, but she included me in an email announcing that they're opening up that inn on the coast like they said. But that's not the point." He paused, considering. "Actually, I guess it sort of is. They're happy doing what they want to do, building the life they want to have together—even if it doesn't quite make sense to me."

"It sounds like they decided to never come back to the real world." Julia rolled her eyes.

"But that's just it, isn't it?" He was getting excited now, wanting her to see. "It *is* the real world—for them at least. It's the world they want to be in, the life they want to live. They're not holding themselves back because it's complicated or impractical or not what they were expecting or whatever else people might say. They're doing it. And Jamie and Laura— they're doing it, too."

"You like her? The new girlfriend, I mean," Julia asked.

"They work together. She's brilliant, caring, great for Jamie. Plus she wants to settle down, have a family, travel sometimes but have a home in Australia with him. It's still early, but I've never seen him so…happy. Content. They click in this way that's so obvious. As soon as you see them, you know."

"So you had dinner with them?" Julia prodded, getting him back to that strange revelation that had changed everything for him. Or not changed it, but brought it into focus so clearly that for the first time, he couldn't turn away.

"It's not like I hadn't seen them together before," he continued. "But there was this night when I'd been working late. I'm writing a new show. I kind of thought it up when I was with you, and I've been trying to get it into production." He shook his head. He didn't want to get into that yet. "Anyway, when I met up with them, I was late. Tired. Focused on other things. I got to the bar after them and I was looking around, trying to find where they'd sat, and it was this moment—it's hard to explain, but there was this moment when I saw them before they saw me, and it was so unscripted, so incredibly intimate. So real. I saw the way they were looking at each other, laughing over their drinks, and she touched his arm and I—"

Blake broke off, looking away. He felt his voice catching. It had been ridiculous even then. What he'd seen hadn't been significant. It was what couples did when they were together, in their own little bubble even when they were out in the world.

But it was exactly that normalcy that got to him. How comfortable and happy they were. How they'd found each other at last. He'd walked up to them and sat down and ordered a beer and they were glad to see him; it wasn't like he'd interrupted. But even when they were talking and laughing, he kept thinking about the way Jamie and Laura looked at each other when they thought no one was looking. When there was no one else in their world.

It wasn't just that he wanted that—to love someone, and be loved in return. It was that in that instant somehow it all slammed into him. That he'd had that—once, briefly—and it wasn't with Kelley. It wasn't with any other ex.

It was with Julia, in Brazil. At dinner with her, walking with her, holding hands with her on the beach. It was trembling in her arms after they'd jumped off a cliff and let themselves soar. It was early in the morning when she rolled over, half asleep, and curled her body against his. That wasn't a time-out from the rest of his life. That *was* his life. That was what he'd shared with her.

He tried to explain all of this, but he wasn't sure she understood. It was so clear in his mind and so convoluted when it came out in words.

"You want what Jamie has," Julia finally said.

"No." Blake shook his head. "I want what *I* had but was too wrapped up in myself and my plans to see."

Julia looked at him intently. "What is it that you had?"

"I spent a week in Brazil falling in love with you, Julia. It took me five months to fully accept that that isn't changing, and that nothing I feel for you is going away. That may be five months too long," he said before she could remind him. "It's five months I wish I hadn't had to spend, and that you hadn't had to go through. But that's how long it took me to be more sure of this than I've ever been of anything in my life. That's how long I could hold out before I knew that if I didn't come see you, I'd break."

She took a sharp breath. When she spoke, her voice was pained. "I tried to forget you. I tried to pretend it didn't mean what it did. Because I thought that for you, it was over. You didn't call. You barely wrote. I told myself I had to accept that we were done, because there was no other sign that we weren't."

Blake pulled up a chair beside her and leaned close, taking her hands in his. "This isn't the kind of conversation for the phone. This isn't the kind of thing I could email you and say." He ran his thumb over her palm, wondering how such a simple touch could do so much to him. "You don't have to do anything. You don't have to love me back. But I had to tell you anyway. I'd never forgive myself if I didn't get the chance to look you in the eyes and say I'm sorry."

He looked at her and watched her scan him, trying to read something there. He let himself face her, open, his thumb gently circling the center of her palm. He didn't know where this was going, but he had to wait and see.

"I've missed you," she finally said, when he thought he couldn't take her silence anymore. "I thought, after so much time passed, that you were gone."

Mentally he kicked himself. How could he have let her wait all that time, thinking things were over for them? How could he have made her think her love wasn't the most important part of his world?

"I had a lot of time to think while I was traveling on my own," he said, hoping she would understand. "The whole time

I kept convincing myself that I'd come home and dive back into my real life and, I don't know, snap out of it or something. Like you were someone I could move on from." He shook his head, laughing at the memories because otherwise he would cringe.

He told her about the blurry two weeks in Santiago before saying good-bye to a heartsick Jamie. He'd wanted to believe it was worth it to be there for his friend...and yet afterward, it seemed he was always moving, always trying to outrun his thoughts. If he could keep on the road ahead of his memories of the dark-haired girl with her captivating eyes, who did things that scared her and laughed at her fear, then maybe he'd be able to forget.

But he couldn't. South Africa, Lesotho, Swaziland, Botswana, Zimbabwe... He went bungee jumping off the world's highest jump in South Africa to prove to himself that he could, that he didn't need anyone with him to do it. But while the adrenaline rush was there, the thrill wasn't. It wasn't as fun when he didn't have anyone to laugh with about hollering all the way down.

At Victoria Falls it was like a dam released inside, flooding him with memories. The falls were supposed to be beautiful, but everything in him ached when he stood before the thundering cloud of white spray and wished it would pound him into the rocks, crush him so he didn't have to feel this way. Julia had said she dreamed of falling, the soaring descent of each drop. But Blake only had eyes for the bottom, where the rocks were steadily pounded down until one day they'd be nothing but dust.

She ran a hand through his hair, pulling a curl behind his ear, and let her fingers linger on his neck. Her touch both melted him and turned him to steel. "I wish you'd told me you felt that way," she said with a sigh.

"The postcard," he reminded her.

"I know."

"It wasn't much."

"No," she said. "It wasn't." His stomach tensed with regret, until she said, "At least it let me know you weren't gone."

"I think some part of me hoped you'd come after me. Tell me I was wrong. Make me see the light. That sort of thing."

"I was stunned," Julia admitted. "It was like when you said you weren't coming to Rio. I thought we were doing one thing, we'd talked about doing one thing, I thought everything was fine. And then—"

"And then I messed it up doing something else instead." Blake finished the thought.

Julia sighed. "It makes it hard for me to understand. I don't know how to read you. I don't know what to believe."

"I know that now I'm doing something else unexpected by showing up here like this. But I hope it's different this time. I want to show you that I'm with you, and I mean it. I want to be with you." He took a deep breath and let it all out, and with it the hurt and loneliness he'd held on to his whole time on the road. "I'm here now to show you what that means."

Chapter Twenty-Five

Oh God. That was what the voice inside Julia's head kept repeating. Not exactly helpful, but it was all she had. Oh. Fucking. God.

It should have been impossible, some fantasy she'd dreamed up in her loneliest hours late at night. But it was real. It was happening.

He was here.

And it felt so perfect, so indescribably right to have his fingers circling her palm. Maybe all those months were nothing but a precursor, giving them both the time and distance to know they were ready for this. So that when he finally stopped standing by the kitchen counter and came over to her, his touch, his kiss, told her that no matter where in the world they both were, they were home.

But it was still crazy. It was like they'd skipped ahead five months and he wanted to pick up right back where they'd been.

"Blake," she started, but when he wrapped his arms around her, she found the words wouldn't come.

"I know that I'm saying a lot," Blake said, as though reading her mind. "But I want to be here. I want to be with you. I want to give us a try."

"I need to ask you something," she said before she could get too swept away. The words gnawed at her. She didn't want to address it, but she knew that if she didn't get it out now, it would keep hanging over her, and she couldn't do that. She'd let things slide without voicing her feelings, and if she'd learned anything these five lonely months, it was that she wasn't going to do that with Blake ever again.

Blake pulled away but it was only to see her better as he said, "Of course."

"Your new show that you're working on—who's going to play the leads?"

"I don't know yet," he said, looking confused by her question. "There'll be auditions, but I don't want to be part of the team that picks. Someone else will know the right players. I want them to go with their gut."

Julia took a breath and asked outright what she'd meant. "So not Kelley, even though she's so good in *The Everlastings*."

Blake's eyebrow jumped. "You actually watched the episodes I sent you?"

Immediately the heat rose to her face. "More like every season. Twice."

His eyes widened.

"Okay, you caught me." She sighed. "Maybe three times."

There was a silence. "Wow," Blake said. "That's…a lot."

She winced. "I know." And then, because he'd come all this way and been so honest with her, she admitted the real reason she'd watched it so many times. "I like falling asleep to it playing in the background. It feels like I'm hearing your voice."

This time she was the one who reached for him, running her fingers up his hand, his arm, feeling the faint blond hairs and the trace of his forearms where the muscles disappeared under his sleeve.

Blake covered her hand with his.

"Kelley's not going to be in it. I'm handing over *The Everlastings* to another writer. I don't know how long she and Liam will stay on it, or what they'll be working on next, but the truth is I don't really care. I want them to be happy, to find roles that they like. Whatever they want from their careers. But for me?" He shook his head. "I want actors who are there to work. I'm not worried about anything else."

Right away Julia could hear the different way he spoke about Kelley from when they'd been in Brazil. Then, she'd still felt him wince at the pain.

But now it was as though he were talking about something that had happened to somebody else, a long time ago. She knew now in a way she hadn't before that he was really over her. Everything in his life had moved on.

And in hers. When she thought of Danny and Amy, nothing in her stabbed at the knowledge that he had someone else on his arm. If anything the feeling was akin to what Blake described when he saw Jamie find happiness with somebody new. That she'd had that, once, and let it go. Whenever she closed her eyes, there was one person she pictured, someone who had been far away and was now somehow, inexplicably, sitting right in her kitchen, wrapping her in his arms.

"But, Blake." She leaned close and shook her head into the crook of his neck, inhaling the scent of him, the surprising softness of his skin. "You live in Australia. I live here."

"I can live here."

"What?" She tilted her head to look up at him.

His arms were still around her, running his fingers through her hair. "I can be here," he whispered into her neck.

"But your show," she started—didn't he have his own plans?

"I can write anywhere. I can try to find an American producer. I can—I don't know, Julia. But we can make it work."

She felt him hold her tighter, grazing his lips along her neck, up to her ear, taking his time. Like he knew he had the time. Like he knew he could have forever to kiss her because neither of them were going anywhere.

"I also thought—" he said, but then he stopped and Julia thought that if it was something bad then she didn't want him to say it because it might make him stop holding her, and want to pull his lips from her skin, and she didn't think she could handle that. Not now, not again, not after she'd finally decided to let her heart open to him.

"What?" Her body trembled against his.

His hands found the nape of her neck, fingers buried into her hair.

"I thought since you have some time off...if you're not doing anything this summer..." he began.

Oh.

The trembling stopped.

She brought her lips to his ear.

"Yes," she whispered.

"You don't even know what I was going to say."

"I do. And you know the answer. It's still yes." She relaxed all the way into him. "With you, I always want to say yes."

He held her tighter. "I haven't gotten my return ticket yet."

She bit her lip, and then without fear, without uncertainty, she went for it. "Then get two."

"Do you really think you can come with me for the summer?"

"If you want me to."

His kiss could have been answer enough, but still he whispered, "I want you to."

But Julia was still Julia, ever practical, and she pressed a finger to his lips to stop him. "I can't make any promises, though. I can't just...up and move like that."

"No," he said emphatically, kissing along her jawbone, her chin, her cheek—anywhere but her lips where she wanted him. "I'd never ask that of you. I just want to spend time with you. Here, there—it doesn't matter. I want you to come with me for a little bit, while you have the time, and then we can figure things out from there. We can be together and still take it day by day."

Her lips searched his, demanding the kiss he was keeping from her. "We can go anywhere."

He made a face. "Not anywhere cold."

She laughed. "That's okay, I don't think they need many math teachers in Antarctica."

"I don't have any script ideas set there, either."

"Something tells me you can come up with anything." Then she added, taking his hand, "I have a few last-minute things to do in the classroom, but stay with me until I can wrap things up around here."

"I have a hotel room," he said. "I can stay there as long as I need. I don't want to move too fast. I don't want to be in the way."

Julia hooked her fingers through his belt loops. "Please don't go away tonight."

Blake cradled her head in his hands. When he kissed her, Julia knew that no matter where in the world he was, as long as he was with her they'd be home.

"Do you have dinner plans?" he murmured, still kissing her face, the flutter of her eyelids soft against his lips.

"I used to."

He laughed quietly. "I hope I'm not ruining things."

She touched her finger to his nose. "You once told me you intended to ruin me."

"Mmm." He licked his lips. "Then I'd better get started."

"How about Indian?" she said. "There's a great delivery place down the block, they'll be slow on a Friday night, but…" She let her fingers trace over his mouth, along his clavicle, down the front of his chest where she longed to follow with her lips. "Maybe we could find some way to pass the time."

And then it was as though a switch in him suddenly flipped. Gone was the reserved Blake standing politely at arm's distance, explaining himself to her. Inching forward until he was close enough to stroke her hand. At her words, he reached for her as he pushed back his chair and stood. She leaped up so her legs were straddling his waist. He held her in his strong arms and she kissed him, tugging on his lower lip with her teeth. She wanted this so much it hurt.

Her hips rocked against him as they clung tightly to one another, kissing furiously. He pressed against her through his jeans and she remembered the first time she'd felt him like this, in the pool. Only now it was in her kitchen, nothing magical or faraway about that, and it still turned her on like it had the first time. Maybe even more.

"Blake," she moaned, the thrill of his name pulsing through her body. "I love you, Blake." She kissed him again. "I love you." The words escaped of their own volition before she could think or second-guess herself. But as soon as she said it she knew there was no second-guessing, because it was true. That their time together had been short didn't make it any less real. She wanted Blake, wanted all of him, and she was going to make sure he knew.

Blake wrapped one hand tighter around her upper thigh while the other hand slid up the back of her shirt, the hint of skin on skin making her back arch so that her hips drove harder against him. His kiss was possessive, and she let herself be claimed.

"I love you, Julia Evans," he told her. "There's no way I'm

letting you go."

"Don't," she said, "ever." She tugged on his lip with her teeth. He groaned and kissed her harder.

"I need you," she said, and felt his lips turn in a smile.

"I thought you needed food."

She laughed, heart galloping out of her chest. "Menu. In the kitchen. By the fridge." She couldn't form full sentences while her lips were on his, her tongue searching, tasting, drawing him in.

He staggered backward, spinning her until her back was up against the refrigerator, her legs still wrapped around him. He used the door as a brace to hold her up while he pinned her with his pelvis, leaving a hand free to reach for her breasts as he kissed the side of her neck, making her moan.

"In the drawer," Julia panted as his teeth found her ear lobe and tugged.

He thrust against her to keep her in place against the fridge, and she loved the feel of it, the way he held her there so that she couldn't move. The pressure of him, the pressure against her back, her thighs open and aching for him.

She craned her neck to see into the drawer. "The red one," she said. He pulled it out and then brought his hand back under her ass to hold her up as he lifted her away from the fridge.

"Bedroom?" he asked. She steered him into the room, kissing him, laughing as he bumped her into the table, the edge of the couch, staggering backward as he refused to pull his lips from hers.

He dropped her on the bed and flopped down next to her. "Favorite choices?" he asked, passing her the menu.

But no matter how much her stomach was growling, she couldn't focus on that. She pushed the menu away and swung her leg over him, pulling herself up so she was straddling his thighs as he lay back on the bed and gazed up at her.

"Blake," she murmured as she ran her hands up his chest, first over his shirt and then under, feeling the ripples in his stomach, catching on the button to his jeans before she unhooked it and slid the zipper down. "My favorite choice is Blake."

She dropped down until she was kneeling on the floor before him as he lay there, pants unbuttoned, the bulge of his cock so tempting she wanted to savor it before she slid it all the way out and put her mouth on him. He groaned, his eyes closed, waiting. The sweetness of anticipation. She thought about how nervous she'd felt when they'd first been together in the pool. He'd seemed so sure of himself—and so sure that the next day, he was going to leave.

How much things had changed for both of them.

This wasn't a promise. It wasn't a guarantee. But it wasn't going to be a one-night stand. This was the start of something too big to be contained in a night, in a week, in any set amount of time. It was too big for a postcard, an email. Too big to have in one talk.

It was in all the things that weren't said, all the things that didn't have to be, all the things that shouldn't have been. Maybe they never talked about what had happened between them in Brazil, not because there wasn't anything to talk about, but because there was too much to know how to say it all. Maybe Blake really had been hoping for her to broach the topic first, for the same reasons she hadn't brought it up with him. Who wanted to be the one who didn't understand what the fling was—the one who ruined it by bringing up feelings that weren't supposed to be there? Who wanted to be the one left behind when the other person moved on?

Or maybe it was like he'd said, and he'd simply needed more time to sort out what was in his heart, the same way Julia had. Because it was only when faced with his absence that she truly understood what it had meant to know him by her side. The pain wasn't in leaving, she'd come to realize, but in having to go through every subsequent moment knowing both of them had left.

She slid him out of his pants and pushed his shirt up so she could lick along his stomach, flick his nipples with her tongue. Work her way down with such tantalizing slowness that he was squirming by the time she touched the tip of his cock lightly, teasing, with her tongue. She licked along the length of his shaft, then slid her mouth over him. She loved the feel of him, the taste of him, the way he filled her mouth. The way he filled her, completely.

And then she was standing before him, pulling her clothes off, reaching over to get a condom from her nightstand, climbing on top of him. Murmuring her love to him as her body lowered down. It was different in her apartment, in her home, surrounded by the quietness of her everyday life. And it was different knowing that this wouldn't be the last time.

That should have been scary, but she wasn't afraid. She was on the edge of the cliff and she was running, she was hitting the edge, she was taking the next step with nothing to hold her up, but she already knew that when she tumbled off the edge of the platform, she would feel not the absence of ground beneath her but the thrill of flying with her brand new wings.

If she fell, well, at least the views would be worth it on the way down. But first the wind would catch her and she'd fly.

Acknowledgments

Thanks to my agent, Andrea Somberg, for her wisdom, support, and generosity with her time—I am so lucky to have you! Alycia Tornetta is a dream editor who completely got Julia and Blake and helped take their story to the next level. Thank you to Alison B. and Nora Metzger for their invaluable feedback on earlier drafts, and to Balaka Basu, the best Skype writing buddy, pep-talker, and critique partner I could ask for. Sean Austin doesn't know it, but he gave me the initial idea for Julia's character—thanks for letting me steal from your brain. And of course my deepest thanks to Robert, my first and best reader, who never fails to believe in what I'm writing long before I do.

I was fortunate to spend time in Brazil from 2004-2005 and again in the summer of 2006. While I didn't have *quite* the same experiences as Julia, I did go to all the places she visits. I am especially grateful to the Paiva family in Fortaleza, Becky for jumping off a cliff with me in Rio, and Dzashe for long chats on the beach. Also the random Australian couple that suggested sharing a cab to the Argentine side of Foz do Iguaçu. You never know who you're going to meet or the ways life can change if you want it to.

About the Author

Rebecca Brooks lives in New York City in an apartment filled with books. She received a PhD in English but decided it was more fun to write books than write about them. She has backpacked alone through India and Brazil, traveled by cargo boat down the Amazon River, climbed Mt. Kilimanjaro, explored ice caves in Peru, trekked to the source of the Ganges, and sunbathed in Burma, but she always likes coming home to a cold beer and her hot husband in the Bronx. Rebecca is the author of *Above All* (2014), *How to Fall* (2015), and is currently at work on a series set at a ski resort in Washington. She can be found at rebeccabrooksromance.com, and on Twitter at twitter.com/BeccaBooks and Facebook at facebook.com/rebeccabrooksromance.

Sad to say good-bye to Julia and Blake? Join the email conversation at rebeccabrooksromance.com/newsletter for tidbits about the book, the couple, deleted scenes, upcoming releases, and more.

26536008R00190

Made in the USA
Middletown, DE
02 December 2015